ICEBREAKER

A. L. GRAZIADEI

ICEBREAKER

GODWINBOOKS

HENRY HOLT AND COMPANY

NEW YORK

Henry Holt and Company, *Publishers since 1866*
Henry Holt® is a registered trademark of Macmillan Publishing Group, LLC
120 Broadway, New York, NY 10271 • fiercereads.com

Our books may be purchased in bulk for promotional, educational, or
business use. Please contact your local bookseller or the Macmillan Corporate
and Premium Sales Department at (800) 221-7945 ext. 5442 or by email at
MacmillanSpecialMarkets@macmillan.com.

Library of Congress Cataloging-in-Publication Data
Names: Graziadei, A. L., author.
Title: Icebreaker / A.L. Graziadei.
Description: First edition. | New York : Henry Holt and Company, 2022. |
Audience: Ages 14-18. | Audience: Grades 10-12. | Summary: Mickey
James III is following in his father's (and grandfather's) skates by playing
hockey at Hartland University, but he is not enjoying the situation:
for one thing he is seriously depressed, unsure of anything, even whether
he can make it as a hockey player (or wants to); more troubling his
rival, Jaysen Caulfield, is also on the team and seems to bitterly resent
him—and Mickey actually finds Jaysen very attractive and does not
know how to deal with that.
Identifiers: LCCN 2021030873 | ISBN 9781250777119 (hardcover)
Subjects: LCSH: Gays—Juvenile fiction. | Hockey players—Juvenile fiction.
| Depression, Mental—Juvenile fiction. | Self-confidence—Juvenile fiction. |
Hockey stories. | Young adult fiction. | CYAC: Gays—Fiction. | Hockey—
Fiction. | Depression, Mental—Fiction. | Self-confidence—Fiction.
Classification: LCC PZ7.1.G7363 Ic 2022 | DDC 813.6 [Fic]—dc23
LC record available at https://lccn.loc.gov/2021030873

First edition, 2022
Designed by Liz Dresner
Printed in the United States of America

1   3   5   7   9   10   8   6   4   2

To everyone who's had to tuck
away a bit of themselves every time
they laced up their skates

ONE

o, being both depressed and anxious at the same time is absolutely wild.

I have zero desire or motivation to play hockey or do anything other than acquaint myself with my new mattress, but I also have this all-consuming need to be on the ice. To prove myself worthy of my own name.

At least I have Delilah here to make the whole situation tolerable.

I sit on top of the boards at home bench, taping the blade of my stick and listening to the scrape of ice as my sister teaches her new girlfriend, Jade, how to skate. Don't ask me how Delilah ended up with a non-athlete. Her life is even more hockey-centric than mine, and in the few hours I've known Jade, she's made it perfectly clear that she knows next to nothing about the sport.

Still, the way Delilah smiles, holding Jade's hands and skating backward as she guides her across the ice, it's almost enough to make me smile, too.

I try. Force a little uptick at the corners of my mouth. But with banners bearing my name hanging from the rafters, I feel like I'm suffocating under them.

Well, not *exactly* my name. I'm Mickey James *III*. Hanging from the rafters are two banners that say *James* and *James II* above the now-retired numbers 7 and 13. Waiting for my *James III* and 17 to join them and complete the trio.

At least until I produce Mickey James IV, and IV spawns Mickey James V, and so on until there are no numbers left for anyone else and Hartland University is forced to shut down the men's hockey program.

"Don't let go!" Jade says with the barest hint of a Southern accent, followed by shrieks of laughter as they both tumble to the ice. Thank god Delilah's wearing shorts under her dress, or I would've had to gouge my own eyes out.

I tear the tape off and set the roll next to me on the boards, trading it for my phone and resting my stick across my lap. Obligation forced me up the hill to the arena and into my skates, but apathy overpowers my will to step onto the ice.

There's a couple messages from my best friend, Nova, waiting for me when I unlock my phone.

> **Nova:** Hey babe
> How's day one going

I look out the floor-to-ceiling windows behind the away goal, the gap in the seats offering a view of Cayuga Lake down the hill, sunlight glinting off it like glass. Hartland's old stone-and-brick buildings peeking through masses of trees.

If I were anyone else, I might be thrilled to be here right now. On this gorgeous campus, days before the start of my freshman year of college. My entire future laid out at my feet.

But because I'm me, all I can think to say is:

> **Mickey:** Kill me now.
> I will pay to fly you from
> paris or wherever tf you are
> just so you can kill me

> **Nova:** Sorry your majesty
> You're not that lucky

I narrow my eyes at the *your majesty*. That's a new one. Never should've joined a team called the Royals.

I glance up in time to see Delilah haul Jade to her feet. She brushes snow off her leggings, and I notice paint stains on her hands, vibrant blues and reds on her dark skin. That's right. Delilah mentioned she was an artist. Delilah, my total jock of a sister, dating an artist who didn't even know what a celly was until Delilah demonstrated her go-to goal celebration (the dice roll, because she is *that* kind of hockey jock) ten minutes ago.

It's a side of her I never thought I'd see.

"Think you're ready for some two-on-one?" I call out, my voice rough with disuse.

Jade startles like she forgot I was here, which I can't blame her for, but her shock melts into an easy grin as she holds Delilah's arm for support and stretches her back. "Sure!

I'll just . . . sit in the net or something. Because I can't even *stand* on ice, apparently."

"Once you get over the fear of falling, you'll pick it up in no time," Delilah says. She guides Jade back to the bench for a break and leans against the boards next to me.

"I'm more interested in watching the two of you," Jade says from behind me on the bench. "I want to see real hockey players in action."

Delilah looks at me, the bangs of her excessively long bubblegum-pink hair hanging in her face. I watch her gaze linger on the dark circles under my eyes, her lips pressing together in a thin line. She probably thinks I'll collapse as soon as my skates touch the ice, but really, this is just how I look all the time now.

Ever since the NHL Entry Draft ended in June and the focus shifted over to next year's prospects. Over to me and Jaysen Caulfield, everyone's projected top two. With my anxiety at its peak, sleep's been pretty hard to come by.

But I don't like the concerned look she's giving me. I slide off the boards and out to center ice just to get away from it.

The smell of a hockey rink is pretty much universal. I close my eyes and breathe in the cold, clean, hockey-scented air, and I could be at any arena in the world. KeyBank Center, where I was pretty much raised back in Buffalo. USA Hockey Arena in Michigan, my home for the past two years.

Hartland's Giancarlo Alumni Arena is probably twice the size of USA Hockey Arena, with alternating sections of black and purple seats in two levels and an honest-to-god overhead jumbotron with four screens for replays and live gameplay. I've played in NHL arenas before, but only for special games. This'll be my first season having a home rink as nice as this.

Everything's okay. Everything is going according to plan. I have no reason for sleepless nights, no reason to be so damn miserable all the time.

As soon as the thought crosses my mind, laughter echoes from down the tunnel to the locker room. Like a challenge I have to brace myself for.

My new captains step out of the tunnel first. Seniors named Luca Cicero and Maverick Kovachis, known as Zero and Kovy according to the team group chat I got put in against my will over the summer. I half expect the entire rest of the team to come barreling out behind them, but only one other follows.

The world narrows to a pinpoint as he steps into view, and for the first time in my life, I truly understand how it feels to be stuck between fight or flight.

Jaysen. Caulfield.

I must have committed some heinous crime in a past life to be punished like this. Stuck on a team with my greatest rival. The biggest threat to my number one draft spot. My primary source of heart-wrenching anxiety.

The captains stop at the bench to talk to Delilah and Jade for a minute, giving them hugs and asking about their summers. Jaysen steps past them, looking around the arena, taking it in with pure, wide-eyed awe on his face.

When his eyes lock on me at center ice, the soft curve of his smile sharpens into something wolfish.

I've never worried much for my draft spot. I figured as long as I kept playing my game, I'd be safe. But in this moment, with Jaysen looking at me like he's ready to devour my every hope and dream, I start to sweat.

This is going to be a long year.

LAST TIME I shared ice with Jaysen Caulfield, the National Team Development Program and I routed his Green Bay Gamblers 6–1. I put up a hat trick and he scored the only Gamblers goal. He must still be holding a grudge because he won't get off my ass now.

I pick up a loose puck at the benches, and he's in my space a split second later. I turn to put my body between him and the puck, and he pushes a fist into my back, reaching for the poke check. I turn again, pulling the puck along the boards back in the direction I came from. He recovers pretty quick, but my speed is one of my greatest assets. I make the pass to Delilah at the blue line, and Jaysen shoves me before taking off to backcheck.

The next time, he doesn't bother with the puck and just slams me into the boards. The glass rattles, and I hear Jade's gasp from the bench. I bite down on my mouth guard and trap the puck against the boards with my skate to keep it out of his reach. But I mean, he's more interested in being an asshole than playing hockey at this point anyway.

"When's the last time you smiled?" he says. I shove my hip into him and get enough space to kick the puck out to Zero.

Jaysen doesn't let up, chirping me whenever he's in earshot and throwing his body into me every chance he gets. Delilah bumps my shoulder as I catch my breath after one particularly rough hit.

"I think someone's a little afraid of you," she says with a wink.

I roll my eyes, but she has a point. He wouldn't be homed in on me like this if he wasn't thinking about our draft projections. So I put up with his antagonism, even when he makes a jab at my size and says, "You gotta buy kid skates or what?"

That one almost gets me. It's not like I'm *that* short. Perfectly average, actually.

Okay, maybe a few inches below average. For a nonathlete. Most hockey players have something like eight inches on me. But Jaysen only has six, so it's not like he's the tallest guy on the ice, either.

He gets around me and puts the puck top shelf, right through one of the holes in the corner of the shooting target, and when he looks at me, his smile is small and cocky, his stick resting across his hips as he glides on one foot back to the rest of us. Delilah's on the bench with Jade now, explaining the game to her as it plays out in front of them.

Might as well give her a lesson in chirping.

"Who taught you how to tape a twig?" I ask. Jaysen's got a single strip of black tape along the bottom edge of the blade and white tape from middle to toe. It's the most atrocious tape job I've ever seen.

He plants the butt of his stick on the ice and practically cradles the blade, drawing a finger along the black strip. "This gives me enough grip to catch a pass while also being thin enough to give me a better feel for the puck." He jabs at the white tip. "This grips the puck right before it comes off the shot and gives it a wicked spin."

I raise an eyebrow at him. "Makes you look like a duster."

The corner of his mouth twitches and my heart stutters like I'm in danger. "Makes me play like a first overall draft pick."

I let out this quiet little chuckle and shake my head, looking away from him. He's absolutely delusional.

"So that's what gets a reaction out of you, huh, Your Grace?" Jaysen tilts his chin up, sliding closer. "A challenge to your birthright?"

My eyes narrow at the title. First Nova, now him? Does he not realize he's a Royal now, too?

"Trust me," I drawl. "You're no challenge."

He gets in my space, towering over me so I have to look up at him. He's taken his piercings out for hockey, but I've seen enough pictures of him off the ice to know exactly where they'd go. Black hoops in his nose and lip. The silver chain of a necklace glitters against his dark brown skin, and even though he's sneering at me, he's got dimples that make me want to punch myself in the face.

I refuse to give him ground, even with my heart racing and palms sweating in my gloves.

Before he gets a word out, Zero skates up and says, "This is hockey time, boys. You can make out later."

Jaysen backs away from me so quickly, there's no way he sees how my cheeks flush.

He gets even more aggressive with his checks after that, and I'm just glad we all decided to gear up for this. It takes all my power to keep my expression neutral. I'm doing a pretty good job of it, until Jaysen clips me on the shoulder after a goal and almost sends me sprawling. I barely keep my feet under me and that's about as much as I can take.

"What's your deal?" I ask. I manage to keep my voice just as dead as he expects it to be, but I twist my grip on my stick, heart pounding. "Mad you're not the best player on your team anymore?"

Jaysen tilts his head to the side, putting all his weight on one foot and casually slouching his shoulders. "Nah. Just thinking about how much you don't deserve to be here."

I pull my head back, screwing my face up in confusion. "What's that supposed to mean?"

"I mean there's hundreds of other guys that'll never get to be here because you're taking up their space, with a scholarship you don't need, exposure you don't need. You have no reason to be here."

I scoff. Okay, buddy. I am officially done with this. I turn to head off the ice, but Jaysen hooks gloved fingers under my practice jersey and tugs me back to him. It feels like I'm about to combust. I grip my stick so hard my knuckles ache.

"I worked for this, too," I snap.

He laughs, but it's this bitter, angry sound. I've never dropped the gloves for a fight before, but man, I am so beyond tempted right now.

"Yeah," he snaps back. "You had to work real hard with a name like that."

I shove him. A full-on crosscheck to the chest with all my weight behind it. He barely budges. He pushes his fingers through the cage of my helmet and yanks my head toward him. I keep my stick across his chest, but he pulls me close enough that I can smell his sweat, see it on his face. He's scowling at me, but it's not all that intimidating with the wedge of red plastic in his mouth.

The sound of skates on ice cuts through the adrenaline pulsing in my head as Zero and Kovy pull up next to us. Jaysen and I keep our eyes on each other when they get their arms between us and push us apart. Jaysen doesn't let go of my cage until he absolutely has to, almost pulling my helmet clear off my head.

"You superstars need some privacy?" Zero asks. "'Cause it looks like some kinky-ass shit is about to go down here."

"Or some serious maiming," Kovy adds.

Zero looks at him and tilts his head, shrugging one shoulder. "They're interchangeable for some people." He turns back to us and shakes his head like he's gotta reactivate his captaincy. He holds an authoritative hand out in front of him. "The point is. You two need to drop this ego garbage. Your draft projections mean nothing on this ice, in these jerseys. Capite?"

Jaysen rolls his shoulders back, standing at his full height so he's looking down his nose at me. "Just getting to know each other."

"Save the getting to know each other for when you've got a few drinks in you." Zero heads back toward center ice and motions for us to follow with another head tilt. I don't move until Jaysen does, skating past me with one final knock of his arm into mine.

I roll my eyes and follow them, watching Jaysen in front of me the whole way. Even after all that, he skates with this kind of grace that could almost rival Mom and my sister Nicolette, and they're both goddamn Olympic figure skaters with about a dozen medals between them.

Jaysen belongs on the ice. He loves hockey. It's obvious in

the way he tilts his head back and takes in a long, deep drag of cold air, shoulders relaxing like his frustration with me can be cleansed by the smell of the rink alone.

He wasn't bred to play hockey. He chose it. Absorbed it into his skin, his blood, his bones by his own volition. There's plenty of others out there just like him who could easily be here on this ice if it weren't for me.

Jaysen's right about that, I guess.

Maybe if he wasn't such a raging asshole, I might even tell him that.

TWO

I'm on my phone in the shower on the first day of classes when I stumble upon a picture Jaysen tweeted last night. And by stumble upon I definitely don't mean that I specifically went onto his feed to see if he's talking about the draft. It's a selfie with him, Dorian Hidalgo, and David Barboza sitting together on a couch I don't recognize, captioned *my two favorite blueliners xoxo.*

It's weird seeing the three of them smiling together when all of us spent the last two years battling it out on the ice in juniors. Dorian and Barbie at least have their lifelong friendship to fall back on. They were both born in Mexico and raised in Wisconsin and chose to come to the same college after their time apart in the USHL. If freshmen had a choice in roommates, they'd definitely be dorming together.

Instead, it's me and Dorian. Not that I've seen much of him this past week. Pretty sure he's only been in our room to move in and change clothes, spending all his time with Jaysen and Barbie at orientation events.

I swear I'm not jealous. I've been actively avoiding the

other freshman Royals. They go to orientation during the day and spend their nights drinking at the off-campus hockey house where the upperclassmen live together. I pass the time in my room or at the dock on the lake while Delilah and Jade do their orientation leader duties and hang out with them when they're done, and that's the way I like it.

Making friends at Hartland would be pointless when I'll only be here for a year before the draft. Even beyond that, when Dad was traded to the Hurricanes from the Sabres, he had to leave that same day for a game that night with his new team. Had less than an hour to say goodbye to a team and a city he played for for two decades. That's what I have to look forward to.

The only reason my friendship with Nova has lasted through distance is because I've known her since the day I was born and lived with her after my family moved away from Buffalo. I still have a room at her parents' house. There's no escaping it at this point, and I wouldn't want to.

I scroll through the replies to Jaysen's post as I head back to my room. There's plenty from the rest of the Royals, some of the other defensemen being mock-offended by his *favorite blueliners* comment, Zero saying *my sons* with a bunch of heart emojis. Then there's the random hockey fans vying for a little bit of attention by commenting how they hope they're all having a good time in college.

I'm staring at Jaysen's infuriating dimples on my phone when I walk into my room.

Jaysen and Dorian are sitting on Dorian's bed, a laptop open with angry-sounding music screaming from the speakers.

I jump so high I almost fling my phone into the sun, but

they're too caught up in their conversation to notice. They look like budding best friends with their all black clothes and tattoos.

"Dude, I am so relieved," Dorian says. "I thought I'd be missing out on shows here."

"Yeah, looks like they don't got a barricade, either," Jaysen says, squinting at the screen through black-rimmed glasses. "We can get right up in their faces."

"I've never been to a venue like that. All the ones back home, the stages were shoulder height and barricaded with this huge gap."

"Once you experience a place like this, those other ones won't even be worth it to you." Jaysen nods his head in my direction. "Your Grace."

I clench the towel tighter around my waist. "That gotten old yet?"

He shrugs. "It's fitting. Zero wants to call you Terzo, but you gotta earn it first. It's Italian for third, apparently."

Right. I was Jamesy on my last team. At least Zero's a little more creative, turning that pretentious little *III* at the end of my name into something decent sounding. Still, I roll my eyes. "He google translate that?"

"His grandma's from Italy. You'd know that if you ever joined us for team bonding. He never shuts up about it."

I glance at him. His words are light and carefree, but the pinched look on his face says he'd rather shave with a power sander than keep talking to me.

"Wait, didn't your mom skate for Italy?" Dorian asks. "Do you know Italian?"

I nod slowly and they both look at me like they're expecting me to go into some Italian soliloquy or something. I keep my mouth shut and duck behind my dresser for some privacy as I get dressed. I'll be changing in front of these guys daily once practices start, but something about being in my room instead of the locker room makes it feel, I don't know, weird. Yeah, this is Dorian's room, too, but I've had it to myself while he's been spending his nights at the hockey house, so it almost feels like he's intruding.

"Okay," Dorian says, drawing it out for a few seconds. The bed creaks, and I hear the snap of his laptop closing. It takes a moment for the music to die, and he's quick to fill the quiet. "Terzo's a pretty sick nickname, though. Better than Hildy. Like, I don't get it. There's not even an *L* there! Please, if you like me even a little, just call me Dorian."

"For the record," Jaysen says, "I suggested Doll Face."

Dorian snorts. "That one's actually not bad. I gotta head out, though, man. First ever college class is physics. *Reza por mí.*"

"That's what you get for majoring in astronomy."

Dorian clenches his hands in front of himself and pulls a face that makes the tendons in his neck pop out. "I just . . . love space . . . so much!" he says through his teeth. He heads for the door with his backpack slung over one shoulder. "Why can't I skip the math and just look at the stars?"

There's a panorama of the Milky Way breaking up all the metal bands and hockey posters above Dorian's bed. I've seen it every day for the past week and never realized it was anything more than aesthetic.

I spent two years with the same players in Michigan but don't have a single one of them saved in my phone or added on social media. Honestly, that doesn't bother me as much as the thought of not knowing a single personal thing about my own roommate. Of wasting my one year of college.

It's not until Dorian gets all the way to the door that I realize Jaysen's not following him.

"What?" I ask when we're alone.

Jaysen sighs, long and loud and tortured. "We got algebra together, apparently. Zero and Kovy are forcing me to walk with you."

I blink at him. What is this, the buddy system? "Why?"

He gives me a look as blank as my own, and I can't hold up against it. I turn to the mirror and comb my fingers through my hair in a vain attempt to tame my curls and stick a pen behind my ear. I head out the door without warning and let it close on Jaysen just to buy myself a few extra steps alone. He seems unaffected when he catches up, falling into step beside me.

Delilah and I are taking this algebra class together. We both suck at math, so it's not like it's gonna help either of us, but it's better than suffering alone. Now it's gonna be pure torture.

I'd gotten used to campus being pretty quiet with just the freshmen and fall athletes here for the most part. Now we have to squeeze past other people crowding the narrow, curving paths from the dorms. Hartland's small for a D-I school, but there's still enough people screaming at the sight of one another and laughing and hugging like they've been apart for years that it gives me a headache.

Seniors are gathered on the hill outside the Sommer Student Center in their black robes and ridiculous costume sunglasses, drinking alcohol out of their class mugs and heckling the freshmen. I keep my head down after spotting Zero and Kovy doubled over in laughter, already wasted at ten in the morning.

We're past most of the noise and starting up the hill to the Stratton science and math hall when Jaysen finally speaks up.

"So, what're you majoring in?"

You know what sucks the most about this? I know he doesn't really want to know. His voice is so dead. He doesn't even glance in my direction as he asks. I know he's only here because our drunk captains want us to stop being so hostile before practice starts. But that doesn't stop my heart from stuttering or my palms from sweating at the weight of his attention.

"Nothing," I say.

"So, what, undecided for now? Testing the waters?"

I look at him. He's got a tight grip on his backpack straps, chewing hard on his gum. There's this heavy feeling in my chest, like I know exactly what he's getting at.

"Not here for a degree," I say slowly, keeping my eyes on him the whole time.

He reacts exactly like I expect him to, finally looking at me with disdain all over his face. "Shoulda gone CHL, then. Why bother coming to college if the NHL is such a sure thing?"

He kinda has a point. Playing in the CHL would let me focus solely on hockey instead of wasting time on classes and homework. But Hartland is a James family tradition. I didn't have much choice.

I adjust the pen behind my ear and turn my eyes back

to the sidewalk. My face is starting to feel hot, and not just from the late-August sun. "I could ask the same of you."

"The NHL has never been a given for me."

I scoff. "You've been a top prospect for years. It's a given."

"James." He says my name like it causes him physical pain, all strained and raspy. "I already had one career-threatening injury. One bad hit's all it'll take for me to lose this. Then there's the fact that less than one percent of men's college hockey players and two percent of NHL players are Black. I haven't been set up for superstardom like you."

I take a deep breath and let it out heavily through my nose. I can't argue with that.

"You realize like half our team's been drafted, right?" Jaysen goes on. I wonder how he would've gone about flipping out on me if I'd answered that first question differently. Because this was obviously his plan from the start. "Hell, Dorian went second round to the Kings, and he's still declaring astronomy. You might as well have a backup plan for when that legacy blows up in your face. One bad attitude can sink an entire team. No one's gonna risk that for your name."

I roll my eyes and stop walking. "Listen. Jaysen."

He faces me with his arms crossed and eyebrows pinched.

"We don't have to do this," I continue, voice hoarse. "You don't have to remind me how much you hate me every time you see me. I haven't forgotten."

He bites down hard, the tendons in his jaw popping out. I don't give him time to come up with another insult before I walk away.

The air-conditioning in Stratton hits me like a wall, and I take in a relieved breath of cold air, wiping sweat off my forehead. I should've brought a backpack just to carry around extra deodorant.

I take a desk at the back of the lecture hall and sink low in my seat, leg bouncing as I watch people come in. Jaysen trails in right behind me, but he sits closer to the front, thank god. I prop an elbow on the table and scrub at a drawing of a dick in Sharpie with my thumb while I wait for Delilah to show up. Good to know college students are no more mature than the ones in high school.

The slap of a notebook on the table next to me makes me jump. "We're sitting up front next time," Delilah says, Jade sinking into the seat on her other side, wearing a T-shirt that says *Seventeen* on the front and *Woozi 96* on the back. They must've gotten together because of K-pop. It's the first thing I've seen them have in common so far. "I need to pass this class."

I sigh. "Fine."

She takes her seat next to me and slides over a sweating plastic cup. "You're in college now, kid. Time to caffeinate."

"Thanks," I mumble, and take a small sip of some kind of bitter iced coffee.

She laughs at my grimace. "You have to stir it first." She jerks her chin toward the front of the room. "Try not to make so many ugly faces—you've got an audience."

A few people quickly look away when I follow her gaze. "What the hell."

"They're selling these in the Sommer Center." Delilah reaches into her backpack and pulls out a magazine, tossing it onto the table in front of me. *The Hockey News*. The cover photo has me in full gear, my new purple-and-black Royals jersey, completely unsmiling.

"The Dynasty Continues: Presenting His Majesty, Mickey James III."

Suddenly, Nova's *Your Majesty* and Jaysen's *Your Grace* make a lot more sense.

My eye roll and sigh combination is a work of art perfected by years of practice.

"Wait till you read it," Delilah says.

I grumble as I flip through until I find my face again, surrounded by my sisters on the couch at Mom and Dad's house in Raleigh. My face is as blank as always, but my sisters stare at the camera like they're trying to break it.

At the time of that photo shoot, I'd been bitter about a lot of things. My parents have lived in Raleigh since I was ten years old, but that was only the third time I'd ever been there. I got to see my sisters for a day, and it was all about hockey.

Mickey James set NHL records, the article says. *Mickey James II broke them. Mickey James III was bred to shatter them entirely. His five older sisters are a testament to their parents' desperation to have a son to continue the James family's hockey dynasty.*

I blink. Read that last line again. Then a third time before I push the magazine away from me. "Fucking seriously?"

Delilah nods. "That's the only mention of any of us. I mean, they do say Bailey and me are at Hartland, too. But they don't talk about Mikayla's SID job, or Nicolette's medals, or Bailey's lacrosse championship, or Madison's coaching."

"Or your Patty Kazmaier?" Delilah was literally named NCAA women's hockey's MVP last season. This is *The Hockey News*. They should probably mention something like that.

Delilah shakes her head. "Nothing we do matters. We

only exist because Mom and Dad were desperate for a child with a Y chromosome."

Jade *tsks* from her other side, stirring her own iced coffee with a metal straw. "That is an inaccurate indicator of gender and you know it."

"Speaking from their perspective," Delilah amends. The two of them start talking about a gender studies class they're in together, and I drag the magazine back to me to give it a rage read while waiting for the professor to show up.

I skim through comparisons of Dad and me, how we were both too young for the draft coming out of high school, spending a year at Hartland in the meantime. Of course it has to bring up my height, because the hockey media is so obsessed with how tiny and adorable they think I am. The writer seems confident that my name and skill will be enough to secure the top pick in June despite my size. The third Mickey James to be taken first overall.

I only start really absorbing the words when I stumble on Jaysen's name.

They seriously interviewed him for this?

Kill me now.

I'm not letting him take that spot without a fight. Teammate or not, I'm coming for him.

"This dickhead," I mutter.

"What, you scared?" Delilah says. She raises her hands in mock surrender when I glare at her. "He's sitting right there. Want me to get in his head? Throw him off his game?"

"No." I want to *earn* that first overall spot. I need Jaysen at his best when I beat him. Prove I didn't get here on my name alone. Prove that I'm just *better* than him.

"I don't get how he's even up for the draft?" Jade says. She takes a small sip of coffee and goes back to stirring. "He plans on graduating, right? How can someone be drafted if they won't be available for four years?"

Delilah sits up straighter, ready to dispense some hockey knowledge. "Whatever team drafts him will hold on to his rights until the August after he graduates. He gets his degree, his draft team gets some free development, everyone wins."

Jade looks unconvinced, but my phone vibrates, distracting me from the rest of their conversation. The official NHL Twitter just tagged me in a post with a picture attached. The preview shows a row of gray tables and half a person slouched over a notebook. My stomach bottoms out before I even click on it, expanding the picture to reveal this very classroom. I glance up, but the room is filled in enough now that I can't pinpoint exactly who took it. All I see are the backs of heads bent over cell phones and a math textbook I didn't bother to buy.

I take a better look at the picture. It shows Jaysen looking down at his phone and me in the back of the room turning a page in the magazine with a scowl on my face, Delilah and Jade smiling at each other as they talk.

Jesus. Social media is scary.

The original poster only tagged the NHL account, but whoever runs it added the comment *who will get the better grade?* with a thinking face emoji, and tagged both me and Jaysen.

It's impossible to miss Delilah with that hair. They just don't care about her. So I retweet it and say *obviously @LilahJames23*.

The professor shows up as the notifications start pouring

in. My follower count has been steadily rising ever since the focus shifted to my draft class. I barely even use the thing, but I'm gonna have to turn off notifications soon. For now, I silence my phone and take the syllabus the girl a few seats over passes to me. We don't do roll call. Instead, the professor goes around and makes each of us introduce ourselves.

In a class this size, it'll take almost the whole hour.

Everyone's giving their year, their majors, what they plan to do with their degree. My hands are clammy, my chest tight. What the hell am I supposed to say without making myself look like an ass?

Jaysen's right. I don't belong here. I should be on some CHL team, not wasting my and everyone else's time in this classroom, taking up space on this campus.

Jaysen turns in his seat to face more people when he's up, eyes skipping right over me as he says, "I'm Jaysen. Freshman soc major. Thinking about working in a law firm someday."

Not a word about hockey. Jaysen Caulfield is made up of more important things.

Now I have to make it look like I am, too. Just to get him off my back.

I drown out the rest of the intros, scrambling to come up with something meaningful. Anything I like that I could make a career out of. Something I'd be happy to get out of bed for.

My mind comes up startlingly blank. Nothing makes me happy, really. Getting out of bed is a chore.

"Hi!" Delilah says, all loud and bubbly, jolting me out of my thoughts. "I'm Delilah James. Sophomore sports management major. I'm playing for Team USA women's hockey in the Olympics next year and working for them after I graduate."

There is no hoping or planning about it. She talks like it's already a given. I mean, of course it is. She's a James, after all.

Then it's my turn. Forty-something pairs of eyes on me is nothing compared to the thousands when I'm on the ice. But this is way more stressful. Talking is not part of my skill set.

My mouth is so dry that my tongue makes this gross sticky sound as it moves. "I'm, uh . . ." My eyes dart around the room, looking for someone safe to focus on so it's not like I'm talking to all of these people. It'd be weird if I stared at Delilah right next to me. So of course I home in on Jaysen. He watches me through heavy eyelids, head tilted back like a challenge.

I clear my throat. "Mickey. Freshman. Marine science major."

And that's all I got. Jaysen raises one eyebrow so it arches above his glasses. I look away.

The room is quiet for a beat before some guy shouts, "Go Sens!"

The Ottawa Senators are a favorite to tank this season and win the draft lottery for that coveted top pick. I sigh heavily and barely catch the way Jaysen's face sours as he turns around. He's a top prospect, too, but nobody made any comments like that for him.

JaysenCaulfield @jaycaul21 · 32m
Replying to @NHL
Note how @mjames17 is behind me,
just like he will be on draft day

THREE

I get through the first few weeks of college without dropping out, but that's only because I don't want to deal with Dad whining about it for the next twenty years.

We got team lifting in the morning, followed by team breakfast in the players' lounge. Team lunch in the dining hall after morning classes and suffering through afternoon classes just to get to team captains' practice and team dinner and team Saturdays at the rink and team study hall on Sunday afternoons. But even with all this team bullshit, I still feel no closer to any of them.

Well, maybe Dorian a little, but that's only because I live with him and he's at least tolerable. Still, it's not like I go out of my way to talk to him. There's a lot of awkward silences in our room at night.

Practice gets more and more serious as the season approaches, and the captains work us hard, running through Coach's practice plans. I leave the rink every night gasping for breath and go to the weight room every morning so sore I can barely move.

And I've been doing this my whole life.

Maybe I should call Dad. Ask if he felt this out of shape at this point, too, or if I'm just hopelessly unprepared for college hockey and everyone will finally see I'm not worthy of my own name.

My entire body shudders at that betrayal of my mind. Let me just call up my dad and fuel the fire of his disappointment. Right.

It's not that he's a terrible parent. It's just . . . everyone says he had five other kids just to get to me. I'm always afraid my sisters are gonna resent me for it. Then there's the fact that Delilah is a better hockey player than me, but Dad refuses to admit it.

With both of us playing at the same level this season, no one will be able to deny it.

The energy in the locker room is completely different before the first official practice toward the end of the month. The guys are pretty quiet as we suit up, this nervous excitement radiating off of everyone. No matter how hard we worked in captains' practices, how seriously we took Zero and Kovy, it's not the same as answering to the coach who's going to determine your ice time.

We get a few minutes to warm up and stretch on the ice before Coach Campbell blows his whistle and calls out, "On the line."

There's a collective sense of *ugh, here we go* as we take to the goal line and another blow of the whistle sends us sprinting to the lines and back. I have a distinct disadvantage with my shorter legs. I might be quick in-game, using my size to duck around bigger guys and get the jump on them, but when it comes to a dead sprint, it's harder for me to keep up.

It's a flaw that NHL scouts will no doubt agonize over when they start getting nitpicky between Jaysen and me. I'm not about to let him show me up here. I push myself to the point of collapse, the taste of iron in the back of my throat, but I still end up a couple strides behind him. We both gasp for air, bent over with our sticks across our thighs, but when he looks up and catches me watching him, he looks so pleased with himself I could smack him.

Our starting goaltender, Colie, is on a whole other level when we move on to shooting drills. He was pretty good during captains' practices, but under the scrutiny of his Olympic gold-medalist goalie coach, he's stepped it up. His reflexes are so quick it's mildly frightening, and he makes it look so easy, I'm half-tempted to put on the pads and try it for myself. I'm so impressed I can't even get frustrated when he blocks most of my shots.

It helps that Jaysen's not having any better luck. The upperclassmen have been playing with Colie long enough that they know his weaknesses and are able to exploit them a bit before he shuts them down, too.

After that, we move on to three-on-twos, with Coach Campbell shouting out real-time feedback, like:

"Cicero, keep your head up!"

"Caulfield, more pressure on the puck along the boards!"

And, "James, you had a lane! Take the one-timer next time!"

I huff, far enough away he can't hear me. I can wrist a one-timer all day, but I was at the point for that one, and I've never been confident in my slap shot. Especially not on a moving puck. I'd rather take the time to set it up than risk whiffing on it and making a fool of myself.

We get in a good hour and a half of ice time before Coach calls it quits. As we head off the ice, Coach says, "Cicero, Caulfield, James. Hang back a minute."

"Oh boy," Zero says, nudging me with an elbow. "You two try not to get your egos too close together. We don't need any concussions."

Jaysen *tchs*, and I feel myself frowning. I've been able to avoid him through most of practice, but as I hoist myself up onto the boards, my feet dangling over the ice, he stops right next to me. He leans back against the boards with his elbows hiked up onto them, almost touching me. Zero stands straight to my right, holding his stick across his shoulders to open up his lungs.

Coach stops in front of us, flipping through some notes he made on a clipboard. He's my dad's age, drafted in the same year but nowhere near as high as him. I think he was fourth round or something. He didn't last long in the NHL, but he's made a name for himself in coaching. Dad's happy with him at least, or he would've been more worried about me coming here, alma mater or not.

My favorite thing is that Coach doesn't coddle me because of my name. He's shared ice with plenty of stars, including Dad, so he's not fazed by it. To him, I'm just another one of his insolent players who basically needs to be retaught how to play hockey from scratch.

I like him. He makes me feel like I deserve to be here, no matter what Jaysen Caulfield says.

But then Coach goes and says, "I want you three on a line together," and all my respect for him goes out the window. Before I can voice my concerns, he adds, "Cicero, left wing, Caulfield, center, James, right wing."

Okay, wait a minute, what? I didn't hear that right. I've been playing center since I first learned that not everyone is supposed to chase the puck at once. I am a center. I'm the best face-off guy in the NCAA. I have the best hockey sense of anyone on this team. My name might as well be written on the ice in the slot and behind the net, that's how much I own those spaces. Center is mine.

"You mean—" I start, but Coach shoots me a look like daggers and I clamp my mouth shut.

"Caulfield is stronger on the backcheck," he says. "I need someone with size and a good defensive mindset centering my top line. James, you'll be in a better position to break out on the wing, which is something you're especially good at. You can still have your place in the slot. Cicero, you know what you're doing."

"What about face-offs?" I ask. I don't even care that I sound like a brat right now; he can't just take away the position I've been playing my entire goddamn life and hand it to Jaysen. He might as well be handing him the top pick while he's at it.

"We'll see," Coach says. He gives me a look like he's daring me to keep challenging him. I bite my tongue.

Coach goes on to giving us our roles on power plays and penalty kills, and I'm on the second PK unit, like what the hell? I twist my grip around my stick and refuse to look Coach in the eye. I can practically feel the smugness radiating off Jaysen.

I need someone with size, he said, like teams haven't been relying on me in spite of my size my entire life. As if I'm not the NHL's top prospect at five foot five. That's unheard of, but here he is acting like he knows better than NHL Central Scouting.

It eats at me for the rest of the day and well into the next. What gives Coach Campbell the right to decide where I play, how I play? He didn't even make it five seasons in the NHL. His team is nothing more than a stepping-stone for me.

Now I know what people mean when they say their blood is boiling. We might as well be walking through drills at practice the next day, but my face burns and sweat prickles my forehead. Rage goes through me in waves. I have never been this angry in my life.

I keep as much ice between me and Jaysen as possible, but he's determined to make my life hell. It's probably twenty minutes into practice when he shoulders into me between drills and taps my skate with his stick. "Serious question," he says. "How long's your twig? Thirty-eight, right?"

"Yes," I deadpan. Sure. Of course I use a stick sized for actual children. If I play along, he'll get bored and leave me alone. That's how it works, right?

Except he smiles. Leans back so his weight's on one foot, all casual and cocky. "I'm thinking about shortening mine a bit." He tilts his head and looks at me out of the corner of his eye, his smile turning vicious. "Might help me out at center."

Hatred surges through my chest, a flash of heat that has me seeing red. I lash out before I can think better of it, the satisfying crack of Jaysen's stick breaking under mine almost enough to calm me down. He wanted it shortened, well now it's fucking shortened.

He gapes down at the snapped shaft in his hands, the other half on the ice at his feet. Someone's shouting, "Hey, hey, hey!" as the team closes in around us, but all I see is Jaysen. He slowly lifts his eyes to me. His lip curls a second before he throws down what's left of his stick and shoves me so hard into the boards my breath wheezes out of me. His hands twist in my jersey and pin me back against the glass. I reach up, heart thundering, and grab him by his cage, pulling down hard enough to break his neck.

"You little shit," he snarls.

"Fuck you!" I snap.

Someone tries to pull him off me but both of us tighten our grips, not even really fighting, just pushing and pulling and raging and hating until arms loop under his armpits and haul him back, both of us holding on until we can't anymore. The guys fill in the space between us, holding us back, forcing us to glare at a distance.

I know Jaysen hates me. He's made it perfectly clear from the moment we met. But I've never seen it like this, written so obviously on his face. The tendons in his neck popping out, his whole body straining like he's ready to lunge as soon as someone gives him some slack.

There's a flash of something hot and dangerous through my chest. I feel my eyes widen, my heart stutter.

Jaysen makes being violently pissed off look *good*.

I shove down the thought as Zero pushes through the team and stands between us, red-faced and fuming. "The fuck is your problem?" he shouts at both of us. Neither of us answer. "Forget you're on a team now?"

He looks back and forth like he's waiting for one of us to speak up just so he can cut us off and yell some more. He'd make a good coach. I glance past the crowd of my teammates to see the real coaching staff gathered at center ice, arms crossed as they watch their captain handle this.

Jaysen drops the sneer but keeps his eyes narrowed and focused on me.

Zero scoffs with disgust. "I can't believe I have to share a line with a couple of children. Get off my ice."

There's a moment of disquieting silence, a lack of sound fully out of place in an arena this size. Jaysen keeps looking at me with a murderous intensity I do everything in my power to return with apathy. I get more satisfaction out of seeing him turn away first than I ever have from anything else.

He shrugs the arms off him and grabs for the broken halves of his stick. I let him get a few strides ahead of me before following, keeping my eyes down as we pass the coaches. They let us go without a word, apparently trusting Zero's judgment. We keep our backs to each other as we strip off our gear in the locker room.

The sound of him losing that smooth, quiet cockiness and throwing his gear into his stall is the most soothing thing I've ever heard.

NOVA VINTER

Mickey: Have you ever hated someone
so much you wanna suffocate
them with your own tongue

Nova: Do you not remember
eighth grade?

Mickey: Fair point

Nova: Who's earned your
hate lust this time

Mickey: You act like it's
a common thing

Nova: You hate everyone mj
So it's an every time thing

Mickey: Whatever
Just promise not to laugh

Nova: Oh this is gonna be good

Mickey: I regret this already
Jaysen Caulfield

Nova: No way
Lmaoooooo

Mickey: I hate you.

Nova: I know
Do we need to talk about
eighth grade again?
Never thought i'd see the day
you fall for a hockey player

Mickey: I didn't fall for him
He's just hot
And infuriating

Nova: Right
Can i officiate the wedding?

Mickey: K bye talk to you n ever

FOUR

Even with headphones over my ears and my three oldest sisters talking over one another on the screen of my laptop, I still hear the thump of bass-heavy music coming from all directions. Across the room, Dorian has his own headphones on, head bobbing slightly along with whatever screaming mess he's listening to while doing homework.

My oldest sisters are *a lot* older and we don't get to talk much, but we're still pretty close thanks to group chats and Snapchat. Mikayla's the oldest at thirty, born when Mom and Dad were still teenagers, less than a year after they met in the hospital at the Olympics when Mom twisted her ankle in training and Dad took a puck to the face in a game against Finland. Now Mikayla's a sports information director at a university in Arizona, engaged to Spencer Brimm of the Arizona Coyotes with a baby on the way. Her life is disgustingly put together.

Nicolette and Madison are twenty-eight, identical twins who I probably wouldn't be able to tell apart if it weren't for their haircuts, that's how little I see them. Nicolette keeps hers long and braided, always looking like she's ready to hit Olympic ice all over again. Madison has hers cut to her chin. She went to school for teaching and got a job right out of college and has coached her school's varsity field hockey team to three state championships since.

I am constantly overwhelmed and astounded by how incredible all my sisters are in all the things they do. The list of their successes is never-ending. But nobody seems to care about them. Because they're women. Because women kicking ass in their sports means less to them than an unproven seventeen-year-old boy with nothing to show for himself but a name.

Sometimes. A lot of the time. I really hate myself.

I pull my knees up to hide my frown from them. Now's not the time to get into one of my moods. I have plans tonight, and I'm not about to let my brain ruin my fun.

On the screen of my laptop, Nicolette's eating pizza and drinking wine in her apartment in Colorado Springs. Madison's curled up in bed at Mom and Dad's house with a blanket pulled up to her chin, and Mikayla's in her office at the university.

"If you had a real job, you'd understand the struggle, Cole," Mikayla murmurs. Her eyes are fixed on her work computer, fingers flying over the keyboard. Madison's squeaky yawn sounds like an agreement. "This school's top sport is volleyball, and I'm leaving my athletic department in the hands of a guy who doesn't even know what a libero is. For six weeks! I'm seriously considering giving birth in my office."

"And that is precisely why I will never have a real job." Nicolette raises her wineglass in a toast with herself before swallowing a mouthful. She still has glitter on her eyelids from her day at the rink. "Look at this, what is it, nine on the east coast? And Mad's half-asleep? It's Friday night, dude, fuck a real job."

"And you're drinking wine alone," Madison says, voice as sweet and soft as always. "None of us are winners here."

"I am choosing to drink wine alone," Nicolette insists. "I had options. This was the most enticing."

"What about you, Mickey?" Mikayla asks. "Aren't you supposed to be at a party with Bailey and Lilah?"

"I'm waiting for them to get here so we can walk together," I say.

"Is that what you're wearing?" Nicolette leans in closer to her screen, squinting at me with a slight curl to her lip.

I look down at my plain gray T-shirt and jeans. "What's wrong with what I'm wearing?"

"Boring," Nicolette says, drawing out the vowels. "How are you gonna pull college girls looking like that?"

"Nicolette," Madison scolds her.

"I'm not trying to *pull* anyone," I say.

"Ah, right." Nicolette rolls her eyes. "Hockey over everything. No distractions."

There's a knock on the door, loud and sharp. Before either Dorian or I can get up to answer it, the door opens and my other sisters, Bailey and Delilah, come striding in like they own the place, Jade following behind them. Bailey's cheeks are red and her hair's a disaster. She's been pregaming hard. The smell of alcohol wafts in after her as she takes one look at me and goes straight to my closet without a word, pulling out shirts and dropping them on the floor.

I haven't seen much of her at school so far. She's a thesis-ing senior with two boyfriends—Sidney and Karim—who spent their summer in Europe with USA Lacrosse, so she's been busy catching up with them when she's not working. But I was in Buffalo with her for a couple weeks over the summer, helping her run a youth lacrosse camp, so I've seen more of her than any of my other sisters recently.

Delilah and Jade cram themselves onto my bed on either side of me, and Delilah unplugs my headphones when she sees who I'm talking to. I hand the computer off to her and climb out of bed to monitor the mess Bailey's making of my closet. She yanks a black-and-red flannel off its hanger and shrugs it on over her black tank top, then digs right back in. She's my only sister who's shorter than me, so the sleeves of my shirt hang to her fingertips.

"What're you doing?" I ask over her shoulder.

Behind me, it sounds like Jade and Dorian are talking about the band posters on his wall, and Delilah is complaining about one of her professors to Mikayla, who had the same major as her.

"Finding you something to wear that doesn't make you look like a slob," Bailey says. After all that digging and throwing clothes all over my room, she finally settles on a plain white V-neck T-shirt. Seriously. How is that any better than what I've got on? She shoves it in my arms before opening the dresser drawers until she finds my jeans.

"We're supposed to stay in tonight," Dorian says hesitantly, like he's afraid to get on their bad side.

"Just tell Zero we took him to the lax house." Delilah

snickers and Jade gives her an elbow to the ribs like she knows all about the hockey-lacrosse rivalry. Delilah doesn't even flinch, just puts an arm across her shoulders. "He'll love that."

"Or don't," I mumble. Bailey throws my tightest pair of black jeans at me and motions for me to change before collapsing over Delilah's and Jade's laps to join the video chat.

I miss having us all together in the same room. It's such a rare thing, even being able to hear all their voices at once makes my heart squeeze.

I throw on the new outfit plus a hoodie for the walk, and Bailey tumbles off the bed to comb her hands through my hair until it meets her drunken standards. She and Delilah blow kisses at our older sisters while Jade waves, and I give Dorian the briefest of glances before saying, "Love you guys, bye," closing the laptop, and rushing out of the room.

I know I'll hear about that display of humanity later.

WE WALK THE two miles to the men's lacrosse house off campus, Bailey's arm linked through mine while Delilah gives Jade a piggyback ride the whole way.

"Sports really are good for something!" Jade cheers, pumping a fist over her head.

I can't help but smile at them. Even with Jade's lack of a sports background, they're so ridiculously perfect for each other it makes me want to puke.

"How are you gonna survive the night surrounded by jocks?" Bailey asks. She leans her head on my shoulder, and even though her legs and words are steady now, she'll be struggling with another drink or two.

"I'm dating a James," Jade says. "I have to survive a lifetime surrounded by you sports fiends." None of us can argue with that.

As soon as we get to the driveway of the lax house, there's the sound of muffled music and shouting. The smell of weed gets stronger the closer we get, until we find six people leaning over the railing on the back porch, passing a vape pen back and forth. A few of them look over their shoulders at the creak of our footsteps on the rickety wood. One of them calls out Bailey's name, long and slow.

"Save some for me," she says just before we go in the house.

We step right into a mass of bodies, people yelling and laughing in every room, the smell of liquor almost overwhelming. The bass makes the air vibrate around us, the music is so loud. One of the lamps is blown out, giving the living room this lowlight, dingy club feel.

The whole house is packed with both the men's and women's lacrosse teams and some of their friends. Delilah and Jade push their way toward the kitchen, but Bailey sticks with me, introducing me to her teammates and the guys. I've met some of them around campus, and they slap me on the back and offer me drinks. They have my sister on a pedestal as the captain of the women's team and a two-time Tewaaraton Award winner, so hockey fans or not, I'm nothing more than Bailey's brother to them.

I have this light feeling in my chest. A rare happiness

that comes from seeing one of my sisters be given the respect and recognition she deserves.

After a couple hours, I end up squished between Delilah and Jade on a couch that sinks so low, we might as well be on the floor. It smells like it's been soaked in alcohol and scrubbed down at least a dozen times over the years. I run a finger along the rim of an unopened beer can while one of my sister's boyfriends, Sidney, leans forward to spread a deck of cards facedown around a *Black Panther* collector's cup, explaining the King's Cup house rules. Bailey and Karim whisper to each other behind his back, all smiles and heart eyes. The three of them are squeezed onto the love seat across from us, and a bunch more people are on the floor around the table, a few lucky ones snagging an armchair for themselves. This isn't even half the people at this party.

But even with this crowd, I can't stop looking over at Bailey, Sid, and Karim. They've been together since their freshman year, and they're still going strong. Not Bailey and Sidney and Bailey and Karim. *Bailey, Sidney, Karim.* Sid and Karim show each other just as much affection as they do with Bailey.

It's so natural and easy with them, and that's the reason they're the only ones I've come out to besides Nova. Not even Delilah knows I'm bi.

Sid and Karim got lucky with the Royals. Lax bro and hockey culture are notoriously homophobic, but the entire Hartland athletics department is super vocal in their support of You Can Play and puts up a zero-tolerance policy for any kind of bigotry. Almost makes me feel like I could be open about myself one day.

Except when the hockey media caught wind of Bailey's polyam relationship, it was the most they'd ever talked about her. Everything she's done on the lacrosse field, all her awards and championships meant nothing. It was only a matter of time before Delilah got outed, too. She got a single sentence in an article about college hockey when she led the NCAA in points last season, but when they found out she's a lesbian, suddenly people knew who she was. Bailey and Delilah, the James family scandals . . . for now.

When Dad jumped in to defend them, it was the closest I've ever felt to him.

I crack open my beer and take a gulp. Then I lower my head and watch Karim lean forward to whisper in Sid's ear while Delilah and Jade flirt back and forth over my head, and take another one.

I swear I'm not jealous. I pretty much have a girlfriend. Kind of. I mean, Nova and I promised to marry each other if we're still single by thirty. It'll never happen, what with Nova being a supermodel with actual celebrities sending her roses and taking her to dinner in different countries every week. But she's my favorite person in the world. I don't deserve her and I'd be beyond lucky to have her.

I take out my phone and send Nova a picture of the table covered in facedown cards and beer cans as one of Bailey's teammates, Marcie, flips over an eight. "Mate," she says, and immediately looks at me. "Mickey James."

Everyone in the room's got something to say about that. I just lift my drink and reach across the table for a cheers with my new mate. Marcie's a sophomore attacker who won rookie of the year last year and will probably take over Bailey's captaincy when she graduates. She's a damn good lacrosse player, and she's got dimples when she smiles at me.

See? No need to be jealous.

BEING PAIRED UP right at the start of King's is a surefire way to get super drunk super fast. Karim makes a rule that everyone has to keep a bottle cap on their head during the game, which Marcie keeps failing at when she tilts her head toward me or laughs too hard. Then Sid makes another rule where we have to say *hashtag* in front of everything we say, which I just don't want to do, so we both are continuously chugging our drinks. Marcie ends up on the couch next to me at some point, probably around the time Jade climbs into Delilah's lap. She's got her arm draped over my shoulder and her head bent against mine.

I turn to say something to her, putting our faces close enough that we're breathing each other's air.

That's when the back door bursts open and Zero shouts from the other room, "Attention, lax bros and brahs!"

Zero. As in Luca Cicero. As in my captain.

"You have something that belongs to the men's hockey team," Zero says. "Please do return it."

"Kill me," I mutter as the clomping of footsteps finds its way into the den. Zero and Kovy stand in the archway, taking in the sight of me with a girl practically in my lap. They look like total opposites, what with Zero in his standard floral print, this time on a button-down and the brim of his snapback, and Kovy in his blue polo and gray chinos.

"Come on." Zero snaps his fingers at me like I'm a dog. "*Andiamo.* You've consorted with the enemy long enough."

I glare at him. I should tell him no, stay right here where I am.

But I can't hide from the team forever. After what happened at practice today, it'd be better to face the drama now than let it simmer till the season starts.

I push myself off the couch and brace for a second as the rush of my drinks finally hits me. My whole body thrums as I stalk toward my captains. They grin at me like they've accomplished some impossible feat and lead me outside, away from my sisters, away from Marcie, away from a night I was actually enjoying.

Kovy shoves a bottle of water at me on the back porch. "Sober up, Majesty. You got a long night ahead of you."

I take the bottle. My stomach is rolling and my tongue tastes like whiskey vomit. At least I'm walking in a straight line. I think.

"Are you hazing me?" I ask as we start down the hill back toward the main road.

Zero looks straight-up aghast at that. "You think we'd risk suspension with a team this good? We've made Frozen Four three seasons in a row. This is my last chance at a championship, and I am not throwing it away over some hazing scandal."

"We don't haze. We bond," Kovy adds. "And you've missed all our team bonding."

"I'm not social," I say.

Kovy gives this kind of bewildered laugh, short and high-pitched. "Which is why we just pulled you out of the lax house. Where Marcie was literally on top of you."

I roll my eyes. "Whatever."

Zero closes his eyes and shakes his head as we pass under a streetlight. "Look. We've got a lot of talent on this team. But that won't matter if one of our best players isn't on board with the rest of us. Is it because of the royalty garbage? If it makes you that uncomfortable, we'll stop."

"That's not it," I say quickly. His niceness makes me feel, I don't know, guilty, I guess?

"Then what is it? We can't fix it if you don't tell us."

I kick a rock down the hill. There's a perfect view of the lake from here. Hell, there's a perfect view of the lake from most places on and around campus. Part of me wishes I could stay here and get a degree, just so I can keep seeing this every day.

"Cauler?" Kovy asks in a way that says they know, they've just been waiting for me to say it.

"No," I say firmly. No way am I admitting Jaysen's antagonism gets to me. "It's not anything you can control. It's just. Sometimes I need a break from hockey. Can't get that hanging around hockey players all the time."

It feels like the wrong thing to say. This is why I usually don't talk. Nothing I say is ever right.

Zero hums. "I'm gonna let you in on a little secret, Mickey. We're more than just hockey players. I'm also a psych student and a volunteer firefighter in the summer. Maverick here? He writes Dragon Age fanfiction—"

"Bro!" Kovy says.

"—and already has a job lined up with a game developer after graduation. And a bunch of us are also huge nerds who play *D and D* once a month."

"I'm a halfling barbarian," Kovy says, tilting his chin up proudly.

"If you spent any time with us, you'd know all this. Because we hardly talk about hockey outside of practice. We need breaks, too."

Kovy sucks air through his teeth with an exaggerated wince. "Yeah, about that. Tonight might be a little hockey-centric. Just 'cause we got some things to work out."

"Great," I mumble.

The hockey house is right on the lake. So close I can hear the water against the shoreline as we head through the front door. It's nicer than the lax house, with an actual entryway and an arch that opens to a living room with a big sectional and one of those curved TVs. The floor looks like wood but feels more like plastic when I take off my shoes. There are so many sneakers piled at the door, I doubt I'll be able to find mine when I leave.

Zero and Kovy head right for the stairs, but I trail behind, taking the place in. I catch a glimpse of a clean kitchen, white cabinets and stainless steel, granite countertops and sliding glass doors out to a porch over the water.

If I stayed here another couple years, I would live in this house. One of the rooms we pass on the second floor would be mine.

I wonder how the hockey media would react to that. If at the draft combine I told every team that interviews me that I'm staying in school another three years. All because I got drunk one night and decided the campus was too pretty and my captains too nice to walk away from.

Talk about a James family scandal.

It sounds like people are wrestling above our heads, and my heart does this anxious kind of fluttering when Kovy opens the door to the attic, as if I'm about to be faced with a room full of strangers. Colie's straight-up cackling up there. I've heard it enough at practice to pick it out from all the other laughter coming down the stairs.

Half the carpet in the attic is painted like a rink. They've got a game of three-on-three knee hockey going. My knees hurt just at the memory of playing with my sisters on the concrete floor of our basement as kids. I wonder if Mom and Dad still have the collection of mini sticks we built up over the years.

The team's crowded onto couches on the other side of the room, cheering and shouting as they watch. The freshmen are all packed onto the smallest one. Jaysen's head is thrown back, laughing so hard he's got his hands clutched in his own shirt.

For the love of god, please kill me now.

There are cases of beer stacked on the floor and a few half-empty bottles of vodka scattered around.

Dorian's the first to notice us. He shoves his fist in the air and shouts, "His Majesty has arrived!"

My face gets hot when they all look at me and start cheering. Doesn't help when I catch a glimpse of Jaysen's dimples before his smile vanishes at the sight of me.

"Put him on the rink!" someone shouts. The knee hockey game has ended with our interruption. A few of the guys who were playing lie breathless on the floor while the rest of them go for the alcohol. "He's used to being that close to the ground!"

They all laugh again. I roll my eyes. Zero shoves my shoulder and says, "Join the rest of the rooks on the shitty couch, if it pleases Your Majesty."

Jaysen keeps his eyes on me as I make my way over, a hint of that burning rage from earlier sparking in them while I try to keep my expression blank. My eyes feel too wide and my mouth is dry, my heart still doing that sick-butterfly thing like a ten-year-old faced with his first real crush.

I blame the alcohol.

I sit on the arm of the couch and try not to act too surprised when Dorian leans over and punches me in the shoulder. "Glad you showed up, bro," he says with his standard level of excitement.

"Sure," I say. Like I had a choice.

Zero claps his hands to get everyone's attention, but it takes a minute or two for the giggling and snickering to die down. "Here's the deal. Season hasn't even started and we're already off to a rocky start. We're taking the NCAA this year, but only if we learn to operate as a cohesive unit. There's rivalries and cliques and crap attitudes all over this team, and we gotta get over it. So we're gonna play a little game, hash out some of this tension. Maverick, would you like to demonstrate?"

Kovy busts out a massive grin. "Of course. Colie? If you'd join me?"

Colie staggers to his feet and almost trips over some of the guys in his haste to get to Kovy. They face each other, holding each other's hands in the space between them. Some of the guys wolf whistle and catcall them, and Colie bats his eyelashes at Kovy to play it up.

Zero's smirking the whole time he explains the rules. "This game is all about honesty. Getting your issues out into the open, listening to what others have to say."

Ugh, god. I can hear it now.

You never smile.

You think you're better than us.

Your dad was a better hockey player than you.

I don't need to hear it all again.

"For every negative," Zero continues, "you have to say something positive to balance it out. When someone says something about you, you can't argue it. You take it in, accept it, and move on. Boys?" He motions for Kovy and Colie to start.

Kovy adjusts his grip on Colie's hands and puffs up his chest. "Colie, when you flop around in the crease thinking you look like Dominik Hasek, you actually look like a halibut in its death throes."

"Of course," Colie says without hesitation, even though it's not at all true. "Sometimes your morning breath is so atrocious, it makes me dream about drowning you in mouthwash."

"I don't doubt it. That new painting you're working on for your portfolio is superb, bro. I'd go to an art museum to see it."

I didn't even know Colie was in any art classes. Is he majoring in it? I'll have to ask Jade.

"I appreciate that, Kovy. That play you made in practice today was a beauty. You should try it in a game."

"I think I'll do that."

They let go of each other and find spots on the couches

so the next pair can go up. I wrack my brain for any compliment I could give Jaysen and come up with nothing. I can almost feel his eyes boring into the side of my head, thinking about all the things he wants to say to me. It's mostly petty things for the rest of them, like, *you took my clothes out of the washer and left them on the counter so they smelled horrible*, and *you're a hockey player, how is your ass so bony*, and *you still owe me five bucks from that road trip to Boston freshman year*. Even when they do get more serious, like a consistent problem in practice or actual hurt feelings, they're followed up with some over-the-top compliment so things don't get too heated.

It's obvious Jaysen and I are the real reason this is happening. Barbie and Dorian stick to each other like glue, and the upperclassmen are closer with the ones they came in with, but the team's not really cliquey.

Sure enough, when Jaysen gets up from the couch and grabs me by the shoulder of my hoodie, the guys go nuts. I've had a few more beers by this point, and it all goes to my head as soon as I stand up. My vision lags behind my eyes as I follow Jaysen to the center of everyone's attention.

"The moment we've all been waiting for," someone calls out from the couches. They quiet down while Jaysen and I stare at each other. His black jeans are so tight, I don't know how the hell he managed to get them on. He's cut the sleeves off his band tee, so I get a good look at his skin through the open sides of his shirt, the bold black tattoo along his rib cage. A dead-looking tree rising from overgrown black shrubbery, the shadows of more dead trees in the background, crows rising from the branches. It looks like scenery from a horror movie, but it's also kinda hot.

That on top of the black hoops in his nose and bottom lip, the black-rimmed glasses, the stretched ears, and oh my god my mouth is dry and he is literally watching me check him out.

I avert my eyes down to the floor between us, clear my throat and try to build up some saliva in my mouth. And that's when Jaysen's hands come forward, palms up, inviting me to hold them. He's got calluses on his palms, right below his fingers. His fingers are long enough they could probably wrap all the way around my wrist, and the veins in his forearms stick out, drawing my eyes right up to the curve of his biceps and— This is not the time.

His hands are warm, his grip strong when I finally reach for them. God, I hope he can't feel me shaking.

"Your Grace," he says. I look up at his face. "Your slap shot is the most pathetic thing I've ever seen in hockey."

Okay, yeah, I can't argue that.

I lick my lips. Try not to let my voice croak too much when I say, "Right. Jaysen, your hesitation to go for loose pucks along the boards is going to lose us games."

His eyes narrow. I've hit a sore spot right out of the gate.

"Of course," he says through his teeth, like he has to keep himself from snapping it at me. "Delilah is a way better hockey player than you."

I scoff. That's the truest thing anyone has said tonight. "Obviously. You're weak on the backhand."

"Sure. You skate like you're trying to chop the ice with your blades."

"Totally. You're way too overconfident in your stick-handling skills."

"You have the worst case of little man syndrome I've ever seen."

"You chew your gum too loud."

"You're soulless."

"You're an asshole."

We rattle off one jab after the other, barely pausing to catch our breaths, hardly taking in each other's words before throwing our own back. By the time we get all our hatred out, our hands are sweaty and we're both breathing like we've been hurling fists instead of insults. Jaysen is glaring with narrowed eyes that are probably a mirror of my own.

The rest of the team is quiet around us. There was none of the laughter or goading like there was when everyone else was up here. If it weren't for the pop of beer cans opening, I probably would've forgotten they're even here.

Someone clears their throat, but Jaysen and I only have eyes for each other.

"You guys owe each other, like, thirty compliments now," Zero says.

Jaysen swallows. I watch his throat move with it as he adjusts his grip on my hands. I almost try to pull away, to wipe the sweat on my jeans, to make this less awkward. But he's not letting go. My hoodie's not doing me any favors, trapping the heat that flushes my body every time I acknowledge the fact that I'm holding Jaysen Caulfield's hands. I just hope they all blame anger for how red my cheeks must be.

Neither of us says anything for a minute. I'm not about to go first. He started with the insults, he can start this, too.

"You, uh . . ." Jaysen shifts his weight from foot to foot. "You got a decent wrister. I guess."

"You're pretty good on the backcheck," I say slowly.

He clears his throat. "Your passes usually go tape to tape."

"Sometimes you make pretty good plays."

"You got okay presence in the slot."

The insults came rapid fire, but this is like pulling teeth. There's a good five-second delay between every compliment, and Jaysen's got sweat springing up on his forehead from the strain of it. We run out of things to say about hockey after a few slow, torturous minutes, and then we stand there in uncomfortable silence.

I glance over at Zero like *please let this end*, but he raises his eyebrows and twists his wrist like *you're not done yet*.

Kill. Me. Now.

I take a deep breath through my nose and let it out in a huff before looking back at Jaysen. He sniffs, scrunches his nose, and keeps his eyes on the ground between our feet when he says, "Your eyes are a nice color."

Um. What?

"Now we're talking!" Kovy shouts. There's clapping, and the catcalling starts up again and my head feels like it's about to spontaneously combust. My stomach twists and I have to swallow hard so I don't throw up all over Jaysen's chest.

"Uh . . . ," I start. How am I supposed to follow that up without giving myself away? Because the only compliments coming to mind right now are things like those piercings *do* things to me and those jeans fit you way too nicely, please take them off.

Jaysen chews his gum almost aggressively, avoiding my eyes at all costs. Right. The gum. That's a safe one, yeah?

"Your breath always smells like cinnamon?" I try.

Colie's wailing cackle starts up again, and I'm pretty sure my face is literally on fire right now.

"Your haircut works for you," Jaysen says.

"You have decent style?" Everything I say comes out like a question, which I guess helps the illusion that I have no idea what I'm talking about. Maybe. Probably not.

"The gravelly voice kinda suits you."

"Your tattoo's kinda cool."

Jaysen lifts his eyes a little. I swear they latch on to where my sleeve is pushed up just below my elbow, then slowly follow my forearm down to my wrist and back up again, to my bicep. "You're pretty fit for being so short."

I think I might pass out. Was he just *checking me out*? No. Of course not. He was just looking for something to say. That was definitely not the same kind of eye-sweep I did to him minutes ago in a *damn you're hot* kind of way. Not even close.

"You have . . . dimples?" I kind of splutter it out, and that's it, I am done. I pull my hands out of Jaysen's and scrub them against my jeans. He's quick to turn away from me, and I keep my face turned toward the ground in the vainest attempt to hide my blushing ever.

The guys cheer and clap for us like we've reached some kind of stunning breakthrough. Zero holds out shots for both of us and I toss mine back as soon as it's in my hand, then hold the glass out for another. Zero pours it with a proud smile on his face. I find an empty spot on a couch away from the other freshmen and drink in hopes of forgetting this ever happened.

Honestly, I would've rather been hazed.

FIVE

'm stuck here for the night, so I might as well have some fun.

Dorian and Barbie end up on the couch with me, crowding me so close between them I can hardly move my arms. My vision lags as I look around the room at my teammates, laughing and drinking.

I dance. Someone dances with me. I think it's Barbie, judging by how tall he feels against my back. For a second I'm sure Colie's gonna suffocate he's laughing so hard.

We all stare at Dorian when he shouts, "Hey, listen. Guys, listen! Rude-ass bitches. Anyway. Space. Don't give me that look, bro. Fucking space. Think about this. The universe is never-ending, yeah? That's terrifying. But it's gotta be never-ending because if it ended, what would be on the other side? Scary, right?"

And I say, "No, you know what's scarier than space? The ocean, dude. It's what, like, seventy percent of the planet, but we've barely seen five percent of it. There could be sea monsters everywhere and we wouldn't even know it."

"Speaking of the ocean," Colie says. "You know how salt water burns your eyes? And sweat? But our tears are salty, so why don't they burn our eyes, too? Wicker, you're premed. I need answers!"

I play a few games of knee hockey, giving it just as much effort as I put in on the ice.

I stand up and fall on Dorian and Barbie and everyone laughs.

I think I might be happy.

I don't fall asleep on a couch with Jaysen.

But that's where I wake up. We're facing opposite directions with our legs tangled together, his toes digging painfully into my inner thigh. His face is buried in the back cushions, hands tucked into his armpits.

The upperclassmen must've all found their way down to their rooms, because it's only freshmen and sophomores on the floor and couches up here. Dorian and Barbie are on the same couch I shared with them most of the night, Dorian curled into a ball to make up for Barbie's size.

Everyone else is still asleep. Someone's snoring.

My tongue feels thick and dry and my stomach rolls as I slowly push myself upright. Jaysen shifts when I try to move my legs, so I stop. I'm not ready to face the awkwardness when he wakes up. My head must've been wrapped in a blanket and bludgeoned repeatedly with the way it throbs. The raging hangover still doesn't cover up the aching in my knees from the knee hockey.

But the most concerning thing is the fact that I am half-naked tangled up on a couch with Jaysen Caulfield. And I really have to pee.

I find my T-shirt and hoodie in a pile on the floor a few feet away. My jeans bite painfully into my hips as I try to get up again, careful not to jostle Jaysen too much, stopping whenever he stirs.

How much time am I missing? Did I stumble over to this couch after falling on Dorian and Barbie? Or was I still up for hours after that? It's the last thing I remember, but I don't even know what time it was at that point. As much as I love to drink, I don't ever black out like this. I hate it. I hate not knowing. What'd I say? How much did I embarrass myself? What kind of secrets did I give up?

As soon as I get free from Jaysen's legs and my bare feet touch the floor, he startles awake with a sharp breath and a hard kick to my hip. I hiss at the pain and slap his foot away while he looks at me with bleary eyes. He blinks a few times, and I drop my face into my hands, rubbing my temples. This whole house is spinning.

"Morning, Jesus," Jaysen says, voice all sleep-rough. I turn my head and give him a *what the hell* look. He rolls his eyes. "C'mon, you don't remember that? You climbed on the back of the couch, claimed to be Jesus, and demanded to be crucified just so you could rise again. Then you passed out."

Okay, first of all, I need to stop drinking. But also, if I passed out on this couch, that means I was here first, so Jaysen chose to share it with me.

"Well, shit." I clear my throat. Reach for one of the full bottles of water littering the floor. "I'm way too white to be Jesus."

"That you are." Jaysen sits up and stretches his arms above his head. I chug my water and keep my eyes fixed on the wall. "You're also way more tolerable drunk."

My face burns. I don't know if it's humiliation or anger or maybe a little bit of both. I stagger to my feet and go for the rest of my clothes. It takes five tries to get my head in the right hole of my T-shirt.

"Good news is you've earned the right to Terzo," Jaysen adds when I stay silent. His voice is a little softer, like he actually feels bad for insulting me for once.

"No more 'Your Grace,' then?" I ask roughly.

He shrugs. He's stretched himself out on the couch now, one hand behind his head, the other resting on his stomach. I try not to look at him directly. "I still like it," he says. "But Terzo looks good on you."

Okay, yep, he's definitely still drunk. Or maybe sleepiness makes him weird, because this is not normal Jaysen Caulfield behavior.

I pull on my hoodie and shove both hands through my hair as I look around for my socks. They may be a lost cause. For a second I think about throwing myself back on the couch and getting more sleep, but that would mean setting myself up for even more awkwardness once everyone else wakes up.

Doesn't matter that I don't know my way back to campus from here. Doesn't matter that every step feels like I'm walking through sand. I need to get as far from this house and Jaysen and last night as possible.

Jesus. *You have dimples.* I really said that, didn't I? And Jaysen likes the color of my eyes, and my haircut, and my voice. Now I'm gonna be thinking about that all day.

"Hey." Jaysen stops me halfway to the door. He's quiet

enough not to wake the others, but honestly with how out they all look, I could probably start screaming right now—like I kind of want to—and they wouldn't even flinch. "Sorry for being a dick all the time."

I blink at him. "Okay?" I croak.

He tilts his head a little, scratches his chest. Looks at me like he's waiting for something.

I frown, but it only takes a second before I realize what he wants. "Sorry for breaking your stick."

Jaysen blows air through his teeth. "You're lucky this school's paying for my equipment now. Oh, and stop calling me Jaysen. You sound like my mother."

I am out. I slip from the attic and ease myself down the stairs, as much as I'd love to just throw myself to the bottom at this point. I put a hand over my mouth and squeeze. I feel beyond sick. Like I've died a thousand times over.

At least when Jaysen . . . or Cauler, I guess, is being an asshole, I have something to temper my attraction to him. If he starts being nice to me, it's all over.

A few of the upperclassmen are in the living room when I make my way down, slumped on the couches watching cartoons, eating cereal, and drinking coffee.

"Yeah, Terzo!" Zero says through a mouthful of cereal. Milk dribbles down his chin.

"Jesus has risen!" Kovy calls.

They all laugh. The sound is a drill into my skull. I keep walking, groaning out some kind of unintelligible hungover greeting that only makes them laugh some more.

And with that, I leave my team behind.

My team.

Shit.

JUST BECAUSE THEY'RE my team doesn't mean they're my friends. They seem to have missed that memo.

I don't know if there's some big heart-to-heart buried in my blacked-out memories from last night, but the others don't look at me like they're waiting for me to leave so they can talk crap about me anymore. They act like they want to talk to me. Like they want me to sit with them in the dining hall and hang out in the team lounge between classes. And like they want me on the ice for more than my wrist shot.

It's absolutely horrifying. Whenever one of them calls me Terzo, I get heart palpitations.

Cauler bumps my shoulder as he skates up beside me at practice one night. His grin is less vicious than it used to be, but it's still just as smug. He leans down to say, "I've noticed something about you, Terzo."

"What's that?" I keep my tone flat and bored, but he's got my attention.

We look out over the ice together from the blue line as drills go on around us. Cauler shifts his weight from skate to skate, knocking into my shoulder repeatedly. I don't know if he even notices, but it's got my nerves all coiled up inside me, heat flushing my cheeks.

"You'd rather party with the laxers than us," he says. "And you play hockey like it's lacrosse."

I scoff. "How?"

"You camp behind the net half the time. And your favorite trick shot is the Michigan. I think . . ." He taps a gloved finger to the cage of his helmet, right over his chin, looking up at the rafters. "I may have stumbled on something you like. Shame it had to be lacrosse. The boys'll shun you for sure."

I scrunch my nose at him, and then it's my turn on the give-and-go drill. I work through it effortlessly, passing to Dorian at the goal line as I sprint for the hash marks. I get the return pass from Dorian and change directions seamlessly, curving toward the low slot with my eyes fixed on Colie's through his mask. I fake one way, then put the puck over his other shoulder with a wrist shot so quick it has the whole team whooping. I take my spot in the feeder line at the back of the net and wait for Cauler to make it back over to me.

My heart is hammering against my rib cage.

Cauler's shot rings off the pipe on his turn, but he doesn't seem concerned when he rejoins me.

"You're reaching," I say. "Even Gretzky camped."

"You would compare yourself to Gretzky." That touch of disdain is back in his voice and my heart sinks with it. He's been less obvious with his hatred since Saturday, but it still comes through every once in a while. "But it doesn't help your case. He played box lacrosse, too."

"You saying you never pick up a lacrosse stick in the summer?"

"'Course I do." He shrugs dismissively. "Lot of hockey players do."

"So what's the problem?"

"Loyalty, Your Grace."

I take my turn receiving the pass and giving it back

before heading to the blue line. My pulse is still buzzing under my skin by the time Cauler is beside me again.

"So," he says. "You like my dimples, huh?"

I almost choke on my own saliva. "What the—" I splutter, sliding back from him a step. Talk about an abrupt and ridiculous topic change.

Cauler laughs, just this single *ha!* at my reaction. His smile puts those dimples in his cheeks, and I have to look away. "That game is made to embarrass people into getting over themselves. All that blushing proves you've got a soul at least."

"Do I?" I keep my voice level, scrambling to reassemble whatever's left of my dignity.

"It's very small and tarnished beyond repair, but yeah, it's there."

He slings his stick across his shoulders and drapes his arms over it. I put mine butt-down on the ice, hands clutching the blade, and rest my chin on my gloves. We stare at each other. Cauler chews on his mouth guard, half of it wrapped around his cheek like a fishhook. He's one of the few Royals who choose to wear one. Probably 'cause of that bad concussion that almost ended his playing career a few years ago.

Even with all those insults I threw at him the other day, the caution he plays with now is really his only flaw as a hockey player. He's still got grit and can take a check as well as anybody, but he doesn't like to risk a check from behind and go for loose pucks along the boards unless an opponent gets there first. Especially by the benches.

Not that I really blame him. When you take a hit from

behind so bad the sound of your head ringing off the stanchion can be heard throughout the arena, fracturing a vertebra
and putting you out for months, it'd be more concerning if
you didn't have some lingering fear.

Cauler takes in a long breath, shoulders rising with it,
and opens his mouth to speak.

"Will you two dusters stop making heart eyes at each
other and shoot some goddamn puck?" someone calls from
the goal line.

The others join in the chirping until Coach can get them
back under control. I use the distraction to put some distance
between me and Cauler. I swear the air between us was
starting to feel dangerously electric for a second there, but
I know it's all in my head. A few forced compliments aren't
going to make him suddenly fall in love with me. There's
still barely restrained malice behind every look and word he
has for me.

But I catch him looking at me again a few minutes later.

SIX

OCTOBER

The first week of October officially brings the coaches into our daily lives. Our strength and conditioning coach takes stock of our progress in the weight room in the morning. We start having all our meals in the players' lounge with the assistant coaches to make sure we're sticking to the nutrition plan and not gorging on bacon and home fries. Colie's goalie coach, Coach Hein, sticks her head into our classes throughout the day to see if we actually go to them.

The temperature outside has been creeping steadily downward all week, to the point where it's not a relief to step into the cold arena anymore. Still, October is my favorite month of the year, not only because it's the start of the hockey season. The woods are turning red and orange, and the air smells like Halloween.

I have a meeting with Coach a few days before our opening exhibition to go over progress and lay out expectations, and he tells me I need to put in more effort in the weight room. I have to restrain myself from rolling my eyes. Not like Dad's been telling me the same thing every single phone call or anything.

I just don't see any room to improve there. I'm plenty strong for someone my size. Then Cauler skates up to me at practice one day and says, "Y'know, I can bench a hundred pounds more than you."

I narrow my eyes at him. Has he been talking to Coach or something? Conspiring against me?

"NHL Network," Cauler explains when I say nothing. "Their latest comparison."

I squeeze my fingers around my stick and make a point of looking up at him, then down at myself, like, hello? He's twice my size, of course he can lift more. "I mean . . . duh?"

Cauler laughs, all dimples and crinkly eyes, and I just about melt into the ice. It's nice, making him laugh. He can make any emotion look good, but this is my favorite.

As much as I brush it off to his face, though, it still gets under my skin. Dad and Coach pointing it out is one thing. Once the NHL Network and the hottest guy I've ever seen latch on to it, it's enough to get me out of bed on Sunday morning, the only day I have to recover, to go to the gym.

I add more weight to the barbell and lie down on the bench, curling my fingers around the bar. The gym is quiet. Even those people who basically live off protein shakes and post daily locker room mirror pics don't wanna be here this early on a Sunday. The student worker is falling asleep behind her desk.

I close my eyes and take a few deep breaths, and when I

open them again, just as I'm about to lift, Cauler steps into view above me. He looks down at me and frowns. I relax my grip on the bar, but the rest of me stays tense.

"I know you're not about to lift without a spotter," he says. He moves to help me lift the bar from the rack, like he actually cares about my safety or something. I'd let myself be crushed under the barbell before admitting it, but he's right. Lifting alone was a bad idea. Especially with the added weight.

I keep my eyes on the ceiling past Cauler's head and try to keep the strain off my face as I go through the set.

"Why are you here?" he asks.

"Why not?" I say on a heavy exhale.

"I'm here most Sundays this time. You never put in these extra hours."

I finish my reps and let him help me replace the bar on the rack. My arms are jelly. I rest my hands on my chest to let them recover. My heart pounds in my fingertips, and I stay focused on the ceiling as I catch my breath. Cauler keeps his hands on the bar, leaning over my face, looking down at me, waiting.

He's probably expecting me to ignore him. Which is probably why I don't.

"You know why."

Cauler's eyes on me are heavy. I'm distinctly aware of the rise and fall of my own chest, the sweat on my skin showing through the cut-off sides of my shirt, the goose bumps rising on my arms when one of the oscillating fans blows over me. I feel more present in my body than I have in weeks, with him looking down at me.

His eyebrows are thick. Jaw and cheekbones sharp. The hoops in his nose and lip are just as eye-catching as the holes in his earlobes. His face is schooled and calm now, but I've seen how intensely expressive he can be in glances at practice and across campus. I get a whiff of that cinnamon gum he's always chewing, and I swear he could drop the weights right on my throat and I wouldn't even notice.

When I finally look at his eyes, he is not looking at my face. There's this split second where I swear he's actually full-on checking me out, taking advantage of me being laid out like this, but then his eyes are locked on mine, and he's looking at me so blankly, I must have imagined it.

Wishful thinking and all that.

"Why do you hate it so much?" he asks. I don't need to ask what he's talking about.

I tear my eyes off him and look back at the ceiling. "I don't."

Even in my periphery, I see his face change. Soften into something almost like understanding. Like for a second he realizes I'm not just some asshole taking his glory from him without earning it.

"Media's gonna get a riot out of us on a line together," he says, standing up straight to spot my next lift. He waits till I'm too busy with the weights to respond to add, "First time someone tries to give you credit for my success, I'm putting you on blast."

I CAN'T FOCUS at study hall that afternoon. I sit at my carrel scribbling lazy circles in the margins of my Italian homework. I took it for an easy A while brushing up on my mother's first language, but it's bad for my attention span.

Especially with the exhibition in a couple days. The moment of truth. A sneak peek at the season that will make or break me when it comes time for the draft.

I hold my head up with an elbow on the desk and start scribbling furiously on my homework. It doesn't matter how ruined the paper is. I'm never gonna be able to focus enough to finish it.

One of the boys snickers, most definitely *not* at his homework, and Zero yells at him, "Working hard or hardly working?"

I sigh and open my laptop to pull up the NHL's prospect rankings. I'm still at the top of North American Skaters, with Cauler right under me. Number three is a guy named Alex Nakamoto. His position is pretty much secure, but below that, guys are always shifting. I click on height to sort the list tallest to shortest, and now I'm dead last. The next shortest guy is five foot eight, and he's ranked in the two hundreds. The shortest European skater is five foot nine.

I don't know why I do this to myself.

My phone lights up on my desk, silenced to avoid Zero's wrath. I squint at the notification that pops up, because there's no way I'm seeing that right. A message. From Jaysen Caulfield.

Jaysen: Lets try to find some
common ground Terzo

I swallow hard, resting my head on my arm on the desk and holding my phone in my free hand. I could ignore it.

Should ignore it. I'm supposed to be doing my homework, keeping myself eligible to play.

But apparently I'm a masochist.

Mickey: Why

Jaysen: So we don't kill each other before draft day

Mickey: Pretty sure competing for top pick is common ground enough

Jaysen: Outside of hockey

Mickey: Zero and Kovy put you up to this?

Jaysen: ... maybe Zero said coach threatened his captaincy if he couldn't get us to get along

Mickey: Dramatic

Jaysen: His job to bond the team

Mickey: I didnt think there was still a problem after that party

Jaysen: He wants to be sure i guess

I close my eyes and take a deep breath. At least talking to someone will pass the time until study hall ends. Even if that someone is Cauler.

Mickey: Ugh.
Fine.

Jaysen: K so
Favorite band?

Mickey: Tragically hip

Jaysen: Are you kidding me?
You hate hockey
But your fav band
Is the hip

My eyes narrow. Just because they're Canadian and have some songs about hockey and they're a staple in arenas and just about every NHL team honored Gord Downie when he died does not mean I wouldn't be able to like them and hate hockey at the same time. Why is he so convinced I hate it anyway?

That would take too long to type out.

So I just say:

Mickey: I told you
I don't hate hockey
Whats yours i guess

Jaysen: The amity affliction

Mickey: Never heard of em

Jaysen: Bc your uncultured obvs
Your turn

Mickey: Color?

Jaysen: Black.
Duh

Mickey: Blue

Jaysen: Movie?
Don't say miracle or i will end you

Mickey: Idk
Spiderman with tom holland

Jaysen: Now we're talking
Thor ragnarok

Mickey: Tv show

Jaysen: I don't watch much tv
But
FMA:brotherhood

Dammit. That's my favorite, too. But I don't wanna admit that to him. I kind of want to stop liking it altogether. First he takes my hockey position, and now my favorite show, too?

I'll never watch it again if it means separating myself from him.

Mickey: idk I mostly just
watch hgtv

Jaysen: what's your middle name?

Mickey: You really think we're
gonna have the same middle name

Jaysen: No
Just curious
Mine's daniel

Mickey: Liam

Jaysen: That the same as
the mickeys before you?

Mickey: Ya

Jaysen: Damn.
Individuality is really frowned
upon for you james men huh

Mickey: You think

I stare at my phone until it relocks itself. Then I stare at my reflection in the black screen. He doesn't respond. I guess it's technically my turn to ask a question, but I don't know how to . . . get to know people, I guess? How to make friends or what to do with them after. I have Nova, yeah, but that's because we were forced into each other's lives as infants and I lived down the hall from her throughout puberty. We couldn't get rid of each other if we tried at this point.

But I mean, it's not like Cauler's trying to be my friend here. And I'm not trying to be his. We just have to get along for Zero's sake.

SEVEN

y entire world narrows down to hockey on the day of our exhibition.

My body carries me to classes and gets me to the rink and puts me on the bus to Ontario for my first college hockey game, but my head plays no part in any of it, only coming alive when I step onto the ice in my black-and-purple uniform. Hartland across my chest above a crown. *James III* across my shoulders over the number 17.

It's just another hockey game.

It doesn't even count toward stats.

I just have to play my game and everything will be fine.

It's a mantra I repeat to myself through the warm-ups, all the way to puck drop to keep myself calm. Every time I catch a glimpse of Cauler, sharing my ice and uniform, I have to start over.

The real hockey media isn't going to bother with an exhibition, but some student-looking reporter with a Mustangs mic pulls me aside in the hall outside the visitors' locker room after a scoreless first period. My hair is slicked with water, and sweat that drips from my chin and stings my lips and burns my eyes, but they stick a camera in my face and start rattling off questions like they expect it to be second nature to me.

Most of the Royals keep walking by like this is normal, but Cauler and Zero both pause behind the camera guy. Cauler looks about as irritated as he always does when I get special attention, but Zero crosses his arms and watches me closely as I assure the kid with the mic that twenty minutes of hockey isn't going to determine the entire outcome of our season.

The rest of the questions are easy to answer with minimal brain power, and after a while, I realize I've been staring over the camera guy's shoulder as I speak. Right at Cauler. I blink back into focus, and he smirks at me. Raises one eyebrow. I clear my throat and look back at the interviewer right as he tilts the mic back in my direction.

"Sorry," I say. "What was that?"

He fumbles for a second before taking a breath and starting over. "Analysts have been saying recently that Jaysen Caulfield's stock has been rising. Does that make you feel threatened at all?"

My face twitches. I see Cauler shift out of the corner of my eye, but I refuse to look at him. I don't wanna see how smug that made him.

"Of course not," I say slowly, shrugging a shoulder. "He's a great hockey player and whatever team gets him, first or second'll be super lucky. It doesn't matter what order we're drafted in. He's my teammate; all that matters is how we work together on the ice."

Cauler's laugh draws my attention back to him just as he and Zero step around the camera guy. Zero grabs my jersey and starts pulling me away. "What does matter is that you're missing Coach's intermission speech," he says. The student reporter is too caught off guard to say anything.

Zero leads us the rest of the way to the locker room, and Cauler crowds against me as the door closes behind us. I can feel him against my back, hovering over my shoulder as he says, "I'm a great hockey player, huh?"

I roll my eyes, even as my heart clenches with his voice almost right in my ear. "Gotta play nice for the cameras."

He laughs again. Sometimes I can't tell if he's mocking me or if he just really enjoys seeing me get taken down a notch. Probably both.

"Nice of you three to join us," Coach says as I sink into my borrowed stall. I don't respond, keeping my eyes on the whiteboard he's used to draw up a new play.

"Wannabe sports reporter was attempting to render him comatose," Zero says, motioning to the muted TV on the far wall playing a delay of the interview. I hardly recognize myself on the screen. The flush in my cheeks from almost ten minutes of ice time can't hide the sick dullness of the rest of me. The dark bags under my eyes, the hollowness in my cheeks. I watch myself bullshit my way through the questions, and I have no idea how no one else has caught on all these years. My mask is nowhere near as good as I thought it was.

I take in every one of Coach's words and I know I'll be able to pick up the new play when I step on the ice, but I don't exactly pay attention. My heartbeat is a too-fast flutter, breaths too shallow to fill my lungs. Sweat pools in the fingertips of my gloves until I pull them off and wipe my hands on my soaked jersey.

Does that make you feel threatened?

I close my eyes. Of course it makes me feel threatened. I've only been told I'd be the top pick since the day I was born. It's like whatever comes of my career after that day doesn't matter as long as I'm picked first just like Dad and Grampa.

How am I supposed to play normally, on the same line with the guy who has a good chance of taking away everything I've worked for? The thing I was literally made for. Every pass I send him has a chance of ruining my life.

I open my eyes to find Cauler looking right at me. He doesn't turn away when I catch him staring. Just tilts his head and lowers his eyebrows. I don't know what he thinks he's seeing.

We watch each other, Cauler solid and calm and me struggling to keep it together, until our teammates jostle us to our feet for a cheer before heading back to the ice. I score once in our 3-0 win, but my celly's nothing more than a sigh of relief toward the rafters.

Doesn't matter that Cauler has the assist.

MY HEART SURGES when my phone lights up on the bus ride home, and plummets when I see it's Delilah in the group chat. I don't know why I expected it to be Cauler.

Delilah's message is just a string of exclamation points and emojis and *i'm screaming* in the preview. I sigh as I open it. She sent an article with a picture of some old dude in a suit smiling, the headline only showing "Former NHL All-Star Com"—before it runs out of space.

It takes me a second to make the connection between that cut-off statement and Delilah's excitement, because I honestly never thought I'd see the day. I click the link, and sure enough, it's an article about a retired NHL player named Aaron Johansson coming out as gay.

He talks about hockey's macho culture, the rampant homophobia, the fear. He's been retired for more than twenty years and is just now comfortable coming out to the public because of people like Harrison Browne, Jessica Platt, Yanic Duplessis.

I don't bother with the comments. I'm sure there are plenty of people screaming their support like Delilah, but there's always gonna be the trolls. I'm not that much of a masochist.

I skim through the article again, waiting to feel something. Some kind of camaraderie. Relief. Excitement. Hope. I exit back to the group chat as my sisters' comments flood in, all of them saying how awesome it is. I should be agreeing. I should be *living*. Instead, I say:

Mickey: Talk to me when an
active player comes out

Yeah, it's nice we got *something*. But I want more. I don't want to be the guy to find out firsthand if the NHL means it when they say hockey is for everyone. I'm no pioneer. I'm not brave enough. I've heard the way some people on campus talk about Sid and Karim, very obviously and openly bisexual.

But people act like Bailey's some kind of, I don't know, voyeur in their relationship? Like their attraction to each other nullifies their attraction to her. If you're a guy and you're into guys, that's all people see.

All five of my sisters see my message, but the steady stream of replies dies instantly. After a few seconds, it shows Delilah typing, then stopping. Then typing again. And stopping. She doesn't actually send anything for a few minutes.

> **Delilah:** Can you not with
> the hetero hot takes?
> Let me have this

For a second I consider sending back *I am bisexual you jackass how haven't you noticed I am so obvious,* but instead, I back out of the chat and go to share the article on Twitter.

Huge step for men's hockey, I say. Because, objectively, I know it is.

Cauler's the first one to like it.

EIGHT

W e open our regular season with a trip to Colorado. I am at peak anxiety right now. I keep trying to tell myself that this pinnacle season is just like any other season of hockey I've played in my life. Being on a different rink in a different jersey doesn't make a difference. It's still hockey, and I'm still one of the best young hockey players out there.

But so is Cauler. I can't let him be better than me this season.

I sit between Dorian and Barbie on the flight to Denver. Technically I'm supposed to have the aisle seat, but since I'm apparently so freaking small, they stuck me in the middle. The plane is mostly quiet aside from a few whispered conversations, and Cauler is asleep across the aisle, slouched in his seat with his hands folded on his stomach, head tilted back, mouth hanging open. Next to him, Zero highlights a line in his textbook.

I've got a short paper due by midnight, my laptop open in

my lap and dozens of research pages I keep clicking through without a real plan of action.

Dorian is fidgeting beside me. Drumming on his knees, raising the shade to peek out the window for a second before closing it again. He cracks his knuckles and goes back to drumming and tapping his foot.

It's extremely distracting.

I manage two painful, probably incoherent paragraphs before he pulls his headphones down around his neck and says, "You ever been to a concert?"

I shake my head.

"We're going to see these guys in a couple weeks." Dorian holds his headphones out to me. I look at him skeptically. "C'mon, they're good!" He yanks up the leg of his joggers—the same black with ROYALS HOCKEY written down the leg in purple the rest of us are wearing—and twists to show me the black tattoo on his calf. A bomb with a flower in place of the wick. "They got a song called 'Flowerbomb,' so."

He settles back in his seat while I put the headphones over my ears. When he hits play on his phone, I swear my eardrums rupture. There is a man. Literally screaming at me. I pull the headphones away from my ears and glare at Dorian until he grins and apologizes. Barbie huffs a laugh.

"You listen to this shit, too, Barbie?" I ask him once the music is turned down enough that my ears aren't bleeding from it.

"Excuse you?" Dorian scoffs. "Shit?"

Barbie shrugs. He's got his hat pulled down over his eyes,

voice sleepy. "Hard to avoid it with Dori and Cauler around. It grows on you."

"'It grows on you,'" Dorian mocks him. "As if you didn't fanboy when you realized it was Ahren screaming in the background of 'Beltsville.'"

"I prefer my pop punk and banda, thank you."

Dorian plays a bunch of songs by the same band, translating the screaming and growling into spoken words for me. It's a lot more meaningful than I expected. More hopeful than the screaming makes it out to be. It's downright relatable. I can see the appeal. The delivery might take some getting used to, but I mean. People who look like they listen to this kind of music are my type, all those piercings and tattoos, so I might as well give it a chance.

"The screamer, Joel? He writes the lyrics," Dorian explains. "He's got depression and anxiety, so he puts all that into his music."

My stomach flips. No wonder it felt so meaningful. I clear my throat and take off Dorian's headphones.

"So you wanna go see 'em with us?"

"Who's all going?" I ask, voice a little rough.

"Me, Barbie, Cauler, Zero, Kovy." He counts them off on his fingers. "Your sister and her girlfriend might be coming, too, but I guess that depends on how much work Jade gets done on some project she's got."

"Okay," I say, and immediately regret it. Hanging out with Dorian and Barbie is one thing; Barbie's always in our room anyway, so that's basically like hanging out already. But Cauler? At a concert? As soon as I agree to it, I know I'm gonna back out at the last second. Tell them I don't feel good or I got a big assignment or something.

"Nice!" Dorian says. "I'll send you some of their songs so you can get to know them better. More fun when you can sing along."

I get a message full of video links from him later that night, lying in a hotel bed wide awake while Colie snores across the room. I put earbuds in and turn the music up just enough to drown him out. Each song hits closer and closer to home, like I could've written these lyrics myself.

I take a cold shower to wake myself up in the morning, but my eyes still hurt and nothing I do gets rid of that grimy, sleepless feeling around them.

"You look rough, bro," Dorian tells me when we meet the team downstairs for breakfast.

I shrug, pouring myself a cup of complimentary coffee. Ever since Delilah started bringing me iced coffees every math class, I've started relying on it to function. At least I've developed a taste for it, because I desperately need it now.

"Colie's snoring," I say, even though it had a lot more to do with the music. Dorian grimaces. The upperclassmen warned us about it. Kovy survives rooming with him at the hockey house because he'd probably sleep through the apocalypse and make it all the way to his first class before realizing something was wrong.

I'm used to running on little sleep, but this is extreme.

I take out my phone on the bus to the rival campus. Nova posted a picture of herself barefaced, red around the eyes, acne scars visible, an angry-looking pimple in the crease of her nose, messy hair cut to her chin, next to a picture of her all made-up and flawless with her waist-length extensions in. She captioned it *nothing is real,* and she's got thousands of people commenting, thanking her for the transparency and saying she's equally beautiful in both.

They're right, obviously. But it's my job to keep her humble.

> **Mickey:** You look like a swamp hag

> **Nova:** Dammit.
> I was going for more of a
> banshee kind of vibe

As awful as the day has started, as miserable as I feel, it still makes me smile, even just a little.

"You been hiding a girlfriend from us, Terzo?" Zero asks from behind me, leaning over the back of my seat to creep on my phone. I click out of the messages reflexively, like I've been caught looking at something dirty.

"Not my girlfriend," I mutter, but it's lost in Zero's shout of, "Nova? Nova Vinter? Terzo!"

"What's your deal?" Kovy asks beside him.

"This asshole's literally texting Nova Vinter!"

"I lived with her," I try to remind them. I figured it was common knowledge I stayed with the Vinters after my family left for Raleigh, but the whole team's yelling about it now. I roll my eyes and sink low in my seat, unlocking my phone again.

> **Mickey:** Thanks a lot
> You sent my team into a frenzy

Nova: Watch them have the
best game of their lives

When we get off the bus to head into the arena, the boys make me take a selfie with them in our suits to send back to her, Dorian and Kovy smiling on one side of me, Zero making what he probably thinks is a seductive face on the other side, and Barbie towering over me from behind, looking slightly less bored than usual with one side of his mouth turned up.

Nova: Who's the tall one???

Mickey: They're all tall to me

Nova: Mickey.

Mickey: Barbie.

Nova: Hmmmm

We make it to the locker room before she can add anything else. I shove my phone into my duffel bag and start getting ready for the game.

We're up against a brute of a team. I've got this same massive blueliner on me all game, straight up trying to kill me with the way he throws his weight into his checks and toes the line with what should've been a thousand slashing and holding penalties. It's annoying, but I don't let him instigate me into retaliation. I've never been one to sit in the penalty box.

Halfway through the second half, Kovy dumps the puck along the halfboards and I pick it up behind the net, turning away a check before passing it along to Zero. I make my way to the top of the goal crease, screening the goalie and fighting for position with the aggressive defenseman. Cauler slides to the point, taking Kovy's place. I see the one-timer coming as soon as Zero makes the pass. As Cauler winds up, I shove my hip hard into my defender, turning my body and reaching out with my stick. The puck tips off my blade and rings off the pipe on its way into the net. The goal light flashes red, and my teammates crowd me against the boards to give out fist bumps and helmet pats.

The blueliner doesn't take it well. Next time we're on the ice together, he gets the blade of his stick shoved into the holder of my skate blade as I'm crashing in on his goalie. He pulls my legs out from under me, sending me sprawling. I hit the ice forearms first, and the rest of me follows so hard, it knocks the breath out of me. I slide headfirst into the goalie's pads, tripping him so he falls right onto my back.

For a second, with his weight on me, unable to breathe, I swear my back's broken and I'm dying. Whistles blow and guys are shouting and the goalie's pads push harder into me as he struggles back to his feet.

The asshole blueliner gets banished to the box, and I'm stuck on the bench for the power play as the trainer fusses over me.

We win the game 5–1, and all I want to do is get to the next hotel and crash for the night. But the boys have other plans. We have an early team dinner at a restaurant with high tables and barstools with no back support, then head to a plaza with a movie theater and what looks like a closed-down department store holding a haunted house for the season. I'd rather go to the movies and sit in a comfortable chair for a few hours, but most of the team and coaches head for the haunted house instead. Dorian doesn't give me much of a choice when he says, "I'm hiding behind you, Terzo. The monsters'll probably be more scared of your glare than you are of them!"

He's not wrong about the last point at least. I've never scared easily. And when I do get scared, I don't scream or jump, just kind of freeze up. I might look unfazed, but that lack of a fight-or-flight response would get me killed first in any horror movie situation.

They try to put me up front, but Cauler argues against it because apparently I'm so short, they'd just end up trampling me. So he takes the lead while Dorian stretches out my Royals Hockey zip-up, choking me with the collar of it and hunching over to bury his face in my neck before we've even run into an actor. The most startling things that happen are when Barbie full-on screams bloody murder from the back, and when Cauler reaches behind himself to grab at me as a little girl in a tattered, bloody dress comes shambling out of the darkness ahead of us.

His hand around mine sends my heart lurching more than any jump scare this place could throw at me.

Is it legal to have an actual child working in one of these things?

Out of all the zombies and killers and demons this place has thrown in front of us, *this* is what finally gets him?

Does he even *realize* he is *holding* my hand right now? He doesn't let go the rest of the way through the house. I hold my body so tensely that by the time we come out of it, I'm positive I've tripled whatever damage that goalie did to my back. It feels like pins are being shoved between all my vertebrae.

As soon as we step out into the crowd, Cauler lets go of me and puts at least three steps between us. I rub my hands together, trying to get rid of the feeling of his hand on me. Dorian doesn't loosen his grip on my jacket until we're out in the open middle of the building, away from the house and actors terrorizing the people still in line. He tries to smooth it out for me, but at this point it'd probably need a full-on dry-cleaning service to fix it.

Dorian and Barbie talk in Spanish behind me on our way to meet up with the rest of the team, and even though I only understand a few words here and there—mostly the bad ones—I get the feeling they're making fun of each other's reactions. They didn't notice Cauler's death grip, and he seems ready to pretend it never happened.

I STEP UP to Coach Hein in the lobby of the hotel with her hat full of paper slips and reach in.

Anyone but Cauler.

Please, for the love of god, anyone but Cauler.

I'd even take Colie's snoring over the awkwardness that would be sharing a room with Jaysen Caulfield.

I unfold the little slip of paper, and written there in Coach Hein's looping handwriting is *Caulfield.*

Why does the universe hate me?

One of the assistant coaches hands me a room key, and I

look over to find Cauler already looking at me. Anxious heat creeps up my spine and I jerk my head toward the elevator, flashing him the paper before shoving it into my pocket.

I can feel his presence at my back. Hear him breathing next to me on the elevator to the fourth floor. My heart throbs as I unlock our door.

Stepping into a hotel room with him feels like crossing into uncharted territory, and I am being absolutely ridiculous. I've shared hotel rooms, even *beds* with plenty of teammates before. There is absolutely nothing different or special about this.

I need to stretch out my back, get it to crack or something, and relax enough to fall asleep so I'm ready for tomorrow's game. But I can't do any of those things when I'm so hyperaware of Cauler's movements through the room.

Even he seems tense, practically tiptoeing as he gets ready for bed. Like he's trying not to draw my attention. Which is weird because usually he fills every space he occupies like he owns it. It doesn't work anyway, because he has my full attention, even if I keep my head down as I get my toothbrush out of my duffel bag.

I have to squeeze past him on my way to the bathroom, our chests inches apart, both of us holding our breath and leaning away with our heads turned. I brush my teeth slowly, glancing toward the door every few seconds. As if he's gonna burst in here at any moment and shove me up onto the counter and make out with me and my mouthful of toothpaste.

My face burns and my stomach flips at just the idea of it.

I splash cold water on my face until my heart slows back to normal and my stomach settles, then head back into the room with my eyes on the floor. I wait for him to take his turn in the bathroom before pulling off my shirt and changing into gym shorts. I'm in bed with my laptop open, pretending to read for an assignment, by the time he comes out.

God, this is the most uncomfortable hotel stay ever, and I once had to room with an NTDP teammate a night after hooking up with his twin sister.

Cauler settles into his bed and opens his own laptop, popping in headphones without a word to me. Still, the weirdly tense silence is better than the bloodbath this would have been if we'd roomed together even a couple weeks ago.

Sitting hunched over my computer doesn't help the stiffness in my back. I pull it into my lap and lean against the headboard, but it's not much better. I've been holding my body too tensely since that collision on the ice and I know there's nothing actually wrong with it, but if I don't crack my spine in the next five seconds, I'm gonna lose it.

I set aside my laptop, sit up straight, and twist, using my hands on my hips to pull myself farther. It doesn't work. So I push my fists into the small of my back and arch it. Still nothing. I feel like I'm eighty years old.

"Need help?"

I freeze with my back arched and my face strained, sure I'm hearing things. But when I relax and glance over at Cauler, he's looking at me. I blink. "Huh?"

"I spent enough time at the chiropractor to pick up some tricks," he says.

I just kinda ... stare at him for a second. What, is he planning to break my back or something? Put me out of the draft running?

He raises an eyebrow.

"Okay?" I say.

Cauler pushes aside his laptop and untangles himself from the blankets, motioning to the floor between our beds. "Lie down."

I get out of bed slowly, my heart rate picking up like something a lot more monumental than having my back cracked is about to happen. I wipe my hands on my shorts and swallow hard before lying on my stomach on the rough carpet, folding my arms under my head and burying my face in them so he can't see the flush in my cheeks.

"Put your arms down."

Shit. Okay. I straighten my arms by my sides and lay the side of my face on the floor. I keep my eyes open. Is that weird? Would it be weirder to close them? God, I hope I don't have any bacne going on.

I hold my breath at the first touch of his hands on my skin. He rubs circles between my shoulder blades with the heels of his hands, then pushes down. The entire upper half of my spine pops like bubble wrap. I close my eyes and straight-up groan.

My eyes shoot open.

Cauler hesitates.

Kill me now.

But then he moves his hands and does the same to my lower back. I manage to hold it in this time. It feels like his fingertips linger on my skin for a moment before he stands up, but that's definitely my imagination.

"Better?" he asks as I push myself to my knees.

I stretch, the pins and needles feeling in my spine gone for the moment. "Yeah." My voice is strained. "Thanks."

I stand up, but he doesn't go back to bed. We face each other, crammed into a space the width of a bedside table for what feels like minutes but is really probably only a second and a half before Cauler clears his throat.

"I, uh . . ." He scratches his jaw. "I'm leeching off my brother's Netflix. I was gonna fall asleep to *Spider-Man* if you wanna . . ." He trails off and avoids looking at me.

I swallow again. What is happening right now? "Tom Holland version?"

He rolls his eyes, smirking. "Are there any others?"

I ease onto the edge of his mattress and keep my arms crossed, legs hanging off so I'm not fully in bed with him. He unplugs his headphones so the sound plays from his laptop and sets it up between us. He actually gets into the bed, under the blankets and everything.

"You need the screen tilted?" he asks.

"No," I say, even though the movie is shadowed when he hits PLAY. I really should go to my own bed. This isn't comfortable, it's probably undoing all the work he just did on my back, and it's just plain weird.

"You can get in the bed," he says after a few minutes. "It's big enough."

I hesitate for a second before slowly pulling my legs up, keeping them angled away from him. Arms still crossed and my back straight against the headboard. I'm not even paying attention to the movie, really. I've seen it so many times, I could probably act the whole thing out on my own. I'm paying much more attention to Cauler, with one of his arms behind his head and the other hand resting on his chest.

That's why I see it when Zero sends him a mirror selfie in a white hotel bathrobe and slippers, a towel around his head and his foot propped on the edge of the bathtub, throwing up a backwards peace sign.

Cauler's grinning as he types something back.

"Didn't realize you and Zero were so close," I blurt out.

He doesn't stop typing, unfazed by my nosiness. "That's 'cause you don't pay attention to anything other than yourself," he says, but there's no heat in his voice.

"Why, though? He's a senior."

He locks his phone and sets it on his chest. "His dad coached my squirt team. Taught me how to skate."

Of course. They're both from Boston. Both have a slight New England accent after years playing hockey away from their hometowns.

I hate being reminded that he didn't even lace up a pair of skates until he was nine years old. That he's been playing hockey for less than nine years and is just as good as me. Maybe even better.

I don't know if it's hatred or jealousy or a little of both clawing into my chest, but I do my best to bury it.

"Did you come here 'cause of him?" I ask, forcing myself not to shut down while we're making progress in tolerance.

There's this long beat of silence between us. His breath sounds shallow. On the screen, Tom Holland's Spider-Man is giving an awkward speech at his aunt's shelter.

For a second I'm afraid I crossed some kind of line and Cauler's not gonna say anything else the rest of the night.

He swallows thickly, like he's preparing himself for something.

"I got over my crush a long time ago, if that's what you're asking," he says quietly. He holds his voice in the back of his throat as he adds, "Mr. Cicero's like my second dad. When I told him I got scouted by Hartland, he basically wrote a thesis on why I should come here. Number one reason was Zero. Mr. Cicero thought it'd be easier if we were on the same team so he didn't have to travel all over the place to see us play."

I hear his words but my brain keeps short-circuiting, replaying that first sentence over and over again. Crush. Cauler had a crush on Zero. I mean, it could be nothing. Straight girls have their girl crushes; what's to say a straight dude can't have a dude crush?

Cauler's done talking, but I have nothing to say in response. I stare at the computer screen without really seeing it. I'm thinking way too much into this. Cauler is my sworn enemy and would never reveal something to me that could hurt his chances of taking away my spot.

This awkward silence grows between us, to the point where I could cry with relief when my phone vibrates in the pocket of my shorts. It's a notification about the picture I sent to Nova hours ago. I open my messages with her and say:

Mickey: Did you really just
screenshot that

Nova: Eye candy purposes

Mickey: I could just
Yknow

> Give him your number
> He's alot like me though i feel like
> Just a lot taller
> And a little less grouchy

> **Nova:** You realize i love you right?
> So being like you isn't
> necessarily a turn off
> But yes please
> Slip me his number

I'm sending over Barbie's number when Cauler says, "I can't believe you're on texting terms with Nova Vinter."

I frown at my phone. I'm not about to explain my history with Nova again. Instead, I turn it on him. "What, you're not friends with any of your exes?"

"That's not what I meant. But yes, I am."

"Then what did you mean?"

"She's famous."

"Y'know, some people would say the same about us, right?"

Cauler makes a face. "Hockey's not popular enough to consider us famous."

"Famous with hockey fans."

"Barely counts."

I roll my eyes and go back to messaging Nova. She's in Australia for the week, on location for a show she's guest-starring on. I kind of get why people are surprised by our friendship. I mean, she's way out of my league. But I've seen her in all her worst, most embarrassing moments. We shared all our firsts together. I was there when she got the call that she'd landed the spread that got her where she is now. She almost strangled me to death with how tightly she hugged me.

I miss her. God, I miss her.

"He might come visit on spring break," Cauler says.

"Hmm?"

"My ex I'm still friends with."

I stop in the middle of my message to Nova. Did I hear that right? I mean, I wasn't really paying attention, but I'm pretty sure he said *he*.

Is he, like, trying to come out to me right now?

There's no way.

I turn my head and look at him. He just raises an eyebrow and waits for me to break the silence. I close my mouth and swallow, holding eye contact with him longer than I ever have before. "Are you . . ."

"Am I what, Mickey?"

The sound of my name in his voice is almost enough to make me jump him right here. It's the first time I've ever heard him say my first name, and he makes it sound rough, seductive, infuriating.

"Are you gay?" I breathe. It feels wrong to ask it so bluntly. But I'm pretty sure he *wants* me to ask. He's been leading this conversation here from the beginning.

His eyes rove over my face, hesitating over my lips before he meets my stare again. "What would you do if I said yes?"

There is *no* way.

No way he'd give me that kind of ammunition against him. No way he would ever look at me like *that*. Like if I leaned in just a little he'd kiss the living daylights out of me.

When have I ever given him the impression that I'd be into it anyway? I mean, I'm obvious, but am I *that* obvious?

Do not look at his lips. For the love of god, Mickey, do not look at his lips.

I look at his lips, parted slightly, just waiting for me.

I bite my own lip and look back up at his eyes. He's still watching me, waiting for an answer. Imagine allowing myself this. Someone in hockey who really *knows* me.

Someone I can have fun with in between running myself ragged for this sport.

But. Hockey's not the most welcoming environment for people who aren't straight white guys. I at least have one of those things protecting me. Cauler's got neither.

It would be a bad idea for both of us.

I clear my throat and look away, back toward Tom Holland and Zendaya, a bisexual's dream. I can almost hear the tension between us snap. "I mean," I say. My voice sounds too high. "I wouldn't be weird about it, if that's what you're asking. My sister's gay, and Bailey's boyfriends are bi."

I don't see his disappointment, but I hear it in the way he sighs, short and soft like he's trying to hide it. "I know," he says. "Why do you think I felt safe telling you?"

It's a lie. It might be part of the reason, but it's not all of it.

Jaysen Caulfield is into me. Maybe just as much as I am into him.

Who would've thought?

IT'S DANGEROUS TO let myself fall asleep in the same bed as him, but I do. We stay up too late, talking about Nova and his ex Jisung and what it's like to stay friends after breaking up.

I wake up facing him, the laptop open between us, screen dark. I check my phone to see it's just after five in the morning, still an hour left to sleep. But I won't be able to fall back asleep now. Not in this room, this bed, next to him.

I let myself look him over for a moment, the way he hasn't moved except to turn his face my way. One hand still on his stomach, the other behind his head, probably numb by now.

I could've kissed him last night. I *should've* kissed him last night.

With a sigh, I ease myself out of the bed to use the bathroom and take my laptop to the small table by the window.

It's dinnertime or something in Australia. Nova has to hear about this.

Mickey: Hey so problem

Nova: Oh boy
Lemme get my therapist glasses on
What's up

Mickey: Okay so
Cauler
Jaysen
Remember him
Well
He's like
Totally into me

She starts typing and stops a few times before a message finally comes through.

> **Nova:** Sorry but I'm failing to
> see the problem here?
> He's into you
> You're into him
> So do the thing

> **Mickey:** Nova
> You realize he's a hockey player
> And like
> MY BIGGEST COMPETITION HELLO

> **Nova:** Still not seeing the problem.
> Mickey.
> How many times do I have to tell you
> Let yourself have something
> that isn't hockey

> **Mickey:** That would be
> easier if what I wanted
> wasn't a person who could
> ruin everything

> **Nova:** you're being dramatic

> **Mickey:** you're underestimating
> the power of the homophobe

It's not that I think Cauler would out me. That would put him in the same position as me. But people have a way of finding these things out. I mean, look at Bailey and Delilah. Word about them got out because of assholes who posted their business online.

My phone buzzes on the table, and a moment later Nova's picture pops up on a video call. I glance at Cauler, still asleep, and head into the bathroom.

Nova's in sunglasses and a bathing suit when I answer. I hear the faint crashing of waves in the background and the sound of people laughing.

She's on a beach in Australia, and I am instantly jealous.

"I'm gonna need you to do something for me, Mickey," she says before I have a chance to say hi.

"Okay?" I say.

"Think about your happiness, for one second. What would make you happy right this very moment? Don't think about the consequences or what could go wrong. Just think about what you want."

"I mean, it's not like I'm miserable right now."

"But you're also not happy."

"I'm never happy, Nova," I say. I poke at the bruises under my eyes in the mirror, permanent physical evidence of the years spent lying awake at night, staring at the walls, the ceiling, the insides of my eyelids.

When it's real bad, I swear I look like a corpse. And people still don't realize what's going on. I guess I can't really blame them. Sometimes I even sit there and tell myself I am way too privileged to be depressed and that I need to suck it up.

Nova adjusts her sunglasses, shoulders slouching when

she leans forward over her phone and looks down at me. "What would help get you there? Doesn't have to be something huge, doesn't have to cure you of your depression here and now. Just, what would make it easier to handle?"

Out in the room, Cauler's alarm goes off. I glance at the door.

"Like, it would make me downright giddy if you were here on this beach with me," Nova adds. "Or if I had a loganberry in one hand and a Tim Horton's iced capp in the other. It can be small things like that."

Nova is backlit by the sun, her pale skin turning pink. Laughter spikes in the background, and she glances up for a second before looking back down at me. I'd be happy if I were on that beach with her, too.

I'd be happy to be on the ice without the weight of the draft hanging over me.

I'd be happy to go out to lunch with all five of my sisters.

I'd be happy to get an A in a class other than Italian this semester.

The fact that I can think of things that would help is a good sign, right? If I was a lost cause, nothing would come to mind.

I open my mouth to say as much, but before I can, there's a knock on the door.

"Terzo?" Cauler says, voice sleepy. "You almost done?"

"Just a second," I answer too quickly, suspiciously.

Nova puts a hand over her mouth for a second before waving it around excitedly and mouthing *is that him?* I nod, and she bounces on her heels, smiling wide. "I'll let you go," she says quietly. She blows me a kiss and the call ends.

I sigh, taking another look in the mirror at my tired eyes before giving the bathroom to Cauler. I'm getting dressed for breakfast when Nova messages me again.

Nova: I want you to do one
thing for yourself today
Promise me

We have the last game of this roadie today, then we're on a plane back home tonight. Tomorrow, it's back to school, where midterms are coming up fast.

But today, I think I can manage.

Mickey: I promise.

CAULER AND I work damn good together.

Even with our positions switched up, we weave around each other and swap places and know exactly where the other is without planning ahead and barely speaking. Zero adapts to us easily, but opponents can't keep up.

I'd honestly hate to play against us.

Still, the game is tight, and I have my promise to Nova stuck in my head the whole time. I'm thinking about it when I get slammed into the boards hard enough my bones ache. I'm thinking about it when I deke around a defender and ring a shot off the pipe.

Do one thing for myself today.

I'm still thinking about it when Kovy scores. When he

and the other boys on the ice skate by to knock fists against ours on the bench. I'm too busy thinking to even smile.

When I was a kid, I was always smiling at the rink. No matter what I was doing, being on the ice made me the happiest kid alive. It was fun. It made me like Dad.

Maybe that's the thing I can do for myself today. Have fun on the ice again. Don't treat it like a job or a birthright. Have fun on the ice with the first friends I've made in years.

The next time my line goes over the boards, I throw myself into the play with the kind of feverish intensity I used to play with on the pond with my sisters when we were kids. Like it's new and exciting and I don't know what it means to be a Mickey James yet.

I laugh when I strip a guy of the puck with this smooth blindside pickpocket and he takes two strides before realizing it's gone. I smile when Cauler offers me a fist bump afterward. I grin and bear it when I block a shot with my ankle that leaves me limping for the rest of that shift. I call out to my teammates on the ice and shout encouragements from the bench. Coach claps me on the shoulder after a shift as I'm spraying water on my face and shakes me a little, yelling in my ear, "Great job, James!"

It feels good. It's not perfect—I rip a second shot off the post and have to close my eyes and breathe to keep from internally berating myself—but it's something.

"Becoming a man of the people, Your Grace?" Cauler asks me as we skate to the face-off dot after a whistle. He grins.

I shrug one shoulder. "Spend enough time with the peasants, they start to rub off on you."

His grin opens up into a full-blown smile, dimples in both cheeks, eyes crinkled. "You little shit."

I'm carrying the puck into the offensive zone late in the second period, and I know Cauler's directly behind me. A defender steps in my path, and I act like I'm gonna try to deke around him, but instead I just leave the puck behind me. A second later, there's the crack of Cauler's one-timer. The defender I faked yells "Shit!" as the puck hits the back of the net.

It's not my goal, and Cauler's my sworn enemy. But it was a downright beauty of an assist, and I won't be afraid to acknowledge my good work today. I'll have a crisis tomorrow. For now, I turn to where Cauler's got his arms up, just as Zero and our blueliners close in on him for hugs and helmet pats. Usually I just offer fist bumps after goals. I've never been a hockey hugger.

Now? Now I throw myself into it. I jump to get my arms around Zero's and Cauler's shoulders, pulling them down to my level as my skates hit the ice again.

"What the hell?" Zero says, laughing. "Atta boy, Terzo!"

Cauler doesn't say anything. But he smiles. And, oh, I am so fucked.

His smile has never been more beautiful than it is now. Shy. And genuine. And at least in part because of me.

NINE

've been feeling good lately. Cauler and I aren't at each other's throats anymore. If anything we're circling around each other, waiting to see who'll make the first move.

What is my life, right?

The season's started off great, 2–0, and I'm keeping pace with Delilah in points and trying real hard to have fun. It doesn't always work. But at least I'm not a robot on the ice all the time.

Things have been good.

Which of course means the universe has to go and pull the rug out from under me.

I've got my feet up on my chair in the tape room, hood up over my head, Dorian sitting to my left, and I'm content.

Kovy's going on about a shifty forward in our next opponent's arsenal when my phone vibrates in my pocket. I pull it out, keeping my focus on Kovy until I can check the notification.

There's a tagged tweet from the NHL Network.

I swipe the notification away without reading it and relock my phone just as one of the guys says, "Hey, look at our superstars!" He motions to the muted TV behind the captains. There's an action shot of me in my USA gear opposite one of Cauler when he played for the Gamblers. Below us is a graphic comparing our USHL stats. When it fades, it's replaced by two NHL Network analysts, Hugh and Alyssa, standing in front of blown-up green-screen photos of me and Cauler.

Kill me.

Someone unmutes the TV in the middle of Hugh saying, "—unique situation with the top two prospects sharing a college team. I'm curious to know how you think that will impact their draft stock, if at all, Alyssa."

The thing about Alyssa? She's never been swayed by the whole Mickey James legacy. That's why she's my favorite analyst in hockey. She was on a segment about the future of USA Hockey once, talking about the most exciting talent lined up for the next winter games, and she's the only one who gave Delilah the hype she deserves while everyone else focused on the men's team.

So I know she's going to tear me apart. I just wish it didn't have to be in front of the Royals.

"Honestly, Hugh?" she says. I brace myself. "I think we'll see Jaysen's value overtake Mickey's in the end."

"Really now?" Hugh raises his eyebrows, pretending to be surprised. Like this wasn't all planned in advance. "Why do you say that?"

"It's no secret that Mickey has been . . . distant from his teams in the past."

My heart drops right into my stomach and instantly starts dissolving. So that's where she's going with this.

"Everyone has always given him the benefit of the doubt," she continues, "blamed it on team dynamics. Now that he's sharing a team with Caulfield, same players, same dynamic, there's no excuses to be made. It'll be clear that it's an issue of personality."

I feel my chest caving in, sucked into the black hole opening where my heart was just a few seconds ago.

"Harsh," Dorian says. I would expect a lot of chirping from the guys after a comment like that, but they're quiet, focused on the TV.

"That's a very good point," Hugh says as the screen transitions to game footage. "They have very similar stats. Mickey does have a slight edge, but he doesn't seem like much of a team player."

"Players with his skill are usually looked to as team leaders, but not Mickey," Alyssa says. Right on cue, a clip plays where my linemate scores a goal, and while the rest of the players on the ice gather for the celly, I skate past them to the bench without cracking the barest hint of a smile.

I remember that game. It was the middle of a three-week stretch where I spent every moment of free time lying in bed, staring at the wall. I ate nothing but canned soup and bread and butter, failed two major tests because I didn't even show up, almost got put in the hospital by my billet family, and felt absolutely nothing the whole time.

In that moment, it barely even registered that a goal was scored.

They just had to pick this out, didn't they? Every time

I think about those three weeks, I can feel that emptiness opening up inside me again.

On the TV, it switches over to Cauler grouped up with his team celebrating a win, his teammates looking to him for guidance during a stoppage in play. The captain's C on his Gamblers jersey at only seventeen years old. All while Alyssa and Hugh talk about his leadership abilities and his overall passion for the game and how that makes him so much more valuable than me in the long run. I watch the whole thing unblinking, until my eyes go blurry and I have to close them.

The guys start up now, and even though I know there's shouting and laughter and everyone talking over one another, it's all muffled by the sound of my own breathing, harsh and unsteady.

I lower my head and press my fingers into my temples.

It's so obvious. *I'm* so obvious. Why can't anyone see what's really going on? I love hockey. I do. I swear. My brain just doesn't let me show it or feel it or . . . or . . .

"You okay, dude?" Dorian's hushed voice cuts through my haze, making me flinch. He's turned toward me, leaning in close. The TV's muted again, and Zero and Kovy have regathered everyone's attention, but I notice the sideways glances the boys keep shooting my way.

"I'm fine?" My tongue feels sluggish. Like it takes a whole minute to say two words.

"I mean, I wouldn't blame you if you weren't. Not easy to listen to a couple grown-ass adults tear apart your personality."

I blink at him. He starts fidgeting when I don't say anything, just staring at him blankly. "Not like they're wrong," I say, trying to make it less awkward for him. Judging by the way his jaw slackens, it didn't work.

My phone vibrates again. Dorian looks down before I do, eyes going wide and a smile cracking through that sad look he'd been giving me. "Your dad's calling," he says, all giddy and starstruck.

My brain feels fuzzy.

The phone buzzes two more times before I slowly stand and answer the call on my way out of the tape room. No one tries to stop me.

"Hello." My voice is miles away. I step out into the hallway where all the Royals alum who ever did anything in the NHL or Olympics are honored. Including oversize murals of Dad and Grampa as teenagers.

"Hey, Mick!" Dad says. "How are things going? How's the team?"

"Fine."

"Just fine?"

"Yeah."

A long pause.

"Give me some details, bud," he says. "Tell me about practices. You excited for your home opener this weekend?"

"Sure."

Another pause. "How are you adapting to the wing?" His voice is strained like he's desperately trying to hang on to the conversation.

"Okay."

"Coach Campbell knows the game. He wouldn't put you in a role he didn't think you could excel in."

"I know."

"Your mom and I are planning on coming out to a game next month."

"Oh," I say, a little more life coming into my voice. I slap a hand to my forehead and drag it down my face. Mom and Dad usually make it out to at least one game a season. You'd think being retired athletes they'd have the free time to make it to more than that. But they've taken up youth coaching. I try not to let it bother me, but it was Dad who taught me how to skate. How to put on my gear. How to hold a stick. And now he's too busy to be there to see what came of the work. After Dad, I had youth coaches of my own, and by the time I was ten, he didn't even live in the same state as me anymore.

He's spending more time with those kids now than he ever did with me.

Still, the prospect of them coming out to see me play makes me feel like a kid again, eager to impress my parents, desperate for them to see me succeed.

"Okay," I say.

"Anything you wanna talk about?" he asks.

I think about Hugh and Alyssa analyzing my attitude the way they'd analyze a play. How Cauler said I'm taking up space and money and exposure I don't need. How the god-damn *Hockey News* treated my sisters like setbacks with me as the destination.

"No," I say.

"Okay, bud, well, call me if you need to, alright? Good luck this weekend. I love you."

"Love you, too."

My legs take me outside, carry me to the dock, sit me at the edge, hang my feet over the water. I drop my face in my hands and breathe.

The sun is setting by the time I come out of it. It's like my vision snaps back into focus. Like I've broken through some kind of barrier inside my own head.

I start shaking.

Goddammit. I was doing so good lately, too.

My legs are heavy when I push myself to my feet. I rub my thighs to get some life back into them and warm up my hands. I swipe the back of my hand under my nose before heading to the dorm.

SO HERE'S A thing that happens when my depression gets especially bad.

I start dissociating.

I write my name on my algebra midterm Wednesday morning, and the letters make no sense. Like, how does this mess of made-up lines spell out a word that represents my entire existence?

I spend the whole hour staring at my name and trying to see myself in it.

Delilah bumps me when she stands up and gives me a look over her shoulder as she heads toward the front of the room with her backpack and exam. Jade's waiting for her by the door, and the room is almost empty.

Panic surges through my chest when I look down at my blank paper. "Shit, shit, shit," I say under my breath, scrambling to get something done. I only manage two equations, probably not even right, before Professor Morris calls time. I put my face in my hands and breathe in deep.

Kill me.

There are two other people left in the room, and of course one of them is Cauler. He sets his test on the desk and looks at me. My eyes are heavy with the grimy feeling of unshed tears and lack of sleep.

Still, I manage to hold his stare. He tilts his head and gives this curious, narrow-eyed look to the paper clenched in my fist.

"I'll take that, Mr. James," Professor Morris says.

My heart lurches. I give Cauler one more look like *mind your damn business* and turn to face my first F of the semester.

"So, uh . . ." I start once Cauler's almost out the door.

"I noticed a lot of staring," Professor Morris says when I don't continue. "Not much writing."

"Yeah, I . . ." I look down at all the white space on my exam paper. "I have this . . . this brain thing. Going on. I guess."

"What kind of brain thing?"

I can't meet her eyes. She doesn't look mad or annoyed or anything. More like concerned. It's not something I'm used to.

"I'm not trying to push," she adds. She leans forward and folds her arms on her desk. "Are you alright?"

There's a lump in my throat. Like having this person I've never spoken to care enough to ask if I'm okay has me all choked up. I should lie. I can hardly talk about this with Nova, and I love her. The second I tell a person of authority what I'm dealing with, they'll be checking in on me all the time and I'll never know peace.

"I mean." My next breath is watery. I look down at my shoes so she can't see my eyes tear up. Like she can't hear it in my voice. "Not really?"

"Have you been to the counseling center?"

I shake my head.

"You should consider it. Freshman year is tough, and being an athlete only makes it harder."

I shrug one shoulder.

"There's nothing shameful in seeking help. You can also let your other professors know you're struggling and they should work to accommodate you better. We're your teachers. We're on your side."

"Okay."

She holds her hand out for my exam. I hesitate for a second before passing it over. She doesn't even look at it. Just folds it in half and tears it up. "My office hours on Monday are eleven to one and four to six. Either of those times work for you?"

"Eleven, I guess."

"Why don't you stop by and take your exam then. I'll make sure you stay focused. Sound good?"

I gape at her for a moment before stammering, "Uh, yeah. Good. Sounds good. Thanks."

She gives me this sad smile. "Take care of yourself, okay?"

"Okay. Thank you."

I almost trip over myself in my hurry to get out. I keep my head down and skirt around people on the paths back to my room, heart palpitations making me feel light-headed and nauseous all the way. But at least I make it back to my room before breaking down completely, back sliding against the door until I'm sitting on the floor with my face in my hands, sobbing.

If I can't make it through a semester of college, how am I ever gonna make it in the NHL?

———————

PROFESSOR MORRIS GIVES me the number for the counseling center when I go in to retake my exam. Even offers to walk me there, but no thanks. I have the number typed into my phone later that afternoon, thumb hovering over the call button, but Dorian and Barbie walk in and I clear it out and don't try again.

I went from feeling great, loving hockey, loving the guys on the ice with me, to feeling like I was maybe gonna be okay, to feeling as bad as I have ever felt all in a matter of days. It's like that single day of contentedness sent my brain into self-destruct mode because it didn't know what was happening.

Maybe it's because my grades are so borderline.

Maybe it's because I could've kissed Cauler and instead I bro-zoned him.

Maybe it's because my parents are coming to a game in a couple weeks.

It was supposed to be just Mom and Dad, but then I mentioned it in a group video chat with my older sisters and they decided to crash it. I almost cried. I haven't seen them in so long and I miss them so much and this whole thing will be a lot easier to handle with them here.

The game's being broadcast on ESPNU. NHL scouts will analyze every second of ice time. It should be an easy win, but the final score won't matter as much as my performance.

Cauler's only a few points behind me, with better defensive stats. I can't afford a single bad shift. I gotta take every chance to pad my stats, put flourish in my play, be the superstar everyone expects me to be.

Pretend I'm not dead inside for sixty minutes.

That's barely an exaggeration.

Whenever I think of Alyssa and Hugh, or Dorian's relatable music or Cauler's face when he said *what would you do if I said yes*, I just get so tired, I want to crawl in bed and not come out for five years. It's not even sadness. It's nothingness.

Hockey is the most important thing in my life besides my sisters and Nova, but when it gets like this, the only thing putting me on the ice is my anxiety, my fear of failure.

Doesn't help when Professor Morris pulls me aside after class one day and asks if I ever contacted the counseling office. Pretty sure she knows I'm lying when I say, "Yeah, I got it figured out. Thanks."

For the rest of the week if I'm not in class or on the ice, I'm on my phone reading about depression and anxiety and trying to convince myself that I'm allowed to feel this way even with all the privileges I have, even though nothing really bad has ever happened to me.

I survive our only game of the week on Friday. Even manage to put up a goal. But it's not fun like it was in Colorado. I feel a thousand miles away from my teammates even in the middle of our celly huddle.

I try to force myself out of it on Saturday, at least long

enough to get some work done on a paper I have due on Monday, but I end up with my head in my hands, elbows on my desk, exhausted after a single sentence.

I don't know how long I sit like that before the door opens on Dorian and Barbie, because it's always Dorian and Barbie. I don't remember the last time I saw them apart from each other, which doesn't make any sense with Dorian's science classes and Barbie's language classes on complete opposite sides of campus.

"What're you doing?" Dorian asks, almost frantically, when he gets a look at me. I probably look pathetic, wallowing at my desk, shirtless in sweatpants with books and papers all over the place. "We gotta leave!"

I blink at him. What is he talking about?

He flails his hands at me like that'll—oh wait. Concert. Right. He invited me to this concert. I don't remember agreeing to go.

I practically deflate in my chair. "Kill me."

"It's fun! Even Kovy's coming, and he's into country music. Country, Terzo."

"You get to shove people around and no one gets mad," Barbie offers.

"I don't know," I mumble.

"You don't have a choice," Dorian says, quickly changing his clothes. "You're not rotting in this room for all eternity. Get up, get dressed, brush your hair. Brush your damn teeth. You don't have to wear all black. We're not a cult."

I don't want to go. But I also don't want to work on this paper, or sit in my room, or exist at all, really. So I guess it doesn't make a difference. I sigh heavily and push myself out of my chair to rummage for jeans in the pile of dirty clothes by my closet. It takes a minute to find a T-shirt that doesn't smell like it's been sitting on the floor for weeks, but Dorian still offers me his body spray anyway. I pull on my Royals hoodie and follow them out.

"Why aren't you wearing that Amity shirt I got you?" Barbie asks when we hit the stairs.

Dorian clicks his tongue and points a finger at him. "How many times I gotta tell you this, Barbs? Never wear a band's merch to their show. It makes you look thirsty."

"Or like a fan."

"Being there makes you look like a fan."

From my place a few steps behind them, I watch Barbie turn his head to give Dorian an incredulous look. "I have seen a guy push his way to the stage just so he could flip the band off the whole time. We're bringing people to this show who are decidedly not fans. I don't think a shirt is a bad idea."

"I wore that thing so much it has a hole in the armpit, you really think I didn't appreciate it?" Dorian says.

Barbie hums like he's been appeased, and I feel completely empty inside.

Delilah and Jade are waiting in the parking lot. Jade's wearing faded jeans instead of her usual leggings, and Delilah's typical dress is paired with a black beanie, denim jacket, knee-high socks, and combat boots. Her hair's this pastel kind of blue instead of the pink she's kept it all semester.

"Your hair's gonna fall out," I mutter.

Delilah rolls her eyes like she's already heard this a thousand times. "It's not like I dye it every damn week."

"Only because I bring up pictures of fried hair every time you want to," Jade says. Dorian makes a noise like bacon sizzling in a pan.

Zero and Kovy show up with Cauler, and I shouldn't be surprised to see him because we're literally going to see his favorite band, but my heart still hesitates at the sight of him.

I. Should've. Kissed him.

He was smiling and laughing walking up with Zero and Kovy, but when he sees me he bites his smile back a little, shoving his hands into the pockets of his jacket, not meeting my eyes. I haven't talked to him much outside of hockey this week. He's probably getting so many mixed signals from me he doesn't know what to think.

I'm an asshole. I know what it's like, getting those vibes from a guy, taking a risk in giving them back only to be shut down. I know what it's like and I did it to him anyway.

Because of hockey.

I look back toward the dorm. I shouldn't go to this concert and ruin his night. This is his music, his thing, and my presence will definitely only complicate things.

"Mickey, hey," Delilah says. They're all heading toward Zero's SUV. "You're in the way back with us."

She and Jade climb in before I have time to back out. Dorian and Barbie have already gotten in on the other side, leaving Cauler waiting for me at the door. I look him right in the eye as I walk up to him, like he'll be able to see the truth in my stare. He doesn't look away, but his jaw clenches and he swallows hard. I climb into the back and reach to pull the seat up at the same time Cauler does.

We both hesitate, watching each other in this weird gay

standoff. Delilah and Jade are talking to each other, and Dorian's leaning between the front seats to connect his phone to the car's Bluetooth, and no one is paying any attention to us. So when Cauler finally makes the move, I put my hand right next to his, our skin touching as we pull the seat back.

I feel like I'm in middle school, sharing "incidental" contact with Nova at the dinner table at her parents' house. Little touches that could be shrugged off as accidents if we were questioned.

Cauler sucks his lips into his mouth as he climbs into the car, not looking at me. But I see the smile fighting to pull through.

I'VE NEVER BEEN to a concert before. As soon as I step into the venue, nothing feels real anymore. And I don't mean that in a dissociation kind of way, either. More like a highway rest stop in the middle of the night or a quiet, empty arena with the lights dimmed. It's dark, humid, and a little claustrophobic.

There's no music yet, just the heavy, vaguely creepy hum of ambient noise through the speakers as some people crowd the bar and others head for the stage. Zero and Kovy are the only ones old enough to drink, and they ditch us as soon as we make it inside. I rub absently at the black X's on my hands, but even if I found a way to get them off, the bartenders would probably take one look at me, assume I'm twelve, and kick me out of the show entirely.

"I'll settle for nothing but right up front," Dorian says. "Everybody grab on!" He takes Barbie's hand. Barbie takes

Jade's, Jade takes Delilah's, and Delilah takes mine. Leaving me with . . .

I look back at Cauler. Hold out my hand. He looks at it for a second, then at my face. Delilah pulls me and I stagger along with her, hand still out, until Cauler lunges forward to grab on before we get lost in the crowd. Dorian leads us toward the stage, squeezing between people and straining our grips on one another to the point where I'm pretty sure all our fingers are gonna break before we get to where we're going. I kind of feel like an asshole, forcing my way through a bunch of strangers, but most of them seem unfazed by it.

We line up right against the stage, and Cauler's hand lingers in mine even as the crowd presses in around us, making me feel smaller than ever. I miss it as soon as he lets go, but he isn't exactly far away. There's no barricade between us and the bands. My face is right at waist-level with them.

Dorian said the openers were pretty small names, but the crowd still reacts . . . *violently* is the only word I can think to describe it. I am completely out of my element. The frontman's screaming right in my face, I can feel the bass in my chest like my heart is syncing up with it, I'm being literally crushed against the stage from behind, and I even get kicked in the head by a crowd surfer.

By the time the first band is done, I feel like I've been to war.

"What'd you think, Terzo?" Dorian calls from down the line. His voice sounds muffled.

"It's something," I call back.

"It's fun," he insists.

And he's right. It's different. Takes some getting used to. But I guess it beats sitting in my room wishing I were dead.

I even bob my head along with the beat when the next band comes on. It's nowhere near as aggressive as Cauler beside me with an arm up, punching the air in time with the words he screams along to. I feel kind of bad taking up space at the front from people who could really get into it, but at least I'm short enough for them to see over me. Not the case for anyone stuck behind Barbie.

"Look at Maverick!" Jade shouts. I twist, pushing up on my tiptoes to catch a glimpse of Kovy in the middle of a big gap in the crowd with a bunch of people all shoving one another and swinging their arms around. Kovy's polo is drenched, his hair slick across his forehead as he throws his body around like he's on the rink. Zero's along the edge of the gap, cheering him on.

I smile. Even laugh. And when I face forward again, I find Cauler watching me just like I'd been watching Kovy. He looks away as soon as I notice.

After the second band, with the roadies for the main act doing their sound check, Cauler puts his forearms on the stage and his head down. The crowd's thinned a little with people going for refills at the bar, so I take the chance to stretch my legs behind me. Delilah and Jade are going back and forth with Dorian and Barbie, but my ears feel stuffed and I can't hear what they're saying.

I should swap with Cauler. Let him get closer to them so he can talk, too, instead of acting like a door between them.

I mean, I guess I could talk to him?

There's a thought.

I lean down next to him, matching him with my arms on the stage. I feel him tense against my shoulder.

"Hey," I say. Like we haven't been standing next to each other for the past hour and something minutes. Good start.

He's quiet for a second, dragging a fingernail through a seam in the floorboards of the stage. "Hey."

Okay. Time to put my nonexistent conversational skills to the test.

"So this is the kind of shit you listen to for fun." I cringe at the same time Cauler scoffs. Wow. I am great at this. Might as well keep plowing on. "I mean, not that it's *shit*, just—you know what I mean."

"Actually, that band *was* kind of shit," he says.

I blink at him. "You were literally singing along."

"Well, yeah."

"That makes no sense."

He shrugs. "Maybe not to you. But some of us like to have fun."

I say nothing. He didn't mean to, but he hit a nerve. Of course I like to have fun. It's just that sometimes my brain doesn't want to let me. I expect the conversation to die there, but then he says, "We trended on Twitter for seven minutes on the way here. Got thousands of people arguing over us."

Now I'm the one who scoffs. "Again?"

"I've got a feeling it's gonna be like this till draft day, Terzo. Might as well get used to it."

"Bet you're loving it," I mumble.

"Not really." A loud, steady beat picks up as the drummer starts his check. I lean in closer to hear Cauler better. "People used to talk about me for my skill. Now they just wanna compare me to you. Someone actually sat there and said that if you were a few inches taller, these conversations wouldn't even be happening."

I roll my eyes. For once, my height's got nothing to do with it. Just, you know, who I am as a person. "Lucky for you, I took after my mom."

He ignores that, fidgeting with his lip ring in a way that reminds me we're in his element here. The stretched ears might be out of place on an ice rink, but they're pretty much standard here.

"I've been talking to your sister about you," he says after a moment.

Great.

"I have five of them," I say. "You'll have to be more specific."

He actually laughs. Just this small huff of air through his nose, but still. A laugh, and a slight uptick at the corner of his mouth. "You little shit. The one right next to you. Delilah."

"Okay."

He takes a breath to continue but pauses with his mouth open, like he's rethinking whatever he was gonna say. He closes his mouth and swallows before saying, "What would your parents have done if you just totally sucked ass at hockey?"

Okay, that is not what I was expecting. Talking about my parents? What are we, friends?

"Paid for more ice time?" I say.

"What if you said no?"

I laugh bitterly. "That was never an option."

"C'mon. It's a sport. Not life or death."

"It's more than that for them."

"What's it to you?" He turns toward me, resting his weight on one elbow. "You wouldn't be doing this if it weren't for your name. Everyone knows it. So why bother?"

"Because I was bred for this." I hope he remembers that *Hockey News* article, or I just sounded super creepy.

"I'm serious." Cauler twists the collar of my hoodie in his fist and tugs enough for me to feel it. My breath catches in my throat. I look at him, close enough to smell cinnamon gum and coconut lotion above the sweat and alcohol in the air. I want to close the small gap between us, chase those distinctly Cauler scents with my mouth.

But we're in public, and he's a hockey player, and we're supposed to be rivals.

I lick my dry lips. Look him right in the eyes. "So am I."

The crowd starts pressing in around us again as the sound check finishes up. Cauler lets go of me and I stand up, pressing the heels of my hands into my eyes and taking a deep breath. I feel Cauler straighten up beside me and lower my arms just in time to steady myself against the stage as the people behind us push in closer. The guy at my back is tall enough, he practically leans over me to be closer to the stage, his armpit dangerously close to my face.

Cauler's looking at me. Even as the band we're here for, his favorite band, rushes out onstage and launches into their first song. He keeps looking at me with this wrinkle between his eyebrows.

I lean into him. He ducks his head so I can speak into his ear. "You're wrong, you know."

His breath on my ear is hot, but it sends chills down my neck. "'Bout what?"

"I'd still be doing this without my name. I'd just be enjoying it a lot more."

"So stop playing for your name and start playing for yourself. I know you can. I saw it in Colorado."

I don't really know how to respond, but I don't have the choice anyway with a heavy breakdown in the song sending a surge of energy through the crowd. We're both crushed against the stage so hard I'm afraid I might have to sit out of practice on Monday.

I feel freer, somehow, admitting something like that to Cauler. Maybe it's not the big reveal he's waiting for.

But it's a start.

TEN

'm just getting out of the shower when Cauler sends me a link to a tweet along with the message *how dare you?*

The tweet shows two candid shots side by side, one of me standing next to a girl in line at the crepe station in the dining hall, and another of Cauler and the same girl walking near each other on campus. The tweet itself says *same draft spot, same girl? Must be one uncomfortable locker room.*

I roll my eyes. This is hockey, not Hollywood.

I pull on a pair of gym shorts and collapse into my bed as I type up a response. This has become something of a routine the past week since the concert. Cauler and I send each other everything we find online about us and our rivalry and laugh about it. Sometimes we even go on Twitter and reply to the posts to try to fan the flames.

What can I say? It's fun.

> **Mickey:** I don't even know
> that girls name
> I just wanted a gd crepe

Jaysen: I think it's carol?

Idk

We walk the same way to class t/h

> **Mickey:** Scandalous
> never thought id be the
> subject of tabloid gossip

Jaysen: you sure about that?

I mean

You are friends with nova vinter

> **Mickey:** Shit your right

Jaysen: Either way we're
a special case Terzo
Most interesting thing to
happen to hockey in years

> **Mickey:** Bar was pretty low then

Jaysen: I think you're
plenty interesting

This is another thing that's been happening. Cauler very obviously flirts with me, and I die inside while trying to act oblivious.

> **Mickey:** Pfft
> How

Jaysen: Lots of ways

My chest feels heavy. I shouldn't lead him on. I should leave him on read, make it obvious this isn't gonna happen. But I like it. I like him.

Mickey: you got pretty
low standards then

Jaysen: You sure about that?
What happened with the
algebra midterm?

That guilty feeling is punched right out of my chest. I sit up in bed and look down at my phone, anxiety rising in my blood with a crackle of static. Dorian comes in from his shower, viciously scrubbing his hair with a towel. I try to keep my face as neutral as possible.

My midterm grades weren't great. I mean, I'm still eligible, but they could be better. *Way* better. I ended up with a C in algebra, which I was not expecting at all. A C+ in biology, which would sting worse if I actually planned on staying and doing marine science. An A in Italian, naturally, and a D in college writing, leaving me at a 2.32. Barely hockey eligible, but safe for now.

I want to do better with the second half of the semester. I also don't want Cauler prying about it.

Mickey: What do you mean

Jaysen: Not trying to be like
invasive or anything
But I know you didn't finish it

Mickey: Professor morris
gave me a redo
I already got my ass chewed
out by coach don't worry

"Dude," Dorian says, and I startle a little. I almost forgot he came into the room. "Don't ever be tempted to fill your science requirement with astronomy." His textbook gives a heavy thud as he drops it on his desk.

"I'm in bio," I say, staring at the three dots that show Cauler's typing. "I thought you loved space."

"I do. And I love this class. But there's so many upperclassmen in there just to get the credit 'cause they thought it'd be easy and fun. It's annoying."

He props his head up with an elbow on the desk and hunches his shoulders over the textbook. I have never seen him this grouchy before.

"You okay?" I ask him.

"Fine. Just tired."

There's this pang of familiarity in my gut, but before I can really grasp it, my phone vibrates.

Jaysen: Not gonna lecture
you. I'm just worried.
Would hate to see you not able
to play next semester.

Mickey: Really?
Cause if I'm out that top slot
is yours no contest

Jaysen: I don't want no contest
I wanna bring down the empire

Mickey: Dramatic

Jaysen: Tell that to whoever
crowned your grandpa emperor
all those years ago
but really tho
you ok?

Mickey: I'm fine

I look at Dorian right as it sends. At the way he's slumped at his desk, a hand clutching his own hair. Totally fine.

Mickey: It's just
Hard sometimes

Jaysen: What is?

Mickey: Idk

Life? Living? The pursuit of happiness? Sure, I can open up to Cauler a little bit, but I can't sit here and tell him I'm deeply depressed when I have it so much easier than him. I'm white. Hetero-passing. From a rich family. I have no right to complain to him about how hard life is.

Jaysen: Terzo.

I don't answer. Just stare at my phone until it relocks itself, then stare at my reflection in the screen. Cauler's not an asshole. Okay, not a *complete* asshole. I don't think he'd be rude about it if I told him I was depressed. Still, it seems like too much.

So I take the conversation in a complete 180.

Mickey: Does zero know your gay

My heart pounds. This room is way too hot. I really hope I don't mess this up.

Jaysen: Uhhh idk maybe?
I haven't told him
But I don't think I'm all that subtle
why

My mouth is dry. I lick my lips and swallow hard.

Mickey: He just talks
about us kissing a lot
Like every time we argue
It's like he equates hate with lust

Was that too far? Of course that was too far. That's *my* thing, not Zero's.

> **Jaysen:** Think it had
> something to do with
> 'Your eyes are a nice color'
> And
> 'I like your dimples'

> **Mickey:** I never said i liked them.
> I pointed out their existence

> **Jaysen:** Might also have to do with
> me grabbing your jersey all the time
> Guess that screams sexual tension

> **Mickey:** Weird
> I thought it screamed
> unbearable asshole

> **Jaysen:** Glad someone gets it

Okay. I have successfully bantered with Jaysen Caulfield over text. Now what? Do I leave him on read? That shows control, right? Let him think it was just genuine confusion, simple curiosity that led me to ask that question. He'll never suspect a thing.

But then Cauler double texts, and I swear I have a full-blown heart attack.

Jaysen: To be fair

I do find you pretty okay to look at

That whole dead inside thing

you got going on?

Right up my alley

My soul has ascended. Jesus take the wheel because I. Can't. I'm dreaming still. Dorian's probably lying across the room with his pillow squeezed over his ears so he can't hear my unconscious reactions to this. I am wheezing.

Act. Cool. Mickey.

Mickey: You're ok too i guess

Jaysen: Even with the

tattoos and piercings?

My gma says they make me ugly

Mickey: Especially with the

tattoos and piercings

That's my type

Ask nova

Its why we'd never work out

Jaysen: Good.

Now I know the pain was worth it

Mickey: Howd you even get

them when your not 18 yet

Jaysen: My cousin owns a shop
Does my work for free

       Mickey: Howd the tongue feel

Jaysen: First you're thinking
about kissing me and now you're
thinking about my tongue piercing?
Starting to think you don't despise
me as much as you say

What is the verbal equivalent of a keysmash? Because
that's what I'm feeling right now.

       Mickey: Just trying to get
          you to lower your guard

Jaysen: And you almost had me

We go back and forth like that until I fall asleep holding
my phone. When I wake up in the morning, I expect none of
it to show up in my messages, fully convinced it was a very
detailed, very good dream.

But it's all there. No turning back now.

ELEVEN

Cauler and I both turn eighteen the first week of November, and I get roped into an interview before our next game in honor of becoming draft eligible. With a bunch of recorders in front of my face, one of the reporters says, "There's been whispers of raising the draft age to nineteen. It wouldn't come into play soon enough to have an effect on you, of course, but what are your thoughts on that?"

I narrow my eyes at her. It's the first time I'm hearing about it, but then again, I haven't really been paying attention to hockey outside of my team and our opponents.

Raising the draft age to nineteen. That would be another year with the Royals. Another year at Hartland. Another year to figure out who I actually am as a person. Zero and Kovy would be gone. So would Bailey and Sid and Karim. But it'd be another year with Dorian and Barbie. Delilah and Jade.

Another year with Cauler.

"I like it," I say. The reporters blink at me like it's the exact opposite of what they were expecting. "It's hard enough to be seventeen, eighteen, going into college and being forced to choose what you want to do with the rest of your life before you really even know all your options. Doing it with a contract over your head? Even worse."

"You're saying you'd prefer to stay in the NCAA an extra year rather than go right into the NHL?"

That's a dangerous question. Cauler's already made it clear he's finishing his degree. My answer here could really close the gap in our draft stock. Pretty sure a big part of my appeal over him is that I'll be available as soon as next season.

And the thing is, I do want to stay. But I also want to start my career in hockey. I want them both at the same time, but that's not possible.

"I'm saying," I start slowly, carefully, "I've already learned a lot more in these past few months at Hartland than I did in seventeen years of nothing but hockey."

Cauler locks his arm around my neck and knocks our helmets together on our way out of the locker room, like he's proud of me or something.

Now I'm noticing those sideways looks the boys give us whenever we're within three feet of each other. Like they're waiting for me to leap into his arms or for him to pin me to the wall or something.

My brain's on a constant loop of *you're pretty okay to look at* and *right up my alley* and wow, the smell of cinnamon is now enough to get me going.

I am pathetic.

It's gotten to the point where I don't even care about people finding out. Right now, some mouth-on-mouth action with Jaysen Caulfield would be worth anything and everything.

———

CAULER PLAYS EVEN better than usual that game. He pulls off this one play where he's cutting behind the net and tosses the puck back to me with this sexy-as-hell no-look pass. I almost don't capitalize on it because I'm too busy going *hhnnnngg*. I get it together just in time to wrist a one-timer into the back of the net, and I swear I'm swooning as I meet Cauler against the boards for the celly.

"Holy shit," I breathe, then immediately pull away because can I be any more obvious? Like, chill, James, come on.

We stay right on each other when it comes to points, but he gets more ice time than me with penalty kills. I start putting more effort into defense, in games and in practice, to keep up. It's almost like he's pushing me to do better.

To earn my spot.

But I'd never tell him that.

Barbie sinks to his knees next to me during Saturday's warm-up. He stretches out one of his legs and mumbles, "This is embarrassing."

The tape's reached Kovy's song choice, which I'm guessing is Barbie's problem. It's some kind of country rap, heavy on the country. It's not *terrible*, but definitely not Barbie's style.

"This is Nova's favorite song, dude," I say flatly, crossing one leg over the other and twisting to stretch my back.

He looks at me wide-eyed, mouth guard hanging out of his wide-open mouth. I smirk, and he clamps his jaw shut, glaring. "Since when do you have jokes?"

"Dario and Diana taught me this morning," I say, nodding up toward the stands where Dorian's little brother and sister are arguing over a Nintendo Switch. His family surprised him by coming out to this game, and I swear seeing their reunion almost made *me* cry. Mr. and Mrs. Hidalgo point things out to each other in the arena, waving when they notice me and Barbie looking at them.

Barbie laughs a little. "Yeah, they're funny kids. Little demons, but funny."

"Hey, hey." Dorian skates up and sits on Barbie's other side, sticking his legs out and bending to touch his toes. "Check out the ankles on number eight."

"Be nice, Dori," Barbie deadpans. "We didn't all have someone to teach us how to lace our skates growing up."

Dorian doesn't take the bait. "Dude's playing D-I. He should know how to lace his goddamn skates."

"Maybe he's got weak ankles."

"Maybe he just blows."

Barbie hums, and we stretch on in silence until Cauler joins us. "This is gonna be a blowout," he says as he takes a knee next to me. "Have you *seen* number eight?"

"See!" Dorian says. There's an outburst of noise and cheering from the crowd as the women's team files in to fill the rows right behind the bench. They're coming off a huge win and their energy is high. I need three points tonight to catch up to Delilah.

I push up onto my hands and knees and cross one leg in front of the other for a glute stretch. Cauler clears his throat. His voice sounds a little pinched when he starts rambling about a new Amity song. Dorian and Barbie either don't notice it or ignore it as they join in, but I give him a look over my shoulder.

He's standing, stick across his shoulders, twisting back and forth to stretch his back. As soon as Dorian and Barbie start talking, Cauler's eyes shift down to me. But not incidentally. Not even at my face. I am about 99.9 percent sure Jaysen Caulfield just looked at my ass. My hockey-pants-obscured ass, but still.

I sit back a little in surprise, and his eyes flick up to my face, widening when they meet mine. His mouth falls open slightly, and Coach's whistle blows, calling us in for shots on Colie before puck drop.

We come out viciously and relentlessly the second the clock starts ticking. Dorian has one of his best games so far, blocking shots before Colie can even touch them, stripping Lakers players of the puck whenever they make the mistake of bringing it near him, throwing nasty checks and assisting on goals for me and Zero. Every time he does something impressive while I'm on the bench, I glance over my shoulder at his family.

They're loving every second of it.

Halfway through the third period, I've got two goals and an assist, Cauler's got a goal and an assist of his own, and we're leading 7–0. And I'm having fun. Every time I score and Cauler puts a hand on top of my head and pulls me in for a hug, I feel my heart stop.

The Lakers, however, are decidedly not having fun. Their tempers rise with each passing second. Checks come later and harder, the shoving after whistles more prolonged and violent.

Coach sends our line over the boards with a few minutes left and the words, "Get James that hatty. Don't care how you do it, just make it happen." Cauler and Zero put the puck on my stick every chance they get, passing up clear shots in favor of handing it off to me.

I don't need another point. I'm ahead of both Delilah and Cauler now, and the Lakers are starting to look homicidal. But my teammates want that hat trick for me badly enough, they'll pass up points of their own to get it for me. Even Cauler. My biggest rival. So when a lane opens up, I take the shot, smooth and quick, a laser into the top-left corner of the goal.

The arena erupts, hats raining down on the ice as I turn, throwing my arms up. I'm laughing, expecting Cauler and Zero to lift me off the ice in celebration. Instead, I'm face-to-chest with a red-faced Laker blueliner named Clarkson. He takes one look at my mid-celly smile and crosschecks me hard enough, I stumble backwards, tripping over someone's leg and collapsing in a heap on the ice.

Okay, ouch.

Whistles blow as guys clash above me. I'm sprawled out, breathless, blinking up at Cauler with his hands twisted in Clarkson's jersey, the cages of their helmets pressed together as they hurl insults back and forth. I don't think Cauler will throw a punch, but god, I'd love to see it. Zero helps me to my feet once a ref pulls him away from the chaos, but I don't hear whatever he says to me. Clarkson shoves his fingers into Cauler's cage and shakes him, pushing his head back and refusing to let go even when Cauler holds his hands up in surrender.

I throw myself at him, surprising him enough to break his hold on Cauler. I shove him back another step.

"You're kidding, right?" Clarkson says, catching on right away. "I'm not fighting you."

I shove him again.

"Seriously, I'm not fighting you, James. I'd get shanked by Gary Bettman."

I get close enough that I have to look almost straight up to hold eye contact, saying nothing, just challenging him to back down from a guy damn near a foot shorter than him.

"Christ," he huffs. "Fine! Alright!" He pushes me back out of the scramble in front of the net, the refs distracted as they try to break up four other shoving matches.

Zero says my name, a warning in his voice, but that doesn't stop me from grabbing Clarkson by the jersey and throwing a punch. It's a reach, but I still manage to get him in the cage and bench myself all in one moment of rage. I pull back my fist and do it again, putting all my weight behind it. I've never been in a fight before. I just want to break Clarkson's teeth in, make him think twice about ever putting his hands on Cauler like that again.

He barely reacts to my punches, his helmet and my lack of fighting experience protecting him from any damage. But when he takes a swing of his own, I *feel* it. My helmet absorbs most of it, but it's still enough to stun me for a second, force me to bite down hard on my mouth guard.

I feel the rumble of the crowd more than I hear it, like a bass line pounding in my chest. There's a flash of black and white in my periphery, the refs closing in on us, but I can't let them separate us before I make him hurt. I line up another shot to his chin and take three more to the side of my head.

My face throbs. I taste blood in my mouth. Feels like I took a baseball bat to the skull. The only thing keeping me on my feet is Clarkson's grip on my jersey, my hands twisted into his. I give him another weak shove.

"Thanks a lot, James," he says. His voice sounds like it's coming through water. "Now I'm the asshole that kicked the shit out of the star."

"Fuck you," I spit back.

"Okay, night night, little one." He pushes back on me, easing me down to the ice almost gently and throwing his hands up in surrender when the refs descend on him. "A little late, yeah?" he says as they lead him to the bench.

I swear to god, if everyone doesn't stop screaming, my head's gonna explode.

I brush off the linesman reaching to help me up and roll over to my knees, pulling off my helmet. Blood drips onto the ice, falling from just under my eyebrow. Pink drool dangles from my lips. Everything's rolling like I'm eight shots deep. It's not like I'm used to taking fists to the head. Doesn't help that Clarkson's massive.

An arm falls across my shoulders, and Cauler kneels in front of me. "Terzo, you legend. You need the trainer?"

I shake my head. Bad idea. I'm about to puke all over Cauler's knees and then he'll never look at my ass again. I reach for his arm and let him help me up. He keeps his arm around my waist as the refs follow us to the benches.

"You looked like a Chihuahua taking on a mastiff," Cauler says. "Like an angry little puppy. Adorable."

I can't hold back my grin, even if it hurts. It stays as I step off the ice and stagger down the tunnel toward the training room, slapping my hands against the hands of fans reaching down to me.

The adrenaline starts to fade as soon as I get to the trainer's and she starts dabbing at the blood on my face, the cheering muffled by layers of concrete and distance.

I just benched myself. Because a guy was being an asshole to Cauler. Not even because he crosschecked me. Because of Cauler.

Cauler, my rival. Cauler, who I probably just handed the top pick.

I'VE GOT STITCHES above my eyebrow and a wicked bruise on my jaw, but neither of them hurts as much as my head after dealing with Coach's close-proximity meltdown after the game. That man can yell.

I get a message from Nova once I'm back in my dorm.

> **Nova:** That was almost sexy

> **Mickey:** You saying you liked
> watching me get my ass beat?

> **Nova:** Mickey
> You've seen the fanfic i read

I can't help but snort at that. Nova strictly reads hurt fic involving her favorite fictional guys. If there's any hint of comfort in it, she's not about it. Sometimes I worry about her.

I'm trying to figure out what to send back when the group chat with my sisters pops up.

Nicolette: Dude that was BAD. ASS.

I smile and lie back on my bed, holding the phone over my face.

Mickey: Wouldve been better
if i won

Bailey: If you could've won your
first fight ever against a
guy 20x your size you're
in the wrong sport
Madison: Wait what? Fight?
What did I miss?
Nicolette: Have you not
checked twitter tonight?
Lil bro's a brawler

Mickey: My face hurts

Delilah: don't challenge guys a
foot taller than you dumbass

Mickey: 11 inches at most.

Mikayla: An important distinction

Madison: Explains why dad's
complaining about you not
answering your phone

      Mickey: Oops phones dead

Bailey: You're literally using it
Right now

      Mickey: Oops no service

Bailey: Just call him
He's probably worried

      Mickey: Yeah about my draft stock

Bailey: You know it's starting to
get real old how you whine
about him only caring about the draft

Seriously, I would throw myself in front of a Zamboni right now if it didn't feel like I already got hit by one.

      Mickey: What's annoying is its true

Bailey: No it's literally not

      Mickey: Right.
      Sure.
      K.

Mikayla: HEY LET'S TALK BABY NAMES

Spence suggested Keith.

KEITH.

Can you imagine a newborn

named Keith?

That's the name of a grown

man working in a cubicle

And don't get me started

on his girl names

I WANT GENDER NEUTRAL

I let my phone fall to the floor next to my bed. I don't know why Bailey always feels the need to defend Dad's honor like that. She makes me out to be the bad guy in that relationship and I don't get it.

Maybe because he defended her and Sid and Karim?

Maybe because she's right.

Deep down, I know she is. But I'm not ready to let go of seven years of abandonment issues.

I heave a sigh and reach above me for my planner. Yes, an actual real planner where I write in my homework and due dates. I gotta do something to salvage my midterm grade. I've got readings to do for biology and college writing, and a journal entry to write for Italian.

My phone vibrates on the floor.

I roll off my bed and toss the planner aside, sit down at my desk and open my laptop. But I don't log into my Hartland account and I don't start any readings. Instead, I go to Twitter to read what random strangers have to say about me.

I'm expecting to see things about how I finally showed some team spirit in the form of violent rage and how that's a liability and how maybe I need help off the ice for starters. How I pick fights I have no chance of winning.

But the first thing I see is a tweet saying, *Mickey James III could be named John Doe and he'd still be a #1 pick. He could be 4'11" and still be a #1 pick.* It links to an article talking about why my height shouldn't scare teams away.

My phone keeps going off.

Another tweet says that getting in that fight was exactly what I needed to solidify my hold on the number one spot.

There's hundreds of people talking about how guys will know I won't take their shit now, even if I didn't win. I could've scored six goals in that game and getting beat in a fight still would've been the most badass thing I've ever done.

I poke at the bruise on my jaw and barely feel it. I'm imagining all this, right? I got a concussion and now my brain is seeing what it wants to see. There's even more of it when I refresh the page.

I smile. Small and painful, but still, a smile.

Someone pounds on my floor from below and I almost fall out of my chair, heart jumping into my throat. A girl's muffled yelling tells me to answer my goddamn phone. I practically tiptoe over to it so I don't bother her even more and go to mute the group chat. And yeah, there's dozens of messages from my sisters. But also five from Cauler.

> **Jaysen:** People are saying you
> clinched your draft spot today
> Don't get too comfortable Terzo

> Still got 7 months to battle it out
>
> All i gotta do is get a gordie howe hat
>
> trick tomorrow and it's back on
>
> Kinda jealous of clarkson though

I fall onto my bed and send back:

> **Mickey:** He wasn't too happy
>
> about it so it's not
>
> as great as it seemed apparently

> **Jaysen:** I'm more jealous
>
> of the way it ended

I squint at my phone. I don't get it. It ended with him kicking my ass. Isn't that what we were already talking about?

> **Mickey:** You've had plenty of chances

He reads it immediately, like he hadn't even closed out of the chat, and starts typing. I can feel my heart beating hard, watching those three dots. It's weird. Like when I had a girlfriend for five seconds junior year, the nerves I'd get waiting for her to text me.

We're talking about fighting each other, but he messaged me first. It feels nice.

I am literally a disaster bisexual.

The dots disappear, but no message comes through. He starts typing again before my heart has a chance to drop, then stops before I can get my hopes back up. He does it two more times before I lock the screen and hold my phone to my chest, staring up at the ceiling. When it finally vibrates, I grit my teeth and force myself not to open it right away. I don't want him to think I was sitting here waiting for his response.

I close my eyes and take a deep breath.

Self-control. Don't open it. Don't be suspiciously eager to read his messages. Repress all emotions.

I can't. I don't even last a minute.

> **Jaysen:** You wouldn't say that if
> we were on the same page here.

My thumbs hover over the screen, but I don't type anything. Not yet.

He liked seeing me get led off the ice for the rest of the game? Seeing me get suspended, knowing he's got an entire game tomorrow where he can show off and people can't credit me for his success?

But that wouldn't make him jealous of Clarkson. Maybe it was the way he laid me out on the ice like I was the most pathetic thing he'd ever come in contact with.

Maybe it was just the way he *laid me out on the ice.*

Oh.

My hands shake as I type.

> **Mickey:** I think we might be

> **Jaysen:** Prove it

I tap my phone against my forehead. Am I really gonna do this right now? It could ruin everything.

But I deserve a life outside of hockey, right? Not even just deserve—I *need* a life outside hockey.

I take a deep breath and force it out through my teeth.

Mickey: Meet me at the rink

I'M SHOVING MY feet into my skates when Cauler shows up. He sits in his stall and starts putting on his own. "What're we doing?"

I pull my laces tight. "Practicing one-timers."

He snorts. "It's not gonna help in the draft, you know. They know what they're getting from us at this point."

I glare at him as I push on my gloves. "What happened to seven months to battle it out?"

One of his eyebrows twitches up, and I want to jump him right now. But my nerves are tingling and my heart is barely keeping up with the adrenaline and I'm not ready yet. I grab my stick from the twig rack and head out before I can act on impulse. His footsteps trail after me. I push the stack of pucks off the boards and corral them into one of the face-off circles. I go to the opposite point, and Cauler's standing with the pucks when I look back.

He's watching me curiously, dressed in black joggers and a hoodie, glasses on. My mouth waters at the sight of him. He tilts his head and waits for me to nod before sending me pass after pass.

I whiff on most of them. Slap shots just aren't my thing.

The ones I do get a stick on are high or wide or barely have the strength behind them to reach the net.

To my credit, I am extremely distracted.

Cauler's sending his passes weaker and weaker, drawing me closer to him. My heart races and I can hardly breathe and finally . . . I'm barely a step away. I look up at him, breathless and electric, and he looks down at me with his head cocked to the side.

"Those were some of the worst passes I've ever seen from you," I try. My voice shakes.

"What are we doing here, Terzo?"

I lick my lips. Shift my weight from skate to skate. "I don't know. I just . . ." I feel comfortable here? Don't have to worry about Dorian and Barbie barging in? I look down at the space between us. I swear my breathing echoes through the entire empty arena.

He steps closer, letting his stick drop to the ice. He pulls his right hand out of his glove and reaches up, trailing his fingers across my cheekbone and pushing them back into my hair. Each second lasts longer than the final moments of a tight game. I can smell the cinnamon on his breath, the sweat from inside his gloves.

"Same page?" he asks softly, a slight tremor in his voice.

"Same page," I almost whisper.

He shakes off his other glove and wraps his arm around my waist, pulling me in. I drop my stick and almost trip over it as I step closer, way too eager.

But he doesn't kiss me. He turns us around so my back is to the boards, and I grab hold of his shirt as he guides me until I'm pressed against the glass.

And then his mouth is on mine, his full weight pinning me and both hands pushing into my hair. I feel it *everywhere*. It takes everything in me to hold myself up.

I let go of his shirt to reach for the back of his head and pull him down to my level. His skates scrape against the ice as he struggles for balance, but he doesn't stop kissing me. It hurts, with all the bruises on my face, but the pain is nothing compared to the total ecstasy of his mouth on me. The metal hoop in his lip clacks against my teeth, and it's a little awkward, a little messy, and a lot frantic, but it's easily the best kiss I've ever been given. And I've kissed a lot of people.

I don't know if it's the way he has me shaking, gasping, my fingers numb, or if it's just because it's *Jaysen Caulfield*.

His hands slide down to my hips, slip under my shirt, send chills through my core as they brush against my bare skin. I sigh into his mouth, grab fistfuls of his shirt again to hold steady.

My head is fuzzy by the time he pulls away, my breathing ragged. If it weren't for his weight against me, I'd be melting into the ice right now.

It's a feeling I could get used to. Before either of us catches our breath or says something stupid, I lean up and kiss him again.

OKAY, BUT PICKING up the pucks together after that is extremely awkward. My legs feel weak, like I just did a whole-ass bag skate or something, and I'm doing my best to stay turned away from Cauler. These joggers really don't hide anything.

My mouth still feels numb and dry and my heart rate only slows back to normal when I'm in my sneakers and my skates are put away.

I should say something. It'd be weird to walk out without saying anything. Right? Like admitting defeat. Or maybe saying something would make him all smug. Even more than usual. I should act like nothing happened. Don't change anything. Let him think I don't care one way or another.

"Uh, Terzo?" Cauler's holding the door open, looking back at me. "You plan on staying the night here or what?"

The collar of his hoodie is stretched out from where I was pulling on it. It's obvious what he was just up to. I feel myself blushing just looking at him and tuck my chin to my chest to hide it as I follow him out.

We walk close enough that our arms touch. When he's sure no one's looking, he even slips his hand along the small of my back, sending chills through me.

I've got a thread of messages from Dorian demanding I come to the hockey house.

> **Dorian:** Terzoooooooooo
> Where are you?
> Hockey house now
> You missed team dinner

Which means.

My room.

Is empty.

My heart's straight-up pounding as we get closer to my

building. He has to walk past mine to get to his. My window of opportunity is closing.

How do you invite a boy back to your dorm room? Last time I hooked up with a guy, it was my senior year lab partner, and we were studying in his room while his parents were outside, so I didn't have to do any of this awkward, I don't know, propositioning?

We walk past the front entrance of my building. My room is toward the back, so it's not totally obvious that I'm stalling. I duck my head farther into my hood when we pass by a group of drunk people singing the alma mater in the parking lot.

As soon as they're behind us, I suck it up.

"Do you—" I say at the same time Cauler says, "Are you going—"

We stop outside the last door to my building and face each other. I look up at him and wait for him to finish what he was saying. He licks his lips, glances around the parking lot. Puts his hands in his pockets and hikes his shoulders up.

I can feel his nerves.

He doesn't look at me when he finally says, "Were you gonna go to the hockey house?"

"Nah," I say. "We missed dinner."

He swallows. "Ah."

I shift from foot to foot. "Were you?"

"I don't think so."

The air between us feels dangerously charged. Or maybe that's the anxiety. It's freezing, but my hands sweat in my jacket pockets and my face feels hot.

"Did you wanna . . ." I trail off, motioning vaguely toward the door with my elbow.

Cauler looks at me, meets my eyes. Doesn't look away. I can't breathe. My whole body shakes, and it's not just from the cold. I don't think I've ever been this nervous when it comes to something like this.

Maybe with Nova, but that was because it was the first time. I wasn't even this nervous my first time with a guy. It's not like I have *feelings* for Cauler, either.

He's just . . . really hot.

Cauler nods his head. "Yeah," he says. His voice cracks and he has to clear his throat. "Yeah, okay."

WE BARELY MAKE it through the door before Cauler's pulling off my shirt and putting his lips against my neck.

"Okay?" he asks when my back hits the mattress.

"Can I?" I ask with my hands at the waistband of his joggers.

"Do you want to?" he asks with a wrapped condom in his hand.

A breathless *yes* at each progression. He's gentle when he needs to be. Less so when I ask him not to. He kisses me like he means it. Holds me close to him.

It's enough to rip my empty chest wide-open.

NOVA VINTER

Mickey: This just in
Hooking up with a hot guy
does not cure depression

Nova: I could've told you that

Mickey: Well why didn't you??

Nova: You never asked?
Regret it though?

Mickey: I mean it literally
just happened
Like he just left
And it hasn't come back to bite
me in the ass yet so not yet

Nova: Then what's it matter
Nothing's gonna cure your
depression but
you can find things that
make it easier to handle
If that's Jaysen Caulfield
and you're both into it
then do what you want

Mickey: Who said it was
Jaysen Caulfield?

Nova: Mickey.

TWELVE

auler leaves before Dorian gets back.

I can't sleep. I can hear the music coming from Dorian's headphones all the way across the room, and I don't get how he can sleep with it so loud.

But it's not his music keeping me up. I don't know what it is, I just feel kind of . . . I don't know, lonely, I guess. I'm used to being alone. Not so used to *feeling* alone like this.

A twin-size mattress should not feel this big.

I pull the blankets over my head and close my eyes. I need to sleep. I can't play, but I still have to be at the game tomorrow. Plus I've got two papers to write and I'm dangerously close to academic probation. Coach and the athletics director don't care who I am, they'll still bench me. I'll have to bust my ass next semester if I want to play through the Frozen Four.

Which reminds me. I only have four months left with the Royals. Six at Hartland. Then I'll be alone in whatever city drafts me and determines my entire future.

I throw off the blankets and scramble for a clean hoodie from the floor before racing out into the cold, heading for Delilah's building. I slip in behind a resident before the door can close and lock on me and take the stairs two at a time to the second floor. I pound on Jade and Delilah's door without bothering to be quiet about it.

The RA reacts first, sticking his head out of his room at the end of the short hall and glaring at me. "Seriously, bro, it's three in the morning, can you not?"

I stare at him blankly, holding eye contact as I give the door three more slow, heavy knocks. He shakes his head and rolls his eyes before backing up into the darkness of his room. I wouldn't want to deal with my petty bullshit, either.

Jade answers the door in a sports bra and sweatpants, one side of her hair pressed flat against her skull, the other blown out wide. Her eyes are half-closed, and it takes her a few seconds before she's able to focus them on me.

"Oh," she says. Her eyes trail down to my neck, and she's suddenly wide-awake. "Oh."

I frown, touching my throat. It feels like pressing on a bruise. Oh. No. I squeeze past Jade into the room and run for the mirror on top of one of the dressers. There is a massive, dark hickey on the left side of my throat.

"Kill me." There is no way I'm hiding this.

"Take it you've had a good night," Jade says, yawning. She leans against the dresser with her arms crossed.

"Kill me," I say louder.

"I will if you don't shut up," Delilah grumbles from the giant bed they've created by pushing them both together. She's not even visible under the mass of blankets and pillows piled on top of her. I crawl into the bed next to where I think she might be lying.

"Please do," I mumble.

I can get away with hiding out in my room with a hoodie pulled up over my head most of the day, but there'll be cameras at the game. Cameras and thousands of people with cell phones. Then there's study hall on Sunday and game tape and a light skate Monday. Two games next week, more cameras on me, and my parents here, and no way this'll fade in time.

Jade sits on the other side of me, sandwiching me between them as Delilah wrestles her way out of her blankets just enough to see. She squints in the light and pushes her head back into the pillows for a better angle when she looks at me. She scowls. "That is repulsive. You are my little brother, get that away from me."

I feel like I'm dissolving. I roll over onto my stomach and bury my face in a pillow, arms curled under me.

It's too much. I smell like saliva. I need a shower. I need sleep. I need water. I need to work on my papers. I need to go back to the rink. I *need*.

I spent two full seasons with the NTDP and never grew attached to any of my teammates. A few months with the Royals and I'm already dreading the day our season ends and I lose them. I don't even know how it happened or when, but I care about them.

And soon they'll all be added to my list of former teammates, Dorian and Barbie and Cauler still here, still with one another, with team study halls and parties at the hockey house and I'll be off in whatever city drafts me. Alone.

"I don't want to leave," I say. I pull the pillow up over my head to hide from them.

"What do you mean?" Delilah asks slowly.

"Hartland. I want to stay."

"You can," Jade says. She puts a hand on my shoulder, and I try to stop shaking so she doesn't feel it. Fighting it only makes it worse. "You have a full ride. You can have four years if you want them. You don't have to leave."

"The NHL will wait for you," Delilah says.

But she's wrong. If I stay, there's a good chance I'll lose the top pick. The goal I've had set for me my entire life. The one thing I want more than anything.

I can't give that up for anything.

Not even Jaysen Caulfield.

I'M NOT ALLOWED on the bench with the team for the next game, so I sit with Jade in the row behind where the women's team will sit once they finish changing. All anyone wants to talk about is my fight, and I chew on the rim of my plastic cup like it'll hide me and everything I did last night. Delilah used cover-up on my hickey and honestly god bless her, because I didn't need to add that to the bruises plastered all over the internet now.

Most of the people back off when Jade starts telling me all about her plans for her final art portfolio, but a couple are still rude enough to try to interrupt.

I ignore them.

"I don't know, I'm worried though," she says as the first few women's players start filing into their seats. "I feel like nothing is original anymore, like anything I come up with, someone's already done, and done better, and even if they haven't people will say they did because I'm a Black woman. People don't like to admit when a Black woman can do something better than them."

"Gonna be real hard to deny it with the work you do," I say. I don't know anything about art, but I know when something looks good, and hers looks *good*.

Jade sighs, watching as Delilah makes her way toward us. "They always find a way."

It's weird seeing Delilah in something other than a dress or hockey gear, matching her team in their postgame sweats. She slumps into the seat right in front of Jade, and when I say slumps, I mean she's sunk so low, she's barely on the seat at all. Jade leans forward and offers her the tea she brought in a travel mug and a pill over her shoulders. Delilah tilts her head back and says, "God, I love you. Thank you."

Jade kisses her temple and sits back as Delilah downs the pill with a short sip of tea.

"What's wrong with her?" I ask.

Jade frowns. "Cramps."

I've been in a group chat with my sisters long enough to know that's not something to scoff at. Especially not with Delilah. She's got something called endometriosis and apparently it's worse than a heart attack.

"But you just played a game!" I say. And she straight-up dominated the ice.

"Such is life with a uterus," Delilah grumbles.

I grimace, turning my attention back to the ice where my team is finishing their warm-up. Dorian, Barbie, and Cauler skate toward the bench together. The sight of Cauler makes it hard to breathe, and when he looks up at me and smiles, I think I die a little.

I spend most of the first period talking with Jade and answering questions from the fans sitting around us, to the point where I'm no doubt gonna be chewed out by Coach again for not paying attention.

Seeing the Royals play from the outside is damn near a religious experience. We've settled into something fast and fluid and beautiful and completely worthy of our 10-3-1 record. Our talent is kind of front-loaded on the top line, but the other three aren't far behind. Our blueliners are easily the best in the NCAA, and Colie's been a beast in goal.

My old teams were good. I've lost count of the number of championships I've won over the years. I got a Clark Cup with the NTDP U17s and a gold medal with the U18s in the IIHF Worlds last season. But I never really felt anything from those victories or for the guys sharing them with me. I've never felt pride filling my chest so fully it literally aches, especially not for a team barely halfway through its season.

There's not a doubt in my mind they'll be adding a new championship banner to the rafters next October. I can almost imagine myself standing on this ice, watching the banner go up with Cauler and Dorian and Barbie beside me. In reality, I'll be off in whatever city drafts me in June, watching a livestream on the Royals' website if I'm lucky.

Every time my line takes the ice, my heart jumps. Wicker got pulled up from the second line to replace me, and it didn't take long for them all to adapt. Wicker adds this little extra layer of grit onto the speed and flash style we've developed together. He makes this sick cross-ice pass to Zero in the third that would've been an assist if Zero didn't ring it off the pipe.

I let out a whooshing breath.

"You worried Wicker's gonna steal your spot?" one of the players from the women's team asks, half-turning in her seat to grin at me.

"No," I lie. I am never not worried about someone taking my spot. On the ice, in the draft, on this campus, in the lives of Dorian and Barbie and Cauler. Coach's already given my spot away once, so I know he's not afraid to make changes. God. What if I don't fit in with another line and my play suffers? What if everyone decides it was Cauler making me look good instead of the other way around?

Because Cauler's playing just as good without me as he does with me. I can't stop looking at him even when he's off puck. The way he moves on the ice has my palms sweating so bad, I'm almost constantly wiping them on my jeans. It's worse—better—when he makes this downright nasty play, practically breaking the ankles of two separate blueliners. They look like they've never played hockey before in their lives as he weaves through them on the way to the net. He puts the puck bar down and throws himself at the glass in celebration.

And then. When he breaks away from the boys' huddle, on his way to the bench. He finds me in the stands and points a finger right at me, this smug little grin on his face. And he winks.

I feel it in my soul.

I melt down in my seat and hold my cup in front of my

mouth, face tilted down. I really don't need my blushing broadcasted over the jumbotron.

> **Jaysen:** Did that goal look
> as sexy as it felt?

I lock my phone before Delilah or Jade can get a look at it. It feels weird leaving the arena with the fans, but Coach apparently wants to mess with my head or something, because he banned me from the locker room on top of my one-game suspension.

It's working, too. I used to be itching to get out, away from hockey as fast as possible, to enjoy as much of a break as I could. But now I miss my team. I should be there.

I pull my phone back out and let Delilah and Jade get a couple steps ahead of me.

> **Mickey:** Hard to say
> I mean it was pretty yeah
> But I'm not exactly aroused
> by hockey plays

> **Jaysen:** Lmao
> Explain last night then

I shove my phone in my pocket and hide my burning face in my hood.

AS GOOD AS things have been going, the days are getting shorter, so my depression doesn't give a single shit. It's getting too cold to do homework at the dock between classes, but as soon as I get into my room all I want to do is lie in bed and watch YouTube videos of near-death experiences caught on camera. As soon as I hit the mattress I am just done. I don't even realize how much time I've wasted away until Dorian bursts through the door and throws himself on his bed, groaning. That means it's past noon.

"You ever enter a room quietly?" I ask. It's common enough at this point that I don't have a heart attack every time he comes back anymore, but still.

"No." His voice is muffled by the pillows.

Okay, so I might have zero social skills, but even I can tell when Dorian, literal ball of sunshine, is in distress. Still, all I can think to say is, "You okay?"

Dorian's head pops up from the pillows in an instant, looking at me like he didn't realize I was in the room even after speaking to me. He stares at me for a moment with his mouth open before rolling dramatically onto his back, throwing an arm over his eyes for good measure. "Today has been the worst day of my life. I want to fling myself into the lake."

The room feels stale and depressing and if I don't get some fresh air soon I might suffocate. So it's not entirely selfless when I say, "I don't know about flinging yourself in, but sitting by the lake always helps me. I'll go with. Keep you from drowning yourself if you want."

Dorian lowers his arm to look at me again. I don't blame him for the surprised look on his face. I mean, when have I ever made a sociable suggestion? I'm about to say forget it and go back to my YouTube spiral when he pushes himself off the bed and tilts his head toward the door.

"Okay. Let's go."

We don't talk on the way down to the dock. I pull my hands into my sleeves and cross my arms tight over my chest to block out some of the cold. Dorian lopes along beside me, close enough to share body heat. He shoves his hands into the pockets of his chinos and hikes his shoulders up to his ears. We won't last long at the dock in this cold, even with hoodies under our coats. The sky looks ready to dump eight feet of snow on us.

It's tempting to let the silence stretch on once we're sitting beside each other on the dock. I could use the quiet. The smell of cold air and the time to think with only the sounds of wind on water. But I brought Dorian here because he's my friend and I'm going to help him, dammit.

So I say, "Talk to me."

Dorian's next breath is sharp. He holds it for a long time, watching himself kick his feet over the water, before letting it out in a slow sigh. "As soon as I woke up, I knew it was gonna be a bad day."

"Did something happen?"

He rakes his fingers through his hair. "No. I just woke up so . . . tired. And then it was just a self-fulfilling prophecy from there. I was late to class. Forgot my textbook. Zoned out so bad that I had no idea what was going on when my professor called on me. Got to my next class and realized we had an assignment due that I completely forgot about."

He keeps his eyes on the water as he talks, even when he eventually pulls his legs up and crosses them, even when he starts tugging anxiously on his hair, even when the waves distort his reflection.

"I thought I was doing better," he says, almost to himself. "I don't know what happened."

"It's one rough day," I say, even though I'm pretty sure there's way more to it than that. "Don't beat yourself up about it."

He sighs heavily and drops his hands into his lap, wringing them together. "It's more than that though. Like, I know I seem like a super happy person all the time, but I'm just . . . not. I'm depressed as shit. And it's not like I have any reason for it. My family is perfectly balanced and boring. Both my parents are professors. They've always been supportive and attentive and caring. I haven't gone through any major trauma or anything like that. My biggest dream of being in the NHL is coming true, and in the meantime I get to study something I really love, so why am I so miserable?"

"You don't need a reason to be depressed," I say automatically. "It's chemistry."

Dorian huffs a humorless laugh. "Y'see, logically I know that. But when you're in it, your brain uses whatever it can to beat you down, and that's one of them. That other people have it so much worse than me and I'm being selfish by being so sad."

Jesus. It's like he's taking the words right out of my head. "I know what you mean," I say cautiously. This isn't something I really talk about, but what's the harm when Dorian goes through the same thing?

He pulls his sleeves over his hands and presses them against his eyes. "You, too, huh?"

"Yeah."

"Y'know, I figured. How do you handle it?"

I laugh through my nose, watching a small sailboat with sails in Royals black and purple glide across the lake not far out. "I lie in bed and watch YouTube."

There's a beat of silence before he says, "Better than pulling your hair out."

He reaches up and brushes back the thick mop of his dark hair, revealing a couple patches of nearly bare scalp above his right ear. He holds it there for a second before letting his hair fall back into place, then leans forward with his elbows on his knees, staring off across the lake, fingers clasped in front of him. He presses his thumbs to his lips and speaks around them. "This is what I do when it gets real bad. I can't help it. It's an actual thing I'm diagnosed with. Trichotillomania. So it's not, like, just a me problem, it's a real thing."

"You don't have to justify it to me," I say. "I know depression works differently for everyone."

"You know when it gets bad and it feels like you have no control? Well, this makes me feel like I have just a little bit of control over something, even though I know it's the exact opposite." The words rush out of him like he's relieved just to be saying them. "Half the time I'm not even aware I'm doing it. How is that control, y'know? It's kind of like how I make myself out to be this super happy, bubbly person, so I decide how people see me. But it's exhausting, dude."

"Have you been talking to Barbie about it? I mean, Nova's the only person I really talk to about my issues, and you two seem just as close as we are."

Dorian tosses his head back and looks at the sky, groaning. His jaw clenches and he swallows hard. "Yeah, usually. But . . . I don't want to tell him I . . . relapsed, I guess. It's embarrassing."

"You really think he'd judge?"

"No, but." He shrugs and tucks his hands into his armpits. We really shouldn't stay out here much longer. We're gonna end up with pneumonia. "It's still hard. He tries, but he doesn't understand the way someone else who goes through it would."

I watch him in silence for a long moment. I don't like the helpless tone in his voice or feeling completely powerless to help him. I don't know how to comfort people. But Dorian's done his best for me and I owe it to him to try.

"You should tell him," I say softly. "He cares about you. I'm pretty sure he'd do anything for you."

"I know."

"And, like, I know we're never gonna be as close as the two of you are, but I'll do what I can, too. I might not ever really know what to say, but I can always listen."

He bumps my shoulder with his, giving me this little half smile. "Aw, Terzo. Same goes for you, y'know."

We both shiver when the wind picks up, a couple stray snowflakes floating down to melt in the lake. I don't want to be the first one to move. I offered to sit out here with Dorian, so I'll stay here until we both freeze to death if that's what he wants.

But it doesn't take long before he says, "I'm freezing my nipples off out here, dude. Wanna run to the d-hall first, get some coffee?"

He starts to stand, but I reach for his sleeve and hold him in place. Dorian watches me, waiting. I like Dorian. If there's anyone besides Cauler I'd want to stay in touch with after I leave, it's him. I told him one of my secrets. Why not the other?

"Do you consider us friends?" I ask. My voice is rough, my nerves coming through.

He smiles. It's small and a little bit sad, but it gives me my answer before he even says, "Duh. What kind of question is that?"

"So can I tell you something only a few people know?"

Now his smile opens up and he gets this knowing glint in his eye. My face burns despite the cold. Of course he's figured it out by now. "Absolutely."

I sigh. "You totally know already."

"Maybe. Try me."

"I'm bi." It comes out blunt, all the nerves wiped out by his grin.

"That's great, Terzo." He twists his hand to grab my forearm and haul me to my feet. "Thank you for trusting me enough to tell me."

"How'd you figure it out?"

"Pfft. Have you seen the way you look at Cauler? I'll show you a picture sometime."

He slings his arm across my shoulder and keeps it there as we walk to the dining hall, my hands in my pockets.

"Does this mean I can send you depression memes now?" he asks, and I feel freer than I have in ages.

DORIAN AND I actually act like roommates for once, hanging out in our room just the two of us. He sits next to me on my bed and shows me the project he and Barbie have been working on for their film and media class. It's some fake documentary type thing, like *The Office* or *Parks and Rec*, but with the Royals hockey teams. There's interviews with a bunch of players, even a bit with Delilah talking about me as a little kid and Cauler doing spot-on impressions of our coaches.

Dorian's a wreck through practice that night, plays sloppy, nowhere near as talkative as usual. He can't even look Barbie in the eye. I have to physically push him toward Barbie as we head out of the arena for him to finally pull him aside. He tells him something in quiet Spanish, then gives me a nervous smile over his shoulder and follows him toward his dorm.

I feel a little empty, watching them leave, shoulders hiked up and arms brushing like they're sharing each other's warmth. The boys are laughing all around me as we head down the hill, but none of them are laughing *with* me. Even if I can call some of them my friends now, I don't have anything like they do.

I stand in the middle of our room for a few minutes once I get back there, taking in the quiet. I don't like it. Even when Dorian's here, silently doing homework while I work on my own, at least I know I have someone else around.

He doesn't come back before I go to bed, and I wake up the next morning with a jerk, Barbie flicking my ear.

"You're drooling, Terzo," he says.

I grumble, wiping a hand across my mouth only for it to come back dry. I glare at him as he collapses onto Dorian's bed, pressed up close to the wall with his back to the room. I rub sleep from my eyes and check the time on my phone. Seven a.m.

"We didn't sleep," Dorian mutters, standing nearby.

"You okay?" I whisper.

Dorian lets out a long, slow breath, looking back at Barbie over his shoulder. "Not really. But I will be."

I nod and leave to take a shower. When I come back to the room, Dorian's asleep, too, curled up with his knees and forehead pressed against Barbie's back. I get ready for class as quietly as possible so I don't wake them.

THIRTEEN

The latest NHL Mock Draft has Cauler going first.

I'm not gonna let it bother me. We still got seven months till the draft; it's all speculation at this point.

But then YouTube has to go and recommend a video called "Unpopular Opinion Re: NHL Draft." It's from this hockey vlogger named Rhys Sarnac who prides himself on being a fan of hockey in general and not just one team. He's got a hat for each NHL team hanging on the wall behind him in every video and a closet full of jerseys of all colors. Except ever since Seattle came into the league, he's been buying more and more of their merch and showing hints of the homer bias he always rags on other vloggers for. He also makes a point of talking me down. Like it's too mainstream to think I'm good or something, I don't know.

I subscribe to him anyway, because I enjoy suffering.

Today, he's wearing a Canucks hat and Blue Jackets jersey. He starts the video talking about the latest draft rankings, how he agrees with just about everything except the order of the top three.

"I know I'm gonna get plenty of hate for this," he says. "But people are not paying enough attention to Alex Nakamoto. The guy had 161 points in sixty-eight games last season and is on track to beat that this season. In fact, he's on track to overtake the OHL single season point record Doug Gilmour's held since 1983. He's got Jaysen Caulfield's size and Mickey James's hands, and the only reason he's number three is because everyone is so obsessed with this rivalry they've got going on over at Hartland University."

I lean back on my pillows and prop my laptop up on my knees. This is gonna be a good one.

"This is the NHL we're talking about here," Rhys reminds his viewers. "It's not some reality TV show. There's no such thing as family legacies in hockey. A guy doesn't get to come into the league on his daddy's coattails." He holds his hands up and bows his head slightly like he's already trying to calm the comment section. "I understand James is a good player. But he's not top-pick material. His size might not have been too much of a problem in lower-level hockey, but no one's coming into the Show at five foot five and making a lasting impact. Hockey is too physical. It's one of the most brutal sports on the planet. There are times when someone's coming up on James and I have to look away 'cause I'm afraid I'm about to witness a fatal injury, I'm just saying. I know it's beyond his control, but still."

Okay, so this was supposed to be a video about Alex Nakamoto and it's become yet another roast session. He spends four whole minutes trash-talking me before finally getting to the point. "Nakamoto should be a contender for top pick, but I'd be okay with him taking second as long as it was to Caulfield and not James. He's getting the shaft because people want some kind of fairy-tale story."

I scroll down to the comments while he keeps talking. The first one says *did a short guy steal your girl or?* Another says *you probably got a shrine to mickey james in your closet bro. you talk about him enough.*

There's hundreds of comments, some of them like that, some of them agreeing with Rhys. There's a whole essay predicting how Nakamoto's gonna sneak up on us while Cauler and I are too busy insulting each other on Twitter and a full-on thesis about how overrated I am.

I've gotten better about not letting things like this get to me as the season's progressed, so I'm only mildly annoyed when the video ends. I scroll up to give it my usual petty thumbs-down and am faced with the most personally disrespectful picture of Cauler I have ever seen in my life.

The thumbnail for one of the recommended videos is a candid shot of Cauler. He's got on his glasses and a forward-facing hat and one of those hoodies with the weird, slouchy-looking collars. His head is tilted to the side, showing off the curve of his neck, and his smile is bright and crooked and sexy as all hell. I can still feel that lip ring against my teeth, the way that smile felt pressed against my throat.

Oh *god*.

I click on the video, a roundup of the hottest young guys in hockey. I'm the first one up, which is technically the bottom of the list, sure, but also more than a little surprising. The narrator sounds like a college girl, talking about how

I was both blessed by my Italian mother for my looks and cursed by her for my size and that if I were just six inches taller, I'd be drop-dead. Whatever. I skip ahead to Cauler.

He's number one. Of course he's number one. Beat out a bunch of NHL rookies and guys who've already been drafted.

And I had sex with him. Once, but still.

My face gets hotter with every picture that comes up while the girl talks. Cauler on ice in his Gamblers gear. Cauler in his black street clothes. Cauler with intensity in his eyes, burning through the cage of his Royals helmet. Cauler sweating at the gym. Cauler, for some unknown, completely unnecessary reason, shirtless.

Okay, yep, that's too much. I get up and lock the door for the next five minutes.

I have to go to the bathroom after and splash water on my face to cool down. How am I supposed to look Cauler in the eye now? Having sex with someone is one thing; this is something else *entirely*.

I take out my phone to catch up on Nova's snaps, watching a video of her ranting about an asshole in line in front of her at a coffee shop with a filter squishing her face as I get back to my room.

It's not empty the way I left it. Cauler's standing in the middle of my room. He turns his head in the middle of a smile, thumbs hooked in the straps of his backpack, and for a second he is an exact replica of the photo that just ruined me.

His smile changes when he sees me, like he's not sure what to do with his face. Or like he can tell. My face gets hot. Again. Because I lost my ability to conceal my feelings somewhere back in mid-October.

"Okay, so," Dorian says from over by his bed where I can't see from the doorway. Cauler turns back to him, and I hurry to close the door and get back to my laptop. Thank god I didn't leave anything incriminating up on the screen. "I'm kinda leaning toward the institutionalization of death, but then there's the whole denial of bereavement in late-stage capitalism that's pretty interesting, too."

"You sure you don't want to research the logistics of launching corpses into orbit to save space on Earth?" Barbie deadpans. He's lying flat on his back on Dorian's bed with his phone held right above his face with this giddy smile. I send a quick snap of him to Nova with the caption *wonder who he's texting*.

"Ugh, god, could you imagine?" Dorian grimaces. "We'd be like Saturn but with a ring of dead people."

"Metal as fuck," Cauler says. "I'll be the first to go."

"And now you have your paper topic," Barbie says. Judging by the sly selfie Nova sends back, they're definitely flirting at this very moment. "You're welcome."

"We are not doing our final project on corpse rings," Dorian says definitively, settling onto the floor and opening up a textbook. I pretend not to notice when Cauler glances back at me before sitting on the floor by my bed.

"What is happening?" I finally ask. Coming back from an existential bathroom crisis into a conversation about death and space corpses. Not how I expected my Thursday night to go.

"Cauler and I are doing our Death and Dying project together," Dorian says. "Barbie's here 'cause he's obsessed with me and I can't get rid of him."

Barbie's too busy smiling at his phone to retaliate. He's so happy it makes my chest ache. Knowing it's Nova on the other end of it is enough to make me wanna cry. If just one good, lasting thing comes from me being at Hartland, I hope it's them.

I grab the tangled mess of my headphones from next to my pillow and work on fixing them. "Why do it here?"

Dorian arranges his laptop, textbook, papers, and notebooks around him on the floor in the most precise chaos I've ever seen. His notes are clean and organized and detailed and exactly what I'd expect from an astronomy major who was sitting at a 4.0 at the midterm of his first semester of college.

"Seniors are thesis-ing in the players' lounge, and the library is fuckin' lit tonight for some reason," he says.

"Why?" Cauler asks. He tilts his head to the side, stretching the line of his shoulder and neck long and inviting. "You not want us here?"

His hair is starting to grow out on top. He's got a dark freckle behind his right ear. The plugs he has in today are black roses, a birthday gift he got from Zero. He smells like fresh laundry.

"It's Dorian's room, too," I say. Cauler chuckles and we are so obvious, how have we not been straight-up called out yet?

I get the cords untangled and slip the buds into my ears, plugging them into my laptop. I have an Italian assignment due tomorrow. Something simple that'll take ten minutes and then I won't have to worry about it in the morning. But I can't focus with Cauler literally leaning against my bed when I can't even touch him.

I'M BARELY AWAKE by the time Cauler and Dorian wrap it up for the night. Barbie fell asleep an hour ago, and Nova took to messaging me instead about how perfect he is, which is just plain weird when I can see him sleeping with his hand halfway down his pants and his mouth wide-open just across the room from me.

"Yeah, so, with this outline we could probably turn this thing in early," Dorian says as he gets his books and papers together. "Get that extra credit, boiiii."

"We can work on it after the game tomorrow," Cauler says. He zips his backpack and slings it over his shoulder and doesn't look at me.

"Good idea, dude. Party without guilt after."

I have YouTube open in front of me and piles of homework to do and I feel like absolute garbage. These guys all have a future in the NHL, just like me. They still take college seriously. They're kind of overachievers about it, really.

Dorian shakes Barbie awake. "Get out of here, flojo. Don't you have homework to do?"

Barbie yawns, stretching both arms above his head. "I'm all caught up. See ya, Terzo."

"Bye."

Cauler doesn't acknowledge me as he walks out, which is probably, definitely for the best, but it still feels like a punch to the gut.

"Y'know you guys don't have to hide around me and Barbie, right?" Dorian says when the door closes. "We're not assholes."

"We're not hiding anything," I mumble.

"Sure," he says, drawing it out and rolling his eyes as he turns toward his bed.

My phone buzzes. I look at it, expecting another text from Nova.

It's Cauler.

> **Jaysen:** Can we talk
> Laundry room?

I take a deep breath. Tap my phone against my forehead a few times. My stomach doesn't come with me when I stand up.

"Going to the bathroom," I say.

Dorian doesn't even look up as he says, "Think of me."

I hesitate on my way to the door, blinking at him for a moment before shaking my head and coming back with "I always do."

I feel sick with anxiety on my way down the stairs.

Can we talk.

The possibilities of what he's gonna say are so immense and terrifying I'll probably go into cardiac arrest if I try to grasp on to one.

I hesitate at the top of the stairs leading down to the basement. I can hear the TV in the lounge, just loud enough to know someone's watching *Say Yes to the Dress*. And no, it's not my sisters' or Nova's fault I know that.

I tiptoe down a few stairs and crouch till I can see two girls huddled in the corners of the couch with laptops in their laps, not paying any attention to the stairs or the laundry room. I quietly make my way down the rest of the way and into the room immediately to the right, easing the door closed behind me.

I keep one hand on the knob and the other flat against the wood for a moment, listening. The sound of the TV is muted through the door, but there's no sign of movement in the lounge. I let out a heavy sigh and rest my forehead against the door for a moment before turning around.

Cauler's leaning against a stack of washing machines, arms and ankles crossed, not looking at me. I lean against the door with my hands behind my back and wait. Looking him up and down, the first thing I notice is that he's not chewing any gum. His jaw is clenched tight and he keeps swallowing like he's nervous, which just makes me even more uneasy. My mouth dries out and then I have to swallow, too.

I watch him stare at his own feet, the rushing water of a rinse cycle droning in the background for a solid minute before I can't take it anymore.

"You okay?" I ask.

He startles like he forgot I was here. He uncrosses his legs and shifts his weight and my nerves are crackling. Is he about to cut me out?

"Yeah, just . . ." He takes a deep breath, and on the exhale says, "Where do we go from here, Terzo?"

Oh. That was not what I was expecting. Like, at all.

My breath is audibly unsteady, completely outing the nerves I'd rather keep hidden. This asshole has totally ruined me. Eighteen years and no one could ever figure out who I really was. A couple months on a team with Jaysen Caulfield and I can't hide for shit.

"What do you mean?" I ask.

Cauler scoffs, rolling his eyes. "You know exactly what I mean. I want to know where we stand."

"And it's all on me?"

He pulls both hands to his chest and leans forward into his words. "I know what I want. I need to know what page you're on."

With two sentences, he's pushed me to the cliff's edge. I can either turn around and walk away, keep Cauler at the distance he should've been this whole time, protect myself and my name and my future. Or I could let myself fall, just a little, and hope there's a branch to catch myself on before I hit the rocks.

Or I could do neither. Just keep doing what we're doing, keep emotions out of it, and go our separate ways in May.

I take a step forward. Scrub a hand over my mouth, keeping my eyes locked on his. He straightens up and lowers his arms. I back him up against the washers just like he backed me up against the boards. Wrap an arm around the back of his neck and pull him down to me.

And I kiss him.

Hard.

Hard enough to make him feel all the anger and jealousy and want I've held for him for years. Hard enough that it hurts when our teeth clack together.

His arms slip around my waist and pull me tight against him, curving my spine when he leans farther into me. I bite his lip, feel his piercing between my teeth, and his tongue catches my own.

He pushes a hand into my hair and pulls me back with a fistful of it, just enough that he can say, "I hate you."

"Prove it."

I make this startled, totally not sexy sound when he hooks his elbows under my knees and lifts me right off my feet, and *god*, for once in my life I am thankful for my height. He sets me down on the folding table, pressed up against a pile of clothes someone must've pulled out of the washer and dumped here. They're cold and damp against my back, but that's the last thing on my mind when Cauler kisses me again.

I've given him a total non-answer. I just gotta keep him distracted enough that he doesn't question it.

FOURTEEN

People aren't letting go of this rivalry thing.

There's this hilarious tweet where someone got a picture of me right after sniffing smelling salts, so I'm making this totally disgusted face, and I just happened to be looking at Cauler at that exact moment. Fans are having a field day with that one.

I send it to him. More fuel for our internet rivalry.

My family's coming to my and Delilah's game this Saturday. It'll be the first time I've been with all of them at once in forever, and all I can think about is coming out to them. Social media is still all over Aaron Johansson coming out, and I'm still stuck on Delilah calling me hetero. If I'm gonna live a lie the rest of my life for the sake of hockey, I can at least be real with my sisters.

I stay up the night before the game agonizing over it and scrolling through Twitter till I find another picture of me and Cauler. He's got a fistful of my jersey, as he tends to, bent down so our cages are pressed together, looking like he's bitching at me when really we were probably talking about some sick play he wanted to try.

I send that one to him, too, and he responds with:

> **Jaysen:** Big party after
> the game tomorrow
> Ready to get drunk and tolerable again?

> **Mickey:** Depends how the game goes
> If i need to drink myself
> into a coma or not

> **Jaysen:** Bro.
> This is gonna be a rout
> The eagles goalie is the
> definition of a sieve
> So get ready to drink for fun.

He stays up with me most of the night, talking about everything and nothing.

The kind of talking people do at the start of relationships.

When he finally falls asleep and it's just me alone in the dark, it's not only coming out I'm agonizing over. Now it's him, too.

COACH STOPS IN his tracks when he sees me at our team breakfast in the players' lounge. "You sick, James?"

"No."

Just tired.

He narrows his eyes at me. "Get a nap in before game time."

"Okay."

I don't.

By the time my family shows up, I'm falling asleep on my feet.

I obediently step into Dad's arms in the atrium of the arena and willingly hug Mom, but when it comes to my sisters, I straight-up launch myself at them. I squeeze Madison tight enough to crack her spine, and Nicolette says, "Oh, me next! That was the longest flight of my life, and I've flown to New Zealand." I do as she asks, and she hugs me back roughly enough to do the same. When I get to Mikayla, I put my forehead on her shoulder and take a moment to breathe.

I love my sisters. If I'm being honest, they're the only reason I'm still around. I stopped calling my parents once I realized they were never coming back for me. Dad only calls to talk about hockey, Mom only on birthdays and holidays, putting Dad on the phone, too. But I'm always in contact with my sisters, even when I'm just lurking in the group chat.

I should respond more. It's mostly memes and pointless arguments and tiny tidbits about their days, but they should know I'm paying attention and I care.

Mikayla pulls away only to be immediately replaced by Nova.

Wait.

"What the hell?" I say breathlessly, burying my face in the crook of her neck and pulling her tight to me.

"Surprise," she says. There's a laugh in her voice and a heavy feeling behind my eyes. I hear when Bailey shows up with Sid and Karim, Jade with them since Delilah's already getting ready for her game. This moment would be absolutely perfect with her here. Everyone I care about here in person instead of thousands of miles away, on the phone or my computer screen.

Nova and I hug each other for a few long moments before she backs away and holds me at arm's length, her smile wide and so different from the ones in her modeling photos. She's showing her Royals support in dark purple lipstick and glittery black-and-purple eye shadow. Her waist-length blond hair is braided over one shoulder. She's four inches taller and four weeks older than me, which used to bother me back when we were a thing, before I grew up and realized it didn't matter.

"Not gonna lie," she says. "I'm pretty excited for this."

"When's the last time you saw me play?" I ask.

"In person?" She takes a moment to think, fingers tapping on my shoulders. "At least two years ago, right? I came to Michigan your first season out there."

My sisters have had enough of our moment, crowding in around us to give me a look over.

"New team, new tie, huh?" Mikayla says, flipping the bottom of my purple tie up so it almost hits me in the face.

"Are you doing okay?" Madison asks.

"Yeah, dude, you've been ignoring the chat more than usual," Nicolette says. "And you look calm as hell. It seems deceitful."

I don't feel calm as hell. I kinda feel like I'm gonna cry.

Bailey and the others work their way in, giving out hugs

and *it's good to see yous* as the conversation continues. Jade and Sidney both gush over Nova, and there's a flush in her cheeks from the attention, but her smile's still genuine.

"If it helps," Mikayla says, "we're hitting up a liquor store before dinner. I'll buy you the fanciest scotch I can find."

"Scotch?" Nicolette gasps. "That'll be wasted on him!"

"If he drinks it, it's not a waste."

"After-party's at the men's hockey house," Bailey says. "You're all invited."

"Laxers aren't," I tell her.

"Joke's on you, asshole, Zero already said we could come."

"Breaking his own rules."

"He called it a family event," Karim adds.

Dorian's voice is the last thing I expect to hear in this moment, but the shouting is enough to make me look over my shoulder. My team is descending on my family like a swarm, looking all official in suits and ties and wristwatches and hair gel. They make me feel like a little kid playing dress-up every game.

"Too many famous people in one place!" Dorian yells. "Can't handle it!"

Half my team goes to fawn over my parents—Dad might be an absolute legend, but Mom is still Lucia Russo, Olympic medalist and damn near legendary herself—and the other half surrounds my sisters and Nova.

There's too many people talking at once, and it's only getting louder as fans start to filter in, some of our classmates shouting and chanting at us on their way by, others stopping to openly gape at my family. Just when I think all attention is off me, I catch Cauler looking this way.

I am never going to get used to seeing him in a suit. It catches me off guard every time. All the blacks and grays, with a tie I'd like to pull on. Get him back for all the times he's led me around by my clothes. He gives me that same shy smile that makes me want to die every time.

"Don't tell me Coach was right, Terzo," he says. His voice sounds off. Like he's holding something back. I don't blame him, considering the company. "You sick?"

"I'm fine," I say.

"Which is why you're so pale."

"I'm extremely white, Cauler, this isn't new."

"The greenish undertones are."

I have to stop myself from jabbing him in the arm, because it would come across a lot less bro and a lot more boyfriend. The crowd starts moving toward the rink as the buzzer sounds at the end of warm-ups, swallowing us and putting bodies between us.

Mom and Dad find me in the mass of people, Mom hooking her arm through mine and Dad putting a hand on my shoulder. "Close with Caulfield?" he asks.

My heart skips, but I keep calm on the outside. "Not really. He just likes to chirp me."

"Sounds like a distraction."

I scoff. "Not even close."

"He's allowed to have friends, Junior," Mom says. I can almost hear the eye roll in her voice, and I have never felt closer to her. She rubs my back before they step up to the row behind my team.

Not gonna lie, I'm a little disappointed that I have Barbie and Dorian between me and Cauler. But it's for the best. No way I'd survive forty-plus minutes knocking elbows on the arm rest with him, inhaling cinnamon and coconut. The lights dim before I even get to sit, my team surging to their feet as the women's team lines the bench. The announcer names off the starters as they race out onto the ice to stand at the blue line.

"Hell yeah, Delilah!" Nicolette shouts. I give my own whooping cheer, and Delilah smiles in our direction.

Watching her play hockey and playing myself are two entirely different experiences. Watching has me at the edge of my seat, jumping up and yelling every five seconds, holding my face in my hands after every impossible save by the Royals' goalie, groaning in frustration as Delilah's tip is blocked by a diving defender. I'm on my feet a second before the puck crosses the goal line for us and slumping in my seat when it's the opposite.

Delilah gets an assist in the first period, and during intermission Dorian leans forward and says, "Yo, Terzo, bet you twenty bucks Delilah destroys you in points tonight."

"Why would I take a losing bet?" I call back.

Delilah's behind the net early in the second, eyes up, waiting for someone to get open. She passes it off to the left and slides around to the right. The defense takes their eyes off her, and I have my fists clenched in front of me, halfway out of my seat. The net's wide-open for her, the pass right to her stick, the play perfectly executed and the goal easy. I jump as high as I can, fists thrown in the air, throat going raw from how loud I scream.

I turn to Barbie without thinking and he's just as excited as me, giving me a high five that I have to reach for and makes my hand sting. I high-five all my sisters that I can reach in the row behind us, and when Nova wraps her arms around my shoulders from behind, I lean back into her and hold her hands.

My whole team is going nuts. I don't know when they all became such huge fans of Delilah, but I've never been more proud in my life. I want to stay and watch the rest of her game, but halfway through the second, we have to leave to get ready for our own.

Dad claps me on the back, Mom gives me a quick hug, but I'm sure the one thing all the boys home in on is the way Nova kisses me on the cheek before I go.

THEY'RE ALL OVER me as soon as we're in the locker room.

"You said you weren't with her!" Kovy shouts. Ugh, god, kill me. I glance at Barbie, waiting for him to step in and say something about his constant texting with Nova, but he shakes his head slightly. Apparently that's a secret for now.

"I didn't lie." I get to my stall and step out of my dress shoes, loosening my tie.

"Dude, she literally kissed you!" Kovy argues.

"You act like she stuck her tongue down his throat," Cauler says. He kicks his shoes off with a little too much force, so they slam against the bottom of his stall.

I think I'm the only one who notices. They're all too busy speculating, noisily and without shame. All I can focus on is the way Cauler's got his jaw clenched.

He's jealous.

"The kid has the social skills of a rock, but he's still got Nova freaking Vinter," Colie says at one point.

I'm about to say something like no, you asshole, I do not have Nova, Nova is not a thing to be had, but Cauler beats me to it.

"You realize how creepy you're all being?" he says. He lets the band of his compression shorts snap against his hips, and I look way the hell away.

"Is that jealousy I'm sensing, Cauler?" Zero says. It's a passing comment no one else pays much attention to, still trying to get me to admit to the nonexistent thing going on between me and Nova. I'm almost tempted to tell them about eighth grade, freshman year, the on-and-off summer before I left for Michigan just to shut them up. But that's none of their business and would probably just rile them up even more.

The goal horn and the rumble of a cheering crowd shakes the locker room, muffled, but enough to get everyone to look at the TV where Delilah's got her stick raised above her head as her linemates crowd her against the boards.

"That's three points tonight, Terzo," Dorian announces. "You got your work cut out for you."

That's fine by me. I smile as the camera pans over the crowd, the rows we just vacated the only empty seats in the building, waiting to be filled by the women's team once we take the ice. One thing about the Hartland student body, they come out in support of all their teams, men's and women's alike. The camera homes in on my family for a second, Jade holding her hands over her chest and looking down at Delilah with this kind of adoration that makes my heart clench. My sisters scream around her.

We get our warm-ups in on the practice rink while the women's game finishes up. The energy is high, the guys are ready to go, and even I'm actually kind of excited to hit the ice.

Until we get back to the locker room for our final pregame talk and Dad's in there waiting for us. Coach Campbell's got this smug look on his face, like he's about to bless this team with the greatest moment of their lives.

Judging by the way most of them react, they agree.

"Kill me," I mutter.

Dorian leans over to me and whispers, "If I kill you, can I have your skates? They're sick, dude."

"Your feet would never fit in them," Barbie says from Dorian's other side. "He's got fetus feet."

Coach actually introduces Dad, like it's really necessary, before handing the floor off to him. I try to tune him out when he starts his motivational speech, but there's only so much I can do with my whole team enraptured by him. Most of them have probably looked up to him since they first laced up a pair of skates, same way their parents looked up to Grampa, Wayne Gretzky, Gordie Howe.

He looks so much older than I remember. Maybe because I've seen more of him in tribute videos and on the walls of this arena at my age than I have in person over the past seven years.

It's hard to see myself in him. Not even because I look more like Mom, with her dark hair and eyes and olive skin. But in the way he carries himself, all inviting smiles and squared shoulders.

We don't even play hockey the same. I had to learn to adapt it to my size on my own, and that makes our play styles nothing alike.

People like Dad for more than his name and his skill. They never have a bad word to say about him, because he's not a bad person. Just not a great parent.

By the time he finishes his speech, my teammates are on their feet, thoroughly impressed and ready for puck drop. I'm slower to stand, all the buildup from warm-ups burned out of me. The boys press in close, all reaching a hand into the center of the huddle. The best I can do is a hand on the backs of Dorian and Barbie in front of me as the captains lead us in a cheer loud enough to make my ears ring.

Dad pulls me aside on my way out. "We've got NHL Central Scouting here, and a scout from the Sabres," he says. His excitement is tangible as he puts a hand on my shoulder and shakes.

My heart twists. I feel cold sweat on the back of my neck. Being in Buffalo would make a life of hockey so much easier to cope with. Buffalo is home. It's where I grew up. It's where Nova is when she's not working. It's where I belong.

There's no way the Sabres are gonna get the top pick this year unless they make huge, unprecedented trades. It's not gonna happen. There's no way it's gonna happen.

But I still need to show them I'd be worth it.

FIFTEEN

The world narrows to nothing but the face-off dot and the puck in the ref's hand. The Eagles' center is paying more attention to chirping me than he is to the puck, pretty much handing me the face-off win. I pull the puck back to Dorian on my left and we explode down the ice, our tape-to-tape passes powerful and flawless.

Zero finds an opening within the first ten seconds, firing a rocket through a gap in the defense that goes wide. It rebounds off the glass, right to my glove. I drop the puck to the ice at my feet and send a wrister toward the net. A defender gets a skate on it and leaves it for his goalie to cover as Zero and Cauler bear down on him. Cauler wins the next face-off right to Barbie, setting him up for a one-timer that hits the back of the net a second later.

The five of us go to the bench with the crowd cheering like we scored five goals. Dorian practically punches me in the fist when I offer it to him. "Now that's hockey!" he cheers.

I sit between Cauler and Zero on the bench, all three

of us looking up at the jumbotron replay and catching our breaths. It looks like something off an NHL highlight reel. Not even twenty seconds in and the Eagles are already pulling their goalie in favor of their freshman backup, Ralph Lu.

Cauler elbows me and leans over to say, "'Bout time they replaced the sieve."

The fact that he's acknowledging last night's message at all makes my face flush.

After that first shift, the Eagles buckle down on defense and push back harder than we expected them to. Doesn't help that Ralph Lu is some kind of goaltending prodigy. The scouts have gotta be loving him right now. We throw fifteen shots at him in the first period and go into the intermission with nothing to show for it outside that one goal.

I look up into the stands on my way into the tunnel. The twins are taking a selfie together. Mikayla, Bailey, Sid, and Karim are all huddled in close to talk over the crowd. Jade's leaning forward to drape her arms over Delilah's shoulders in the row in front of her, and Nova's talking to a few of the women's team excitedly. Mom and Dad both look at me, smiling and waving when they have my attention.

I'm walking too fast, and by the time I see them, I'm already stepping out of sight without waving back. I kind of feel bad about it.

We have to reevaluate our entire game plan during intermission. We came in expecting to skate circles around these guys, but the goaltending switch has made them into a completely new team. Like they saw what Lu was capable of after that first shift and it inspired them.

Panic sets in halfway through the second. There are pro

scouts watching us be shut down by one of the worst teams we'll face this season. The Eagles take advantage of our frustration. At every face-off, they've got something to say about my personality, about my face. Every check into the boards is followed by a comment on my height and how easy it would be to break me in half. Every stoppage in play brings on the prediction that I'll never be as good as my father.

My silence only spurs them on, but I've never been very good at chirping.

Cauler finally, finally, puts the puck away with five minutes left in the second, unassisted and absolutely beautiful with a toe drag through the crease and a flick of the wrist that sends the puck straight back and into the water bottle on top of the net, breaking it open so it sprays all over Lu.

It's the most horrible thing I've ever seen. I can imagine him walking to the stage at the draft after being picked first. Holding up one finger in all the press photos to show his rank with me beside him holding up two.

I know it's ridiculous. I know one single goal isn't going to determine our draft order. But when I watch the replay, with Cauler beside me smiling and soaking in the praise of our teammates, I feel sick to my stomach.

IT GETS WORSE.

It's late in the third and I am *desperate*. I have no points and there are Sabres scouts in the stands, and Cauler is showing me up left and right. We got comfortable with our two-goal lead. Sat back on our heels, watched the Eagles come back to tie it up.

The Eagles. The fucking Eagles.

This was supposed to be a blowout. A chance to pad our stats. And now we're about to go into overtime with a team that only won six games last season.

Coach calls a time-out with less than a minute to go, and we gather around the bench only to be bitched at. "We are not going to be a team that plays down to our opponents' level," he shouts, pointing down for emphasis. "We are going to play our game, no matter who we're up against."

Cauler cracks a vial of smelling salts before we hit the ice again, and for once he does not look attractive, grimacing at the smell of it. He blinks the burn out of his eyes and holds the vial up to me. "Here. Wake up before you make both of us look like shit."

He says it without real heat, but it still burns under my skin. I have been a non-factor in this game. I've been doing my part on the draw when I'm called on, but I don't have a point or a hit to my name, only two shots on goal. I need to do something.

I lean in to inhale the salts Cauler holds up to my nose. He might as well have jammed ammonia-laced needles directly into my sinuses. My face scrunches and I shake my head a few times until the burn subsides. It's the most awake I've felt all day.

Our line is sent out with thirty-three seconds left on the clock. We put the pressure on right off the draw, because we are not going into overtime with the *Eagles*. But Ralph Lu isn't breaking. He throws himself around with no regard for his own safety, getting some part of his body on all the shots we pepper him with.

I have never wanted to fight a goalie as bad as I do right now. Can he just. Let. Me. Score?

The Eagles ice the puck just to get a break, and with only six seconds left, Coach leaves us out there.

The crowd is on their feet in anticipation, but my pulse is pounding so loud in my ears, their screaming is a dull hum. The play is for me to tap the puck through the legs of the guy in front of me on the face-off. Tuck my shoulder, skirt around him, make a quick pass to Cauler in the slot.

We've practiced it dozens of times for moments exactly like this. When we're down to the wire and need something. When it works, it's quick and pretty and perfect.

The puck drops. I get a stick on it, tap it through. Step around the Eagle center. And the puck is back on my stick. Cauler is open in the slot, the defense collapsing in around me, Lu squared up and ready for a shot.

If I get it to Cauler, we'll win this game. Still get ripped apart by Coach for putting ourselves in this position, but at least we won't be the team that lost to the Eagles. Cauler will leave this hell game with two goals. Two beautiful goals. One game winner. He'll be all the analysts talk about.

If I take this shot, at this angle, the chances of it going in are about zero. But if it does, I'll have that game winner. I'll be the one in highlight reels. The scouts in the stands will give impressed nods as they jot down notes about my daring and confidence. I'll even give them the most passionate celly they've ever seen from me.

Cauler is open in the slot. I keep my eyes on Lu.

Somewhere behind me, Zero shouts "No!" like he knows what I'm going to do before I've even decided myself.

I take the shot. Aim for the short side, where there's this tiny little gap in the top corner.

Lu gets a glove on it. Of course he does.

The entire arena deflates as the horn sounds on regulation. There's none of the excitement from the crowd that usually comes with overtime. They know we screwed this game up.

They know *I* screwed this game up.

I let my momentum carry me backward into the boards and stand there staring blankly out over the ice as the Eagles celebrate keeping up with us. They look like they just won a championship. Someone in the crowd pounds on the glass by my head. I still don't move.

Until Cauler skates up in front of me. I push off the boards before he can say anything. He stays with me, grabbing my jersey to slow me down.

"Forget the play, Your Grace?" he asks. There's full-blown malice in his voice again.

I don't say anything. Don't feel anything. I tug out of his grip and skate to the bench with my eyes forward.

Jaysen Caulfield and 271 others liked
a tweet from Paul Duggan • 41 min
Paul Duggan @duggerfest
Caulfield—charismatic asshole
James—socially inept asshole
Cicero—clueless asshole
The Royals top line is just
a line of assholes.

SIXTEEN

 bad bounce loses us the game two minutes into overtime. I don't hear anything Coach says in the locker room. All I know is it involves a lot of screaming.

The boys are quiet. Judging by the quick glances they keep shooting me, a lot of them blame me for this. But we were all off our game. Screw them.

I don't shower at the rink. I'm gonna hear it from them eventually. Doesn't need to be when we're all naked.

I pull my hood up and hunch my shoulders, keeping my head low when I step out of the locker room. I just want to get out of this arena without anyone talking to me, looking at me, breathing in my general direction. Take a shower and convince my sisters to get drunk at the lax house instead of the hockey party.

"Mickey!"

Oh god, kill me now. Haven't I been tortured enough today?

I stop in the middle of the Hall of Champions and take a deep, deep breath before turning to face my father. He closes the glass door to Coach's office and heads toward me, passing the mural of himself and his name on the walls under every honor.

"Hey, bud," he says softly once he catches up to me. He drapes an arm over my shoulders and we head out. "How're you doing?"

"Fine." I can't see him with my hood up, but I'm sure he's giving me those fake concerned eyes, the ones he uses to mask his disappointment.

"You sure? That was a rough game."

"It's one game. Not the end of our season." Doesn't matter that I embarrassed myself in front of Sabres scouts. ESPNU. My family. Nova. Doesn't matter that the Eagles are probably in their locker room right now screaming about how they beat the NHL's top prospects. Doesn't matter that Cauler hates me again, if he ever actually stopped.

I keep seeing my shot go right into that glove. They probably replayed it twenty times in the postgame report.

"You say that," Dad says as we push through a side exit. "But you look like it's bothering you."

I scoff. Is he serious right now? "How would you be able to tell, Dad? This is just my face."

His arm loosens on my shoulders and I slip out of his grasp, quickening my steps. His longer legs keep pace with me easily.

"Mickey. Hey. Tell me what's going on."

I keep walking.

"Mickey," Dad says again, more firmly this time. His hand closes around my wrist, jerking me to a stop. I yank my arm away from him. I am so *sick* of being pulled around like this.

I turn my back on him and shove my hands into my hair, still wet and gritty with sweat.

I shouldn't be this tired, this sweaty, this sore. I didn't do shit in that game. I handed Ralph Lu a save he'll remember for the rest of his life.

Oh god. What am I supposed to do with myself if everyone decides I suck at hockey?

A hand settles on my shoulder and pushes. I let it guide me without much thought to who it is or where they're taking me. I'm pushed down onto a bench outside the arena, on the hill overlooking campus and the lake.

The trees are almost bare. The bells start ringing out the alma mater from the top of Main Building, announcing the start of the dinner hours. A group of girls march down the hill with their arms locked together, dressed in Royals purple and black, singing one of their class songs. The colors of the sunset reflect off the lake.

My eyes sting. The air feels so heavy all of a sudden.

"Talk to me," Dad says. "What's going on?"

"Please stop pretending you care." It's a fight to keep my voice even. I squeeze my hands together to stop them from shaking and tuck my chin to my chest, hiding deeper in my hood so he can't see my eyes well up.

"What are you talking about? Of course I care."

"You only care 'cause it's affecting my game." My breath stutters. "Just tell me how bad I screwed up today and be done with it. Please. I cannot handle whatever the hell you're doing right now."

"You're fine, bud. Every team has bad games. Every player makes bad plays."

"In front of Sabres scouts. In front of you and Mom."

"Mickey. Look at me." I don't. He takes me by the shoulder again and forces me to turn toward him. I scramble to wipe the tears from my face before he sees them. "It was one shot amongst years of great hockey. You don't need to be this torn up about it."

I finally look at him. And maybe I do see hints of myself in him. In his inability to show how he really feels. He's burning with disappointment and embarrassment inside. I know it. But he's looking at me like he means every word.

My next breath comes in this uncontrollable shudder, and suddenly I am violently sobbing on a bench out in the open next to my father. I drop my face into my hands and hold my breath, trying to make it stop, but that only makes the next sob louder and more aggressive. Dad sits next to me patiently and quietly while I have a complete breakdown, and I don't think I've ever felt this low in my life. By the time I get my breathing under control and the tears to slow, the sun is almost set and my head aches.

"Bailey and I have been talking about you," Dad says while I wipe my nose on my sleeves and pull my feet up onto the bench to make myself as small as possible. "She's worried. Remember the medicine your mother used to take?"

I shrug. I've got this vague memory of stopping at a pharmacy with Mom as a kid, her arguing about the price of a small orange pill bottle. But it's been seven years since I lived with them, so I don't remember much.

"They were antidepressants," Dad goes on. "Did you know depression is genetic?"

"I'm not depressed," I say on instinct. My voice is small and lifeless again.

"You're showing a lot of the signs your mom did."

I don't say anything. I don't have the energy to argue. I watch a few dry leaves scratch against the cement in front of the bench, the breeze pushing them around and making me shiver.

"You have a few days off for Thanksgiving," Dad says. "Why don't you come home? We can get you into a doctor and—"

At least I have the energy to laugh at that hilarious joke.

"What?" Dad asks.

"Home." I scoff. "You mean with the Vinters? Or my billet family in Michigan."

"I mean with me and your mother and Madison."

"When has that ever been my home?"

"Mickey—"

"I don't even have a room in your house, Dad."

He breathes in sharply. Gets out half a syllable before stopping himself. He bought a four-bedroom house when he got traded to Carolina. One room for him and Mom. One for the twins. One for Bailey and Delilah. And one for Mikayla as the oldest. I was ten. But I wouldn't need a room if I never spent more than a couple days there at a time.

"You still have a place there, Mickey," Dad says after a tense moment of silence.

I stand up and start walking. "I need to shower."

He doesn't follow me.

I TAKE MY phone into the shower and open the group chat.

Mickey: Don't forget the scotch
Maybe some vodka too
Actualy the whole liquor
store woudl be great

Delilah: Someone needs a drink

Mickey: drinks.
Plural.
Many of them.

Mikayla: We got you covered kid

Mickey: Nice
Sure you don't wanna drink
at the lax house instead

Bailey: They're not partying tonight
The guys have 6am fall ball

Mickey: Kill me

Bailey: We can just drink in my room?

Mickey: Omg yes pls

I'm pulling on a pair of black jeans when Dorian and Barbie come in.

"Terzo, perfect!" Dorian says, all excited like I didn't just lose us a hockey game an hour ago. "We need your permission for something."

I tense up, turned toward the closet. My eyes are swollen from all the crying and I don't need them seeing me like this. "Okay?"

"Remember that film project I showed you?" Dorian sits on the edge of his bed and runs a hand through his hair, almost nervously. "We need your okay to use anything you show up in."

"For what?" I pull on a black V-neck and look in the mirror. My closet isn't exactly colorful, but I don't usually wear all black like this. I actually kinda like it. Cauler and Dorian still pull it off way better than me though.

"We want to put it online," Dorian says. "Barbie was drafted fifth round by the Flames. This is the only way to make him famous."

I see Barbie give Dorian a look in the mirror as I run my fingers through my wet hair. He mutters something in Spanish that makes Dorian smirk. To me, he says, "Part of it's a compilation of you saying *kill me*."

"What?" I whip around to face them.

"You say it a lot, dude," Dorian says. Then he gets a good look at me and his face drops. "You okay, man?"

Shit. I turn my face to the floor and look for my wallet. "I'm fine."

"No, but you got like, emotions on your face."

"The *aftermath* of emotions," Barbie corrects him.

I close my eyes and take a deep breath. I can't get mad at them when I've made it a point to seem emotionless. Dorian's probably the nicest person to me on this campus. He already knows so much. And Barbie's pretty much attached to him at the hip. If I'm gonna open up to anyone on this team, it might as well be them.

"Been a rough day," I mumble. My phone vibrates on my dresser. A snap from Madison.

"Family issues?" Dorian asks. I raise my eyes to look at him without lifting my face. He gives me this knowing look. "Every time you get a message from your dad, you look like you wanna smash your phone. And now he's here, so I figure you'd wanna smash his face instead."

I shake my head and sigh. "It's not that bad."

"You sure? 'Cause if that's what you want, I'll help you, dude. Don't care that I used to have a poster of him on my wall, I will end him."

Madison sent a picture of Nicolette and Bailey, holding a bottle of whiskey between them, smiling wide. *Hurry up before they drink your alcohol.* I close out of it and slide my phone into my pocket. Dorian and Barbie watch me, waiting.

I rub the back of my neck. "It's fine."

"Okay," Dorian says, but he sounds unconvinced. "Don't be afraid to cry around us, y'know. We won't judge."

"Dori cried when we went to different USHL teams," Barbie says.

Dorian puts a hand over Barbie's mouth and pushes his head away. "And Barbie cried when I went to the Kings and he got stuck with the Flames."

"I was crying for them. Wasted a second round pick on you."

Dorian tries to cover his mouth again, and this time

Barbie ducks out of his reach before wrapping an arm around his waist to throw him on the bed.

They lie next to each other, talking in Spanish and looking at their phones while I finish getting ready. I keep glancing over at them. They're at a level of comfort that can only come from a lifetime of friendship, the way they spend all their time together and drape themselves over each other and don't give a damn what anyone has to say about it. They'll probably dorm together next year, since they'll actually have a choice in roommates their sophomore year.

I have to clear the jealous knot from my throat before I can say, "You guys going to the hockey house?"

They both look at me. "Are you not?" Dorian asks.

"I'm gonna hang out with my sisters in Bailey's room."

Barbie sits straight up, a frantic look on his face. "Wait, is Nova gonna be there?"

"I mean, yeah?" I say.

They share a look, Barbie with both eyebrows raised and Dorian with this smug little grin.

"Uh, did you want to come with?" I ask.

Barbie thinks for a second, then sighs and shakes his head. "I don't wanna intrude on your family time."

"Dude, it's fine."

Dorian stands up from the bed and stretches his arms above his head. "We should at least make an appearance at the hockey house first. Give it an hour, and then we can go hang out with your girlfriend."

Barbie slaps at Dorian's arm, but the goofy smile on his face shows how he really feels.

They transfer the bottles in Dorian's minifridge to a

backpack and we head out. I text Bailey to let her know I'm on my way, so when we make it a short way down the hill to her building, she's waiting at the front door.

Bailey lives in the mansion that once belonged to Hartland's founder, now converted into a dorm for junior and senior women. I've never been inside.

"Hello, gentlemen," Bailey says, wedged between the door and the frame to keep it open. She looks happily buzzed with a beer in her hand. "Will you be joining us tonight?"

"Maybe later, if that's okay?" Dorian says.

"Hell yeah. Our RA is out of town this weekend, and we got plenty of room and plenty to drink." She opens the door wider and ushers me inside as Dorian and Barbie continue on down the hill.

We're in an entryway with a high ceiling and a black-and-white-checkered floor. Up ahead is a staircase that curves along the wall and leads to the widow's watch that's part of one of the many Hartland ghost stories. They say if you're crossing the bridge over the creek just outside and the light in the tower goes out, don't look behind you or you'll come face-to-face with a murderous spirit.

It definitely feels the way I'd expect a haunted house to feel—a little drafty and a lot echoey. Old framed black-and-white photos of what I'm guessing are the Hart family line the walls, and we pass a couple sitting rooms with tall windows overlooking the lake on our way to the staircase.

Bailey's got a single on the top floor, and as soon as I step in, Nicolette slings an arm around my shoulders and plants a drunken, sloppy kiss on my cheek. She pushes a heavy glass bottle into my hand. "Mikayla bought this but didn't wanna give it to you 'cause she's a professional and you're a child," she says, too loud in the relative quiet of the building. I twist the cap off and gulp down a burning mouthful of whiskey.

The room looks like something I'd expect from a fancy old apartment building. Nothing like my freshman dorm with its cold, hard tile floor and furniture pressed up in a line against the wall. Bailey's got a creaky redwood floor, floor-to-ceiling windows, a fireplace that's been bricked up, and even a small balcony facing the lake. The door's open, Nova and Madison leaning against the balcony railing as they talk.

"I'm risking my job just being here," Mikayla says from her spot on Bailey's bed. She's got a bottle of water in her hands, but she watches Nicolette take a swig of her drink with a jealous look in her eyes. "We could be arrested for this, Cole."

"Dude, relax," Nicolette says. "No one's gonna arrest a pregnant lady."

"Are you kidding? I'd get in more trouble than anyone! Bailey's a senior and she was in *middle* school while I was graduating college."

"Jesus," I say. "You're ancient."

"And you still go to a pediatrician!"

It's hard to drink when you're laughing. Delilah pries the bottle from me while I'm distracted and pours a few fingers' worth into a plastic cup. "Take it slow, my dude," she says. "Scotch is meant to be savored."

I narrow my eyes as she's slow to hand the cup over, holding the bottle out of my reach. There's a hard look on her face, her lips pinched and eyebrows pulled together. I take the cup from her and look down at the tiny drop of alcohol she gave me.

A couple miles away, my team is probably talking all kinds of shit about me. Commiserating over an embarrassing loss and pinning it all on me. A couple shots of whiskey aren't going to be enough to loosen the knot of anxiety in my chest.

I toss back the sip of scotch and hold the cup back out to Delilah. She gives me what I'm guessing is supposed to be a meaningful look before pouring me my refill. We repeat the same process until my nerves start to give way to tingling in my fingertips, numbness in my tongue, and a haze in my head. Delilah must see it on my face, because she screws the cap back onto the bottle and says, "Slow down." She takes it with her when she goes to sit on the floor next to Jade.

There's some reality show playing on the TV on Bailey's dresser, but no one's paying attention to it. Mikayla and Bailey are on the bed talking, Nicolette's got her legs crossed on the old wooden armchair in the corner, leaning forward to put herself into Delilah and Jade's conversation. Nova and Madison come in from the cold and close the door to the balcony, rubbing their arms to warm up. Nova's all red in the face, still looking photo shoot ready in baggy sweatpants and one of my old National Team T-shirts cut into a crop top under a cardigan.

I stand in the middle of the room for a second and just soak in their presence. It's a little weird, having them all here in a place I've started to associate with home. Family and home haven't gone together for me in a long time.

They're not leaving until tomorrow, but I miss them already.

SEVENTEEN

Dorian and Barbie showing up is enough of a distraction that I'm able to get the bottle of whiskey back before Delilah notices. I don't remember much of the night after that aside from collapsing face-first into bed.

Now, Barbie's on the floor with his entire upper body tucked under my bed. With the sunlight coming through the blinds and the whiskey headache, I'm about five seconds from joining him when panic hits me so hard and sudden it knocks the breath out of my chest.

I scramble for my phone in my sheets and almost drop it, my hands are shaking so bad.

No messages.

I'm the one who should be apologizing to Cauler, making first contact, so I don't know why the empty screen hurts so much. But it does. Like a sucker punch to the gut.

I'm about to message Nova for help when six bodies come crashing through the door making as much noise as humanly possible.

Barbie whacks his head on the underside of my bedframe while Dorian screeches awake, clutching his blanket to his chest and putting his back against the wall. His horror dissolves into straight-up mortification when he sees it's my sisters and Nova. He pulls the blanket over his head and says, "Terzo, it's your turn to kill me now."

"I think I'm concussed," Barbie says from the floor.

Delilah and Nicolette step over him to jump on my bed. "Get up, get up!" Delilah says while Nicolette groans, "I'm hungry, dude, let's go."

"How are you not hungover right now?" I mumble. I push myself upright, forcing them over the edge of the mattress. Nicolette almost stomps right on Barbie's head.

"We're adults and know how to pace ourselves," she says, maneuvering around Barbie while he curls into a ball to protect himself. He barely opens his eyes when Nova crouches in front of him. "We don't chug entire bottles of whiskey the second we get our hands on them."

"I did not chug that whole bottle." My brain beats against the inside of my skull like it disagrees.

"Only 'cause Madison pried it out of your hands once you started sliding down the wall."

"No, I think it was after he sat Nova and Barbie down next to each other and said *now kiss*," Delilah says. She's got her arms crossed and a disapproving scowl on her face.

"That was after he snuck the bottle back," Madison says. "We had to take it from him several times."

"I was obviously having a good time." I gag at the tail

end of a yawn and have to hold my breath for a second. "Why'd you kill my fun?"

"Alcohol poisoning, that's why."

I almost fall over as soon as I stand up, like my body has to drive the point home even further. I pull on the nearest hoodie I can find, which definitely isn't mine with the way the sleeves swallow up my hands, and the same jeans from last night. I cover my bedhead with a snapback and the hood for good measure. "I got time to brush my teeth at least? Tastes like something died in my mouth."

Bailey hands me a stick of gum from her sweater pocket, hood pulled low over her face and black makeup smudged under her eyes. At least I won't be the only one looking like a wreck at breakfast.

"You can take my bed if you want, Barbie," I say over my shoulder at the door. Barbie makes some noise of gratitude, but he doesn't move except to watch Nova leave.

She walks with me at the back of the pack, looking a little rough herself. She twirls her phone in her fingers with a hint of a smile on her face.

"Barbie kept me up all night with his texting," I tell her.

Her face flushes and she looks at the ground. "It was nice meeting him in person. I like him."

I shrug. "He's not bad."

She sighs, tapping her phone against the palm of her hand. "Either way, I doubt it'll go anywhere. I had to bribe my way into this weekend off."

"Why don't you just quit modeling and acting and stay home?"

She raises one eyebrow and purses her lips. "I'll do that when you quit hockey, babe."

I kick a pebble down the sidewalk. "Yeah, right. Might as well after last night."

"C'mon, Mickey. It was one game. I'm sure everyone's over it by now."

"Not Cauler."

"Oh boy. Talk to me."

I hike my shoulders up to my ears, hands in the pockets of my jeans. "What's there to say? He's pissed and doesn't wanna talk to me."

She clicks her tongue and puts her arm through mine, pulling me closer. "Aw, babe. It'll pass. If he really cut you off over a single hockey play, he wouldn't be worth it anyway."

I heave a sigh. I mean, I'd probably do that if he purposefully screwed me over on the rink, but maybe he's a better person than me. "I guess."

We get to the small café just off campus and sit at a table overlooking the lake. My anxiety kicks in as soon as I sit down.

If there was ever a time to tell them, now's it.

After ordering, I hold my head up with my fist and stare out over the water while Mikayla goes into wedding and baby talk. I've only met my future brother-in-law a couple times, but I'm still standing up as one of his groomsmen. I don't get why I can't be with my sisters, but I'm not about to argue with the bride about it.

And the baby. I'll see them as an infant, but after that they'll probably be talking by the time I see them again. Probably won't even recognize me.

Nova's holding her phone out to Mikayla for approval on her bridesmaid dress when the server comes back with our food. I soak my home fries in syrup and shovel down a forkful, instantly feeling half as hungover as soon as it hits my stomach.

"If your baby's a boy are you gonna name him Mickey to keep up the trend?" Delilah asks. A strand of her blue hair sticks to a spot of syrup on her chin.

"Hell no," Mikayla says, screwing her face up in disgust. "That'd be freaking weird. I want gender neutral. Something like Jordan or Riley. And they're not touching hockey unless they explicitly ask to."

"Yikes. Dad's gonna hate you."

"He's not that controlling," Bailey argues, spooning sugar into her teacup.

Delilah stabs at her French toast. "Only 'cause we're all athletes. Can you imagine if one of us had been into theater?"

"He does say field hockey isn't real hockey a lot," Madison adds quietly.

Nicolette takes a break from cutting up her pancakes to point her fork around the table and say, "How did we go from happy wedding and baby talk to depressing Dad talk?"

"It's one thing we all got in common," I say. Bailey curls her lip like she wants to argue some more, but instead she just shakes her head and sips her tea.

As we get closer to finishing breakfast, closer to when four of them have to leave, I can feel it in my chest. This heavy sense of impending loss and grief. The static cage squeezing in around my heart as the words build up behind my teeth. This is the first time we've all been together in forever, and the next time won't be till draft day and Mikayla's wedding a few months later. After that, who even knows? I don't want to do it over group chat.

If I don't do it now, it'll be on the tip of my tongue—or my fingertips, I guess—till I see them again.

My breathing picks up, heart racing just at the thought of the words coming out of my mouth. And I know they'll be accepting. I mean, Delilah's a lesbian and Bailey's dating two bi guys, for Christ's sake. But it doesn't make it any easier to breathe in and say, "Can I tell you guys something?"

I focus on pushing soggy home fries around on my plate so I don't have to look at them.

"Duh," Nicolette says.

I think I'm gonna be sick. "I am . . ." Nova's knee presses against mine under the table. I look at her out of the corner of my eye. She's grinning as she sips her coffee. "Bisexual," I blurt. "I am bisexual. Or maybe pan. I don't know. Pan fits better, I guess, but bi just sounds better to me. Is that bad? It's just easier. I don't know. But yeah. Not straight. So yea—"

Madison's hand closes on top of mine and I cut my rambling short. I take a few breaths before looking up at them. Bailey's propping her chin in her hand with this smug twist to her lips. Mikayla and the twins have these small, almost proud smiles on their faces.

But Delilah's gaping at me, French toast hanging from the fork she holds over her plate. She closes her mouth and sets it down slowly. "How did I not know this? Mickey! Why didn't you tell me?"

I shrug a shoulder. "Same reason you didn't till you brought your first girlfriend home."

"It's not like it wasn't obvious with me."

"But you still didn't tell."

Her eyes soften with understanding. She nods a little, and goes back to eating.

Bailey clears her throat before saying, "Sid and Karim would be totally willing if you wanna talk more after this."

I give her a small nod and an even smaller smile. My breathing's evened out and my heart's not pounding anymore. I feel lighter somehow.

"You knew?" Delilah demands. Bailey quirks an eyebrow, holding eye contact while she takes a long sip of her tea.

"Anyone else wanna come out today?" Nicolette says. "Now's the time to do it. Nova?"

Nova clicks her tongue and sets down her coffee mug. "Sadly, I am still exclusively attracted to guys."

Nicolette jerks her chin toward me. "Surprised this one didn't ruin them for you."

We all laugh, and I've never been so grateful to have Delilah and Bailey at the same school as me as I am while watching the rest of them leave. If I didn't have them standing next to me as everyone else got in the car with Mom and Dad to head to the airport, I might've dropped out right then and there and gone with them.

Paul Duggan @duggerfest • 1d
Caulfield—charismatic asshole
James—socially inept asshole
Cicero—clueless asshole
The Royals top line is just
a line of assholes.

Mickey James III @mjames17 · 6m
Replying to @duggerfest
If calling someone a little shit and
pulling them around the ice by their
jersey makes someone charismatic, it's
no wonder I'm the socially inept one.

Jaysen Caulfield @jaycaul21 · 6m
Replying to @duggerfest @mjames17
Congrats, you learned how to
use social media. You are now
slightly less inept but still just as
much of a little shit as before

Mickey James III @mjames17 · 5m
If you can teach me how to be
charismatic maybe I'll teach you
how to lift a puck over a goalie pad

Jaysen Caulfield @jaycaul21 · 5m
That might be the funniest thing
you've ever said terzo. @Duggerfest
you might wanna amend your
labels. James is both the socially
inept one and the clueless one

Mickey James III @mjames17 · 3m
I have literally stood open at the post in
practice like 12 times just for you to put

a shot right into colie's pads. Wrists and follow through cauler. Lift. The puck.

Jaysen Caulfield @jaycaul21 • 2m
I take it back. THAT was the funniest thing you've ever said. You're really gonna talk about being open at the post after last night's game? That's bold, Terzo.

Mickey James III @mjames17 • 1m
If I had any faith in your accuracy I would've passed to you no problem

Jaysen Caulfield @jaycaul21 • 36s
Are you for real right now? This is a joke right. This is you trying to improve your social skills by telling terrible jokes. Otherwise nothing you just said made any sense

Paul Duggan @duggerfest • 21s
Is this really happening in my @'s rn

EIGHTEEN

Zero grabs the shoulder of my hoodie and pulls. It's either get choked or follow, so I throw back my chair and stagger after him. My phone drops to the floor with a heavy thud. He doesn't give me time to pick it up, just keeps dragging me along behind him. Some of the guys lean back in their chairs and peek over the walls of their study carrels to watch.

We're heading right for Cauler.

Kill me.

All I see is his back from here, headphones over his ears, but I'm sure he's hunched over his phone waiting for my half-typed reply. Zero grabs him the same way he grabbed me, but it's not so easy to manhandle him. Cauler slides off his head-phones and puts them around his neck.

"Let's go," Zero barks. "Leave your phone."

Cauler sets it facedown on his desk and stands slowly. He gives me a cool look, but I keep my face as neutral as possible as Zero drags us toward the exit.

"You two are gonna sit out in the cold until you stop acting like teenagers," he says.

"But we are teenagers," Cauler says. I roll my eyes.

"Embarrassments to this team is what you are," Zero snaps. "Fighting on Twitter? Seriously? Analysts are already up your asses and now you pull this shit?" He holds the door open and pushes us out onto the bridge outside the library. "Figure your shit out before you ruin my championship season. You have till the end of study hall."

He pulls the door closed behind him and leaves us. It's quiet. Everyone's in the dorms on the other side of campus recovering from last night, and it's pretty much just us overachieving athletes out here. The black wood of the bridge is covered by leaves from the branches arching over it, and I am totally focused on that just so I don't have to acknowledge this awkward tension as Cauler and I stand facing each other in silence.

I pull up my hood and stuff my hands in the pocket, hunching my shoulders against the wind. I hope I get sick just so I can sneeze on Zero as revenge for whatever this is.

I'm not about to speak first. Sure, this is probably my fault. Definitely my fault. But there's no way I'm admitting to it.

Cauler holds out for what feels like a solid two minutes before he says, "They're probably in there making bets on if we're gonna make out or not."

I start walking away before he catches me blushing. I only make it a few steps before leaves start crunching behind me. Part of me is thrilled he's following after saying something like that, but the rest of me hates myself for it. It's not like we're really gonna start making out right now just because the boys want us to.

Great, now that's all I can think about. How are we supposed to figure our shit out if I'm too busy fantasizing to talk to him?

Cauler catches up by the time I step off the bridge, and he seems to know exactly where I'm heading, turning toward the lake without waiting for me. We make it all the way past Main, the dock in sight before he speaks again. "If you really don't trust my accuracy, we can hit the rink right now and clear that up. But I think you're full of it."

I sigh, and mutter, "You're probably right."

"Then what was that about?"

There's more people outside now that we're by one of the dorms and the dining hall. There's some girls sitting under the giant sycamore in front of Main in sweaters and leggings and scarves, sipping from paper coffee cups and looking at us for a little too long as we pass. A guy's crossing the bridge over the creek from the other dorms, tapping on his phone, glancing up to watch his step. His eyes follow when he spots us.

I duck my head. "Not here." I say it as if I'm actually gonna explain myself once we're not being watched.

The dock is empty, and I can't tell if I'm relieved or disappointed that I don't have an excuse to keep quiet. I go to my usual spot at the end and sit, kicking my legs out over the water. Cauler sits too close. For someone who can't stand me, he's got no problem being in my space.

A gust of wind comes in off the lake, making me shiver. I pull my feet up onto the dock and wrap my arms around my knees. My hood blocks him from my periphery, which is fine by me. Can't stare at his mouth that way.

I wait for him to say something. To tear into me for that play, call me out for being selfish. Tell me whatever we were is officially over.

But I want to fix this. I want to get back to the flirting, the kissing, if we can. At least then we were having some fun with each other.

"Sorry for being a little shit," I mumble.

"You're always a little shit," Cauler says. "You'll have to be more specific."

I look down at the lake and sigh. "In the game yesterday. Just now on Twitter."

Cauler hums. I glance over as he brings a knee up to prop under his chin. "That game was a joke all around. I'm over it. Mostly surprised you know how to send a tweet, honestly."

I don't say anything. I've got that same heavy feeling in my chest that I got before I came out to my sisters earlier. Words trying to force their way through my teeth before I've had time to think them through. It's just . . .

"It's hard, playing in front of my dad," I blurt out.

Cauler laughs a little. "I can tell you for a fact it was hard for some of the boys, too. Figured you'd be used to it by now."

I shrug. "He only retired a few years ago. Not like he had time to come to my games. Raleigh's a long way from Michigan. It's just—" I cut myself off. He doesn't want to hear my sob story. I should be grateful I got into the NTDP. It wouldn't have happened if it weren't for Dad pushing me and leaving me in Buffalo.

"It's just?" Cauler presses.

I heave out a breath and tug on the strings of my hoodie to keep my hands occupied. "He expects a lot. Like . . . a lot. Or at least I assume he does? I don't know. I kind of panicked at the end of that game. I hadn't done shit and he was watching and . . . I don't know."

"You realize if you'd've passed to me, you'd've got an assist, right?"

"Yeah. But then you'd have two goals."

"And you would've set me up for a game winner on a beauty of a play with seconds on the clock, and everyone would've been obsessed over our on-ice chemistry instead of pitting us against each other like always."

I press my forehead against my knees. "I know."

"You'll look a lot better to scouts if you focus on the team and winning instead of racking up goals."

"I know." There's this desperate kind of pitch in my voice that makes me squeeze my eyes shut. I am not about to cry in front of him.

He totally hears it, too. He's close enough I can feel him pull his other leg up, his elbow pressing into my arm as he adjusts himself. "If you want a parental figure who'll be disgustingly proud of everything you do, I'll give Ma your number. Go a shift without scoring on your own net or falling on your ass and she'll be blowing up your phone about how great you're doing."

I huff a laugh through my nose and turn my head, resting the side of my face on my knees so I can look at him. He tilts his head back, looking up at the colors of the sunset peeking through gray clouds. My eyes follow the long stretch of his throat, down to the silver necklace resting at the base of his neck.

"She didn't know a thing about hockey when I started," he goes on. "She cried when she saw me standing on skates without falling. Basically called Mr. Cicero a miracle worker, she was that impressed. Never really got over it, either. She's amazed by everything."

"How'd you start playing if she didn't know anything about it?" I ask.

"Kyle Kane's from the same neighborhood as me. We were on our way to my first football practice, actually. Black kid says he wants to play sports, teachers send home football and basketball pamphlets, y'know. But Ma and I ran into Kyle Kane playing street hockey with some kids a couple blocks from home. Black man playing a sport that's not football or basketball with a bunch of little Black kids?" He smiles. Shakes his head a little. "I was instantly obsessed. Dad started working a ton of overtime, and Ma started babysitting a bunch of kids before work at night so they could pay for me to play." He turns his head to look at me. "Don't know if you knew this, but hockey's expensive."

"I know," I say softly.

He leans back, holding himself up with his hands on the cold cement of the dock. "Know what else is expensive? Hospital bills." I can't see his face with him sitting like that, but I hear the bitter change in his tone.

I can still see that hit he took in my head. Hear the sound of his helmet ringing off the stanchion. Picture him facedown on the ice for five motionless minutes before being taken off on a gurney, the announcers so terrified they wouldn't even speculate on how bad the injury might be.

I can't imagine experiencing it firsthand.

"I'm surprised your parents let you keep playing," I say.

"Same, honestly." He's not surprised I knew what he was talking about. It was all the hockey media talked about for months. "It was the worst. Couldn't think straight, threw up all the time, could hardly walk. Felt like I was getting an MRI every other day. But all I cared about was getting back on the ice. Ever since that day, playing street hockey with Kyle Kane, I built my whole life around this sport. I didn't have anything else. Sound familiar?"

"I didn't build this life." I cringe at my own words as soon as they're out.

"Dramatic," Cauler says, but he doesn't sound annoyed about it for once.

We're both quiet. The sun is setting fast, and it's getting colder by the second. I don't feel like moving. When Cauler lies flat on his back with his knees drawn up and hands folded on his stomach, it seems like a good idea. Till I lie back with him and our arms are pressed right up against each other.

He doesn't move away. Doesn't even flinch. The warmth of him is enough to chase off some of the November chill.

"You should go pro next year," I say. It's almost a whisper.

"I should," he agrees.

"So why won't you?"

"Because. I don't ever want to feel like hockey is all I have ever again. My parents are doing okay with money for now, but with my medical debt, they wouldn't've been able to send me to college without this full ride. I'm taking advantage of it."

"What's your backup, then?"

"My brother's in law school. Lots of scholarships and grants. He's gonna start his own firm taking on civil rights violations. I wanna help."

"You're actually gonna go to law school?" I pick my head up off the dock to give him a look. "You tell people that, there's no way you're getting picked first."

He screws his face up at me. "I'm not going to law school, you little shit. You don't need a law degree to be a paralegal. What about you?"

"What about me?"

"You figure out a backup plan?"

"No."

"What happened to marine science?"

My cheeks warm and my heart skips. He remembered that all the way from our first algebra class? Dude. "I panicked when everyone was saying their majors."

"If that was your go-to, you must like it at least. You do spend a lot of time down here."

I shrug. We go quiet again. Like we've reached our working things out limit for the day. I close my eyes, feeling more relaxed now than I have in days. Outside of being drunk at least.

"Terzo," Cauler says, and I startle awake. I didn't even realize I'd been falling asleep. "If I go first, will your dad disown you?"

I blink the sleep out of my eyes. If he'd asked me this same question yesterday I probably would've said yes. Maybe even believed it, too. But today, I say, "Huh? No. He's a fanatic but he's not a total asshole."

"Eh, not so sure about that. But good to know. Now I won't feel so guilty about it."

I laugh. A real, full-throated laugh. "You're delusional, Cauler."

"Hold on to that sense of security, Your Grace. It'll make draft day all the more satisfying."

The sun is almost fully set and I am freezing, but I want to stay in this moment, with me and Cauler getting along and lying next to each other in a silence that's not tense and awkward for once.

Cauler taps his fingers on his chest, and I shiver through my whole body as stars start peeking through wisps of dark clouds. He blows air through his teeth that freezes above his face.

I could kiss him right now. Here, at the dock. My favorite place on campus. It'd be downright poetic, ending a fight with a kiss.

But we're the NHL's top prospects and there's so much attention on us that out in semi-public like this, there's no way it'd stay a secret for long. And when I come out to the world, I want it to be on my terms.

So instead, I say, "Zero gave us till the end of study hall. What time is it?"

"I'm gonna go ahead and say study hall is over by now."

"Think we've worked it out enough for them?"

"You obviously haven't been paying attention. To them, working it out means putting our mouths on each other."

I splutter as my heart jams its way up my throat, but

Cauler just laughs and sits up, stretching his arms above his head. "Chill, Terzo. I know PDA is dangerous." He stands and holds a hand out to help me up, and I want to scream. I kind of just stare blankly at it for a second before reaching up.

He looks me in the eyes. Full-on, deep eye contact as he hauls me to my feet. He pulls me closer than he needs to, holds on for a beat longer than necessary, and for a second I swear he's gonna do it. Prying eyes be damned. I bite my lip and look at his mouth and wait for it.

He turns away just when I'm about to lean in, and I follow him back to the library with my heart in my stomach.

NINETEEN

Cauler and I have sex again a few more times before Thanksgiving break, and thank god we don't have any games coming up over the next few days, because he leaves me with this giant hickey to remember him by the last time.

The boys who stayed behind at the hockey house spend the whole of Thanksgiving dinner trying to figure out who I got it from. The general consensus is that Nova flew in last night for an international booty call. Cauler's name doesn't even come up, and I'm pretty sure it's intentional.

I'm half-asleep on the couch after dinner when my phone goes off, startling me awake with a message from Cauler.

Jaysen: How's zero's cooking

I glance around the living room. There's a football game on TV, and Colie's passed out in the recliner across the room, mouth open and snoring. Everyone else seems to have migrated toward the alcohol in the kitchen.

Mickey: Not bad actually
Turkey's a little dry but i just
drowned it in gravy
How's home?

Jaysen: Nice
If you notice any welts on me when
i get back, don't be alarmed
My cousin rashida takes barbarian
ping pong very seriously

Okay, I have never heard of a version of Ping-Pong that would result in welts, but I can't say I'm not intrigued. Before I can ask about it, though, Cauler sends another message.

Jaysen: Playing cards with the fam
now and shae's kicking my ass
Seems i can't win

He's playing cards with his family and took the time to message me. That's not what friends-with-benefits do, right? That's gotta mean something more.

Mickey: Who's shae

Jaysen: My brother
He asked about you

I look up again, make sure no one's come in the room and Colie's still sleeping.

Mickey: Oh?

Jaysen: Yeah
I mightve talked a lot of shit
about you in the beginning
And my family's been keeping
up wityh draft projections
You're the villain in this house

Mickey: My dad thinks
the same about you
He called you a distraction

Jaysen: Is he right

My palms are sweating. I take a selfie with my neck in clear view and send it to him.

Mickey: You tell me

He sends a bunch of laughing emojis and then:

Jaysen: Looks good on you

Mickey: You would think so.

I glance toward the kitchen again. The only person I can see is Zero, sitting on the counter with a beer bottle in his hand, laughing at something out of sight. Paying no attention to me.

Mickey: Tell me about shae

Jaysen: Dude he's like
One of my favorite people
We're pretty different, like
he's not into sports at
all and he hates my music
but he's so smart
I look up to him a lot but we're nowhere
near as close as you and your sisters
Kinda jealous actually

"Who you texting?"

I swear I almost choke on my own heart when Delilah pops her head over the back of the couch and puts her chin on my shoulder. I slap my phone to my chest to hide the screen and glare at her.

She grins. "I think I can guess."

My phone hums against my rib cage, making my heart skip. "I bet you'd be wrong."

Delilah rolls her eyes. "Deny all you want, Mickey. But I know things."

"Like what?"

She holds up her right hand. "I have been sworn to secrecy."

"Delilah."

"Mickey."

"I'm your brother."

She laughs a little and comes around the couch to sit next to me. She tucks one of her legs under her and turns to face me, cradling a wine cooler. She had dinner with her own team, so she missed the whole hickey conversation. When she sees me now, her nose scrunches in disgust. "Ugh, again? You're such a teenager."

I hike my shoulders like it'll hide it. "Shut up."

"So what's the deal with you two?" She wiggles her eyebrows. "Please tell me you're boyfriends."

"Oh my god." I look around in a panic, but Colie's still snoring and I can hear the bounce of a pong ball off a cup before the boys start yelling in the kitchen. "No. We're not . . . dating."

"Ugh. Men."

"What do you care?"

She shrugs and takes a short sip of her drink. "I just think it'd be good for you. You've seemed better since this started."

I frown at her. "Better?"

"Yeah, like . . ." She points a finger at her own head.

My stomach drops. I went so long without anyone ever catching on, and now it's like everyone can see right through me. It's one thing to tell people myself, but to be confronted with it, first by Dad, now by Delilah?

Anger flashes sudden and hot in the back of my skull. I try to stamp it out before it takes hold, but it settles in and pours out of my mouth anyway. "Better," I snap. "There's nothing wrong with me."

She seems so tired when she looks at me again, pinching her lips together and giving me these sad eyes. "Mickey, I wasn't trying to—"

"There's nothing wrong with me," I repeat. I stand and head for the kitchen.

I need a drink.

THE LAST TEXT I have from Mom is from back in the summer, when I was coaching at that lax camp with Bailey. My thumbs hover over the keyboard for ten whole minutes before I get the nerve to type.

> **Mickey:** Hey mama

She answers right away, which kind of makes me feel bad.

> **Mom:** Topolino! Happy Thanksgiving!

> **Mickey:** Happy thanksgiving

> **Mom:** Mi manchi

> **Mickey:** Miss you too
> Sorry i couldn't come
> Lot of homework

> **Mom:** That's ok. Christmas maybe?

> **Mickey:** Maybe

I rub my eyes with the heels of my hands. I can hear the rumble of the boys talking through the floor of the bathroom, where I sit on the closed toilet. I didn't even drink that much, but I feel sick. Tired. Like I could crawl into bed and stay there for three years.

All because Delilah said something about me getting better. Like her pointing out that I have a problem made it come back, I don't know.

My hands shake when I pick my phone back up and start typing again.

Mickey: So
Dad said something about depression
Like that you have it i guess
I don't remember much from when i
lived with you guys so i didn't know

Mom: Yes. It runs in my
family. Why? Are you ok?

Mickey: No
Not really

Mom: Let me get somewhere
quiet and I'll give you a call.

Mickey: Ok

Mom: Ti voglio bene Mickey.

Mickey: Love you too

I READ THROUGH the medication pamphlet three times before I even touch the pill bottle. It's the same antidepressant Mom takes, at the lowest dosage to start. The list of side effects is so long, my mouth goes dry reading through them. But Mom said she just gained some weight. The only time she's ever had a problem is when she missed a couple doses and started going through withdrawals.

I shake the bottle slowly, listening to the pills rattle as I stare at the ceiling.

Antidepressants.

Me. Taking antidepressants.

Me, Mickey James III, with such a bright, financially prosperous future ahead of me. So many people would kill to switch places with me. And here I am. With a bottle of antidepressants in my hand.

I don't have a right to be depressed, I'd said to Mom. *My life isn't horrible. Nothing really bad's ever happened to me.*

Depression doesn't care who you are or what you've been through, she said. *It's an illness that can happen to anyone.*

She said it, the internet said it, the Hartland counselor said it when I went to ask about medicine. The doctor who actually prescribed the medicine said it. Hell, I even said it to Dorian.

But as much as I logically know it to be true, that it's all in my genetics, my brain won't stop telling me that I'm being ungrateful. Dad didn't abandon me as a kid, he set me up for success. I didn't have this life pushed on me, it's just what I'm good at. I don't hate hockey, I just don't have the energy to like it.

Because I'm depressed.

I close my eyes and breathe slow and deep, tapping the bottle against my forehead.

Dammit.

TWENTY

As soon as Dorian makes it back to campus after Thanksgiving, he motions to my neck and says, "Hope you've got a story spun for that one."

Jesus. It's almost gone by now, how did he notice it? It's bad enough I'm still getting messages in the group chat like:

> **Delilah:** Hey hickey
> I mean mickey
> As soon as the lake freezes
> we're gonna play some pond hickey
> I mean hockey
> You in?

I literally hate my life.

"The boys already decided it was Nova," I say.

"Right. Because you'd really do that to Barbie. Happy for you, though. And honestly impressed. I hear Cauler's hella picky."

I actually splutter at him.

Dorian just laughs. "Now that's a textbook case of opposites attract, huh? Just be careful, dude. League finds out their top prospects are banging each other, shit'll go down."

My face is straight-up on fire. "Oh my god. Dorian. What the hell."

"What're the chances? They'd be all over it."

"I started taking antidepressants," I say just to change the subject, and we spend the rest of the morning cleaning our room and talking about medications and side effects and benefits. Honestly, we get so into it it's like we're bonding over talking about girls or something.

I pull the collar of my hoodie up over my mouth when I step into the tape room that afternoon. I don't need the rest of the boys who went home for Thanksgiving noticing. My stomach does this weird little flip when I see Cauler. He usually sits up front with Zero. Today, he's in the back where I always sit with Dorian and Barbie.

As soon as I sit down next to him, he hands over a stick of gum. I take it from him and glance over to watch him push his own into his mouth. He quirks an eyebrow at me.

This asshole.

As soon as the gum touches my tongue, it's like I'm kissing him all over again. I glare at him. He did this on purpose.

Cauler just laughs as I sink lower in my seat and chew furiously.

Barbie sits on my other side, leg bouncing against mine. He's texting Nova. Not that I'm being nosy or anything. He chews on his thumbnail as he reads her messages and takes his time typing up his own. Things must be getting serious. His leg keeps bouncing even when he puts his phone in his pocket. I wanna push his knee down to stop him, but Dorian presses his leg against him on the other side and that seems to help a little.

My stomach bottoms out when Coach starts the tape and I see the blue-and-gold jerseys of the Canisius Golden Griffins on the screen. Anxiety surges out of my chest all the way to my fingertips. I sink low in my chair and chew on the strings of my hoodie, squeezing myself tight around the middle. We lost this game, and I know I made my fair share of mistakes. Nothing like the Eagles game, but enough that I was grouchy the rest of the night. I hate watching any kind of tape, even from games we won. Dad recorded everything when I was growing up, from games to practice to shooting on a net in our driveway. Showed me the tape to walk me through every mistake I made until it was all I could focus on. I could put up five points in a game and still only remember the one turnover, the lost face-off in the defensive zone.

It's not like he meant it to be like that. Right? He was just trying to teach me.

But I still don't like watching tape.

Whenever my line shows up on the ice, I try to focus on Cauler and Zero, the blueliners, Colie, anyone but myself to keep Dad's criticism out of my head. Being on the ice with Cauler is one thing. Being in the moment, everything happening so fast, mind working out my next steps. It doesn't really give me a chance to fully appreciate Cauler's skill. Watching it happen on a screen honestly scares me. Even with the puck across the ice, he's always moving, always putting himself in the best possible position, always working. He's a full-on two-hundred-foot player. Makes a way better center than I ever could. And when the puck's on his stick, well . . . it's obvious why he's such a threat to my draft rank.

I lean forward and hold my breath when a clean saucer pass from Barbie at the outside hash marks in our zone hits my stick just outside the blue line. I redirect it to Cauler at the opposite blue line with a quick flick of my wrist, and Cauler carries it to the face-off dot before putting it top corner with a hard snapper to tie the game. The play is quick and exciting and enough to get a rise out of the boys even though we all know it doesn't matter. Colie shakes Cauler from where he sits next to him on the other side, shouting, "Top cheddar! Oh, what a beaut!"

"I don't know why you're all so excited when you know how this ends," Coach snaps, silencing everyone's joy. "We can make all the pretty plays we want, but if we can't follow them up with wins, what's the point?"

The energy in the room deflates enough that no one even reacts when I whiff on a one-timer at the top of the left circle. I can see my mistake with startling clarity this time around. On the ice, I thought I had no time. My defender was stepping in, the goalie sliding through the crease, another guy closing in from behind. My lane was closing, and I thought taking time to line up the shot would've been a missed opportunity. But seeing it like this, I can see the defender down low stumble, catching himself on the goalie's pads, tying them both up. I could've waited, deked at the last second to get out of the double, taken a better shot. I had plenty of time.

The worst part is I got over it faster than I have ever gotten over a mistake before. I know I suck at slap shots. I've come to terms with it.

And now it's being shoved in my face.

I sink lower in my seat.

"This is a problem we've been having all season," Coach says, pausing the tape. "We play too fast. There's times when it works, sure. Like that play with Barboza, James, and Caulfield. But the times it doesn't are catastrophic. We need to slow it down, think. We hit the blue line like a wall, all at once. Spread it out, take your time. We only got a few months to get our game settled. Our record's on our side for now, but we keep making mistakes like this, it's not gonna last. We need to play smarter.

"James," Coach calls me out. I snap my eyes to him. "You're better than that. You . . ."

I tune out the rest of his words and keep my chin tucked in the locker room as we lace up. I don't hear anything else until I stand to follow my team out to the ice and Coach calls me aside. Cauler narrows his eyes at us as he passes. It almost looks like concern.

"I want you working on your slappers with Coach Stempniak," Coach says.

My whole body tenses as I look up at them.

"I don't ever take slapshots, Coach," I say after a beat of silence. "That was a fluke."

"It's a skill you should have."

I blink at him. The tone of his voice sounds less like *a*

skill you should have and more like *an embarrassing skill not to have as Mickey James III.* We stare each other down, but I have a lot more practice in keeping my face chilly and unsettling, and Coach cracks eventually. He looks away and says, "Go on, get on with it."

I take an extra few seconds before tearing my eyes away and leading Coach Stempniak to the ice. We take over one of the zones and set up identically to how Cauler and I did. But this isn't Cauler and we're not alone and where each failed shot brought me this weird kind of joy before, now they bring me nothing but rage. I feel eyes on my back. I know the boys are busy practicing behind me, but all I hear is blood rushing in my ears, and I swear they're all standing back there watching me miss every shot.

I wonder what Dad would say if he could see me now. Probably something about my name and my blood and his legacy. He didn't have these problems. He's tall. Strong. Can take a shot from anywhere, slap a puck so hard it breaks the glass. I will never live up to his name.

Sometimes I wonder if he regrets marrying Mom. If he blames her for making me so short.

It takes a half an hour of continuous failure and Coach Stempniak doing the hardest work of his career trying to fix me before I finally connect solidly, accurately, the way a real hockey player should.

And then I'm Mickey James III. A flawless hockey machine who can hit a slap shot as good as anybody.

TWENTY-ONE

J ust because we're regularly having sex now doesn't mean I'm gonna let Cauler off easy. I put up three goals and two assists in our two games that weekend, while he comes away with a goal and two assists, and I am officially eleven points ahead of him.

Twitter loves it. Especially when Cauler tweets:

> **Jaysen Caulfield** @jaycaul21
> Imagine if @mjames17 could add
> those eleven points to his height.
> Maybe then I'd be nervous.

I'm sitting next to him on my bed, sharing a bag of salt-and-vinegar chips, when I reply.

> **Mickey James III** @mjames17
> Replying to @jaycaul21
> Must really hurt your ego for

someone as small as me to be

so much better than you.

Cauler snorts when he reads it. "That the best you can do?"

I shrug. "Not like I can get vulgar on social media."

He pushes me down onto my mattress while Twitter blows up about our rivalry and how much we despise each other.

I wake up on Monday to the alma mater chiming from the bell tower, greeting the first heavy snowfall of the year. My jeans are soaked halfway to my knees by the time I make it to class, only to find a sign taped to the door saying it's canceled.

My toes are frozen solid for no reason. I check my email before I can make the same mistake again and find messages from my professors canceling my later classes, too. Apparently canceling all classes was what the bell was for, and I'm too much of a freshman to have known that. I'd almost forgotten how good a snow day felt. I just wish I hadn't come all the way out here for nothing.

I stop at the dining hall for coffee and a bagel, and I'm on my way back to my room when Zero messages the team group chat.

Luca Cicero: Lax team heading
to fall ball in twenty minutes
It's snowing
You all know what this means

I have literally no idea what that means. I watch the replies come in as I change out of my wet socks and jeans and after a few minutes, Barbie's the one to speak up.

> **David Barboza:** Anyone wanna explain whats going on to us noobs?

> **Maverick Kovachis:** Get your asses to the hockey house and prepare for battle.

Apparently, battle means pelting the men's lacrosse team with snowballs as they leave the lax house. It's a full-blown war within seconds, and they have the advantage of lacrosse sticks to launch their snowballs farther and harder.

"We've made a terrible mistake!" Kovy shouts in this awful British accent. "Retreat!"

We all scramble to fall back, but my foot gets stuck in a mound of snow. I fall face-first, sinking so low into the powder, it feels like I'm in quicksand. I watch my teammates leave me behind, spitting snow out of my mouth and trying to push myself up to my knees. Dorian's a few steps ahead before he notices and comes back to grab my wrist and yank me to my feet, screaming and pulling me along behind him. Sid and Karim are on us a second later, tackling us both back into the snow.

"Should've saved yourself, Hidalgo," Sid says, pinning Dorian down.

"Just 'cause you laxers are disloyal doesn't mean we are,"

Dorian says. He gets a handful of snow shoved in his face in response.

By the time we make it back to the hockey house, we're soaked to the bone and shaking from the cold, but the boys are piling into the cars, giving us no time to recover. Cauler's standing by Zero's SUV with the back door open.

"Don't worry, Cauler, I went back to save him," Dorian says, jabbing a thumb at me. He doesn't see the dirty look Cauler shoots him as he climbs into the car.

I stand in front of Cauler, shivering so bad my teeth are chattering. My hair's frozen solid against my forehead, and I feel every change in the wind as it pummels me. "You left me to die," I say.

Cauler scoffs. "You really expect me to go back for my mortal enemy?"

"That's what I am to you?"

"You're a little shit, that's what you are." He grins as he grabs me by the shoulder and pushes me into the car.

I don't know what we're doing until we get to the rink and I see the women's team out on the ice. I practically run to the locker room for my skates and stick. Pond hockey with my sisters was a highlight of my childhood. We had a pond out back, fed by flooding from the creek that snaked through the woods behind our house and curved into our yard. It was a few feet deep, smaller than a standard rink, but good enough for us. In the summer it was full of frogs and turtles and enough mosquitoes that we didn't get to swim in it much. But in the dead of winter, it froze solid and clear, enclosed by snow drifts and backdropped by white-dusted pine trees. A picture so perfect it ended up on postcards in local grocery stores and a western New York calendar or two.

Back then, I'd wake up before the sun just to get out there in my skates with my sisters. They feel like the memories of a completely different person.

The lake here is too big to freeze and I don't have all my sisters here and things aren't perfect. But I don't get to be on the ice with Delilah often, so I'll take it.

Delilah, Barbie, and I are all picked by the women's team captain, but Cauler and Dorian end up with Zero. I kind of wish I could play against Delilah so we could battle for points like we have been all season, but I'm happy to dominate the ice with her instead. We played together often enough growing up to know exactly where to put the puck for the other to appear in its path, no matter how long it's been or how much we've changed as players.

Now we skate circles around our teammates and make impossible passes to one another, burying goals that make everyone scream in frustration and astonishment.

"Okay, who the hell thought it was a good idea to put the Jameses on a team together?" one of the girls on Zero's team asks after a set of filthy passes and a goal by Delilah.

I pull off a goal by picking the puck up on the blade of my stick and throwing it like a sidearm lacrosse shot, and Delilah straight up lifts me off the ice while Kovy shouts, "Oh shit, he's got the dangles!"

Delilah's screeching in my face and spinning me in circles. I roll my eyes. "Put me down?" I say, and she does only to take me by the hands and keep spinning.

"Dangles?" Cauler hisses as he slides up next to Kovy. He

gives me this scathing look with the faintest glint in his eye that gets my blood pumping. "More like betrayal. Might as well dump him at the lax house where he belongs."

I dig my skates in to stop Delilah's spinning and tilt my chin up at him. "You really expect to go Frozen Four without me?" I keep my voice low and even, fighting a smile.

Cauler steps closer, until we're almost chest-to-chest, forcing me to look up at him. "You're way too small to have such a big ego."

I quirk an eyebrow at him, and Delilah lets go of me. "Okay, can I get at least ten feet away before you two do . . . whatever it is you're doing?"

"This is called intimidation tactics, Delilah," Cauler argues. "Get your mind out of the gutter; this is your brother we're talking about."

I laugh. Loud and uncharacteristically, enough to get a bunch of the boys to whip around and look at me.

"What are you doing to him, Caulfield?" Zero skates over with mock concern in his voice and puts a hand on my shoulder. "Is this boy hurting you, my poor grumpy child?"

"Yeah, I think I ruptured something." I clutch my stomach, and Cauler's watching me with this soft kind of look on his face. The kind of look I've seen Delilah and Jade give each other, or Bailey and Sid and Karim.

I choke on my next laugh and let Zero lead me away by the elbow before I can jump to any more ridiculous conclusions.

We don't get far before Cauler calls out, "Hey, Terzo. We should practice our poses for draft day." He holds up his pointer finger, the way a number one pick always poses in photos with the top three. Like he expects me to go ahead and hold up two.

I cock my head to the side. "You wanna try that one again?"

He stretches his arms, pulling them across his chest and shaking out his wrists like he has to limber up for it. He holds up his fist and slowly raises one finger. I lunge forward and grab his hand, trying to force it down. The entire game's devolved into trick shots and hockey players pretending to be figure skaters at this point. Zero doesn't even try to break up our shoving match. He watches until Cauler gets me into a headlock and skates away saying, "Children, all of you."

I should be embarrassed, what with my arms flailing uselessly at Cauler's side, bent over and trapped in the crook of his elbow. But he's laughing, and I'm laughing, and honestly, both teams could vanish off the ice right now, leaving just the two of us, and I wouldn't even notice.

NICOLETTE SENDS A link in the group chat in the middle of my Italian class. I don't usually use my phone in class, but it's just finals review, and Italian is probably gonna single-handedly keep me from flunking out next week, so it's not like I really have to pay attention.

The link takes me to a video that I have to panic mute before it gets me in trouble. It's Hugh and Alyssa in front of another graphic of me and Cauler, this time standing next to each other in our Royals gear during a break in play. He's saying something with his head bent toward me and pointing down the ice, but I'm looking up at him.

I've got this bratty kind of look on my face that makes it seem like I want him to shut up, but it was probably just sweat in my eyes.

Plays perfectly into the *Royals Rivalry Heats Up* banner they've got on the bottom of the screen.

I glance up to make sure Professor Iacovella isn't staring me down, but since she realized I'm nearly fluent and took this class for the easy A, she pretty much started ignoring me. I'm just lucky she didn't get me kicked out and sent up a few levels.

I sink lower in my seat and hide my phone under the table anyway.

"Now, you've always been one of Mickey James III's biggest critics, so I'm sure you have plenty to say about his turnaround this season," Hugh's saying in the captions.

"I do," Alyssa says with a deep nod. "We've really seen him come out of his shell these past few months. You can tell he's bonded with this team in a way he never has before."

"Not to mention how much he's grown as a player as well," Hugh adds. "Going into this season, I would have said it was impossible for Mickey James to get any better than he already was without taking the step up to the NHL, but..." He shakes his head, smiling. "He's become a real two-hundred-foot player. He's always been a menace in the offensive zone, what with his playmaking abilities, that infamous wrist shot, his outstanding hockey IQ. But we've seen him improve exponentially on the backcheck this season. He's tiny, but he knows how to use his body to create offense in the defensive zone. No matter where he is on the ice, he's dangerous. I feel bad for any guy forced to go up against him."

Alyssa shifts her weight from foot to foot as Hugh talks, obviously waiting to say more, and when Hugh's finally done, she jumps at the chance to say, "I'm gonna go right ahead and credit a good chunk of that growth to Jaysen Caulfield."

Of course she would. She's probably right, too.

"James has been touted as the best player on every team he's ever been on," she continues. "He didn't have to put in as much effort to climb above the rest. Now that he shares a team with his biggest draft competitor, he's been forced to improve himself."

"Do you think the same could be said of Caulfield?"

"Of course. They're both gunning for the same spot at the top of their class, so they have to bring their best to the ice every day or else let the other pull ahead. They push each other to do better, whether they mean to or not."

"They have one of the most heated rivalries in sports going on right now, but they're surprisingly good at keeping how they feel about each other off the ice. They're young, but when it comes to hockey, they're professional."

"Well, we can't forget about their behavior on social media."

"Like I said." Hugh turns to face the camera with a full media grin. "They're young."

The clip ends, and I go back to the group chat.

> **Nicolette:** Imagine the fanfic
> this rivalry is gonna spawn.

> **Mickey:** People don't write
> fanfic about hockey players

Nicolette: Ummmmm I'm counting over
12k in this hockey rpf category so
You're wrong

I could have gone my whole life without knowing I could be the subject of someone's fanfiction. I've read my fair share of fanfic, and I know what that tends to involve. I also must truly enjoy suffering, because I barely make it out of class before I look it up.

And oh. My god. Nicolette wasn't lying. There's AUs and slice of life, hurt/comfort and fluff, and just about all of them involve some ship or another.

Jesus.

This is gonna become a thing now. I'm gonna have to check this every day. Maybe twice a day. Just to make sure I don't show up at all, of course.

TWENTY-TWO

There's two kegs at the hockey house to celebrate the end of the semester and a break from games and practices. But I'm over here reading a fantasy AU where I'm some kind of elven rogue sent to assassinate Cauler, a human prince, and instead end up falling in love with him.

I swear it's a hate-reading. I can't stop because I can't believe someone actually wrote this. I am not invested at all.

But oh my god, I have to show Cauler.

Delilah's doing a keg stand in the kitchen when I finally go for a drink, a couple of the boys holding her up. The kitchen's crowded with players from both teams waiting for a turn and cheering her on, so I take a few quick shots with Zero and head back to the living room with a beer in each hand.

I wait until my fingers are tingling and my tongue feels heavy before texting Cauler sitting across the room, a bottle of water in his hands. I haven't seen him drink all night.

Mickey: I gotta show you

something man

It's horrible

I'm slouched in the bend of the sectional between Dorian and Barbie with one of Delilah's teammates, Sierra Browne, sitting on the floor in front of me, leaning against my knees. She's been nearby all night. I don't think she's following me, necessarily. She just really wants to talk about hockey. And the fact that whenever the camera pans over the arena in the Bruins–Sabres game playing on the TV, my dad's name is visible hanging from the rafters.

I chew on the rim of my empty plastic cup. I was raised a Sabres fan. Played with the kids of Dad's former teammates, *lived* with one of his former teammates, Mr. Vinter. Went to every home game, dreamed of lifting the Cup in the blue and gold, having my number retired next to Dad's.

But Cauler's a Boston boy, a die-hard Bruins fan, and watching the way he sits on the very edge of the couch, leaning forward, ready to jump out of his seat at any moment and scream in rage or excitement is almost enough to make me a Bruins fan myself. And that is utter blasphemy coming from a Buffalonian. I watch Cauler more than the game, keeping my face forward while my eyes wander to the spectacle that is Jaysen Caulfield riled up on hockey.

I just wish he would pause for a second and check his damn phone. He's practically levitating from the adrenaline, shaking Colie by the shoulder and shouting, "Shoot the puck, holy shit, you had a wide-open lane!"

"It's not gonna happen, Cauler," Colie says seriously. "The Sabres' PK is filthy this year, and the Bruins' powerplay's been lacking."

"It's a five on three, you mother—AH!" Cauler shoves Colie before putting both hands on top of his head. "Are you kidding me? How did he miss that! God, I'd trade him for a fucking camel right now."

Dorian snorts and Barbie says, "Really, Cauler? A camel?"

"Don't start with me, Barboza." Cauler points a finger in our direction without looking over.

"Dream bigger, Cauler," Sierra says. "They could at least get a fifth-round pick for him."

"Um, excuse me?" Barbie sounds genuinely offended. "You saying I'm not worth more than that?"

Sierra throws her head back in laughter, knocking into my knees. She leans forward and rubs the back of her head, still laughing. "Sorry, bro. Forgot you were a fifth-rounder."

"I might be a fifth-rounder but I still wouldn't've missed that shot. Seriously, he had the top, like, eighty percent of the net."

"Pretty sure you missed a shot on a completely empty net before, Barbs," Dorian reminds him. "Like, the goalie was pulled and everything."

"In bantam! This guy's supposed to be a professional!"

They keep arguing over my head, but I tune it out when Cauler leans back into the couch with a sigh, finally checking his phone. He doesn't look at me when he reads the message, but his eyebrows come together and he frowns as he types something. A moment later, my phone vibrates in my hands. I sink down and pull it close to my face so Dorian and Barbie can't read over my shoulder.

Jaysen: That sounds ominous

Mickey: Ok not horrible

like seriously horrible

Just horrible in a cringey kind of way

Attic?

I have to fight my way off the couch between the alcohol and the bodies pressed all around me, but they're too busy arguing to say anything about me leaving. I stop by the kitchen to sneak another shot behind Delilah's back before heading upstairs. Cauler takes his time, making our mutual disappearance a little less suspicious. He slides into the attic silently, glasses slipping down his nose and his hat crooked. I can't help but think of that insult game we played up here. It's only been a couple months, but I couldn't even imagine saying things like that to him now.

Cauler smiles as he presses me down into the couch with a hard kiss and rough hands under my shirt. The same couch we woke up on together after that party.

We have to take these moments when we can get them. It's straight-up torture how much time we spend together unable to touch each other. We're with each other for hours at a time every single day, but never alone like this.

It'd be easy to get carried away, but Cauler pushes off me after a few minutes, sitting cross-legged on the couch next to me. "Let's see this cringe material."

I sit up, tucking a leg under me and adjusting my hat as a wave of dizziness surges through my head. I rub my eyes and blink a few times before it passes, then pull out my phone and bring up the fic.

Cauler traces a finger around my knee as it loads.

Maybe I shouldn't show him. What if it scares him off? Just the thought of people shipping us for their own entertainment feels a little dangerous when it hits that close to the truth. Like every one of our public interactions'll be scrutinized to the point where someone will figure us out.

But who am I kidding? What we're doing doesn't make for an epic fantasy love story. There's nothing close to the truth about it.

I hand my phone off to Cauler and rest my head on the back of the couch to watch his face as he reads. As soon as he sees the site, his eyebrows go up. "You find Kovy's Dragon Age fics?"

He goes back to reading before I can answer, his face going through phases of confusion, understanding, and then . . . Absolute. Joy. He gives me the most ridiculous smile I've ever seen on him, his nose scrunched up and his eyes half-closed. My heart feels like it's trying to compress itself into nonexistence.

"They made you an elf," he says, laughing. "Perfect."

I glare at him.

He laughs some more. "Oh, that's a good one. Kinda hot. Much hotter than the corpse look you usually got going on."

I narrow my eyes, but he doesn't stop smiling, even when he reaches forward and brushes a thumb over my lip, pulling me in for a kiss. He laughs against my mouth.

"You know you made it big when people write fanfiction about you," he says.

I huff a breath. "We haven't even been drafted yet."

"Even better. We can only go up from here."

"You don't think it's creepy? Like at all?"

"It's hilarious, are you kidding? I can't believe they made me the prince and you the assassin. Amazing."

Oh my god. Is he serious right now? He keeps a hand up by my jaw and goes right back to reading, and I am full of regret. I groan. "Showing you was a mistake, wasn't it."

"Not at all. I'm gonna bookmark this."

I lunge forward and snatch my phone away from him, drop it on the floor, and crawl into his lap. "You were supposed to cringe with me."

He gives me a crooked grin and pushes a hand through my hair, knocking my hat off my head. "We'll see how it goes when I actually read it."

We kiss like that for a few minutes, me in his lap, his hand in my hair, until there's an uproar downstairs that has both of us looking to the door.

"Bruins probably scored," Cauler says all smugly. I roll my eyes and stand up. We've been up here too long already. I adjust my clothes, fix the mess he's made of my hair, and put my hat back on. Make myself look like I didn't just have someone else's tongue in my mouth.

Cauler gives me this soft, almost loving last kiss before heading downstairs, and I just feel so . . . sad all of a sudden. The kind of sad I felt watching Dad go through security at the airport without me when I was ten. My mom and sisters leaving me behind as they drove off ahead of the moving truck.

Cauler and I will never be more than this. And the worst

part is I *know* he wants more. And I think I do, too. But the prospect of what happens when we mess it up is just too much to handle.

I swipe the back of my hand across my mouth like it'll erase the memory of Cauler's lips on mine and go to the kitchen for another drink.

––––––––

FIVE MINUTES LATER, I'm in the longest keg stand of my life. Barbie and Kovy hold my legs up while Delilah reluctantly works the valve, Dorian and Zero screaming right in my face. I'm not in it to break Colie's house record. I'm in it to stop feeling.

The two probably go hand in hand.

By the time I'm back on my feet, barely holding myself upright, my name's replaced Colie's on the whiteboard hanging over the pong table. Might as well replace more names.

"Lilah?" I say, motioning toward the pong table where Dorian and Barbie have already taken a side.

She frowns as she looks me up and down, taking in my probably glassy eyes, the way I can't hold my head up straight.

"C'mon," I beg. "It's the end of the semester."

She lets out a soft sigh. "Fine." She puts a cocky smile on her face and leads me to the table.

"Dude!" Dorian says. "No way, you two don't get to be a team!"

Delilah lets out this absolutely maniacal laugh as she pushes back the sleeves of her dress. She rolls the ball between her hands and sinks a cup right off the bat.

"Ugh, here we go," Barbie groans.

By the time we beat Dorian and Barbie, and Zero and Sierra take their place, I'm at the point where I'd usually be half-naked and dancing on a table or claiming to be the second—or fourth or maybe seventh by now—coming of Jesus Christ. But Cauler's in the living room playing *Smash Bros* and not thinking about me at all, and Mom and Dad are down in North Carolina in their massive house that doesn't have a single touch of me in it, and I am not in the mood to dance or perform miracles.

An hour ago, I was being kissed senseless. Now all I want to do is drink myself senseless.

Delilah and I sink cup after cup, even when I start swaying on my feet when I throw and leaning on Delilah when I watch, to the point where she takes my drink away from me and makes me switch to water. Sierra keeps bending over every time I'm up, trying to distract me with a clear line of sight down her shirt. It only works when I let it.

Cauler literally hates me when he's not touching me. I don't owe him anything.

"Cut it out, Brownie!" Delilah snaps eventually. "That is my brother!"

"It's the nature of the game, Jamie," Sierra shoots back, smirking.

Zero turns and drops his pants to give Delilah a full view of his bare ass on her turn, and now I'm the one to gasp and say, "Luca Cicero, that is my sister!"

"Hey, when you party with your siblings, shit's gonna get awkward," Zero shouts. He scoops up the ball from Delilah's missed shot and buttons his pants. "Where's Jade tonight anyway? I could find a way for things to get real awkward for Terzo if she were here."

"Working on her final portfolio," Delilah says. "I thought art majors had it easy, but I swear she's got more work than anyone else I know."

I don't last at the table much longer. I can't see straight when I throw the ball. The cups multiply and move on their own, and if I keep looking at them I might throw up. I stagger out into the hallway before the game's even officially done and lean against the wall, tilting my head back.

The floor is literally rolling under my feet.

"That keg stand catching up to you?"

I crack an eye open as Sierra leans against the wall beside me, close enough our arms touch. She's got long blond hair and blue eyes, and she's got on this tight white shirt without shoulders, tucked into jeans that go up to her belly button. Not my type at all, but she's cute. "Nah," I mumble. "Feel great." She has a nice laugh. "You play D, huh?"

She turns toward me, face lighting up because she has been trying to talk hockey with me all night and I've been completely blowing her off like an asshole. She's been playing hockey just as long as me, with a Team USA, NWHL end game. I've seen her play. She'll make it. Won't be as successful as Delilah, obviously, but they play different positions anyway, so I guess it doesn't really matter.

I can tell she's being flirty. And I'm being flirty back. I feel dirty about it and I can barely keep my eyes open. Mom and Dad would like her, though. If they can't have Nova as a daughter-in-law, they've always said I should at least seek out a hockey fan. Someone who knows the game and the lifestyle and will help me raise another Mickey James to legend. An actual hockey player would be even better.

But Cauler's an actual hockey player, too. Dad's not a homophobe, obviously, but I can still imagine the lecture he'd give me. Why it's okay for Delilah to be gay but not me. Why women's hockey fans would accept her but NHL fans would make my life hell. How I'd literally never see him during the season.

I don't know what Sierra just said to me. I try to open my eyes to look at her but they feel glued shut. I barely manage to get them cracked when I hear Cauler say, "Where's Terzo?" There's laughter in his voice, and when he steps into the hallway, he's smiling. "Hey. I wanna kick your ass in *Smash Bros.*"

I don't want to play games. I want one of the bottles of liquor stashed in the attic. I want to chug it down until I forget my own name. I want to touch somebody. I want to touch Cauler.

"Um . . . ," Sierra starts, looking back and forth between us. "I'm gonna get a drink." She eases her way out of the hallway like she knows exactly what's going on here.

Cauler and I stare each other down. Or maybe it's just me and he's trying to figure out if he should back up before I puke on him or something.

"Well?" Cauler asks, motioning toward the living room.

That keg stand really is catching up with me. I let myself slide down the wall until I'm sitting. "We probably shouldn't do shit like that," I try to say. I don't know how coherent it is.

Cauler sighs. He sits down cross-legged in front of me, picking the calluses on his hands. Chewing on his lip ring. I try to close my eyes to block him out, but the floor is swaying again and I have to open them.

"Why not?" Cauler says gruffly.

"'Cause. Too close to being something then." I don't know if I'm speaking actual words. I don't wanna close my eyes with the way everything spins when I do, but they're too heavy to keep open.

He doesn't answer right away. My stomach is doing flips. I gotta get out of here.

"You don't think we're past that point already?" His voice is soft, quiet. Almost kind of sad.

I push down the feelings trying to dredge their way up into my chest. "No. If we are, then . . . we gotta stop."

He's so quiet, for a second I'm not sure he's even here anymore. I open my eyes enough to see his shoes before letting them fall closed again.

"Why do we gotta stop?" he asks eventually.

I laugh, a delirious, drunken sound that I instantly feel guilty for. "Because. Too danger—"

My stomach lurches and I clamp a hand over my mouth. Cauler jerks away, then comes back to help me to my feet. "Bathroom?" he asks. I respond with another dry heave.

Cauler straight up lifts me off the floor. I let my head fall onto his shoulder as he carries me down the hall.

Seriously though. Kill me.

I hear Delilah's voice but can't understand what she's saying. Cauler's voice vibrates through his chest when he says, "I got him."

Everything's quiet after that.

TWENTY-THREE

I wake up hating myself.

It's not an unfamiliar thing, but it's not welcome, either.

Same goes for the pulsing headache and sour taste of vomit in the back of my throat. I lurch out of bed and stumble out of the room, into the bathroom to throw up.

Last night was a total shit show. Why am I like this?

Cauler carried me to the bathroom and stayed with me while I puked. Then he took me out to someone's car. Drove me back to campus, carried me to my room, and helped me into sweatpants. Made me drink water and lie down and stayed with me until Dorian came back.

We didn't talk.

I lay on my side, facing the wall, listening to his steady breathing and holding back tears.

How embarrassing.

I wish I could just take apart my head and carve out every part that makes me like this, really. It's exhausting being inside my own head.

Dorian's up when I get back to the room. I stagger my way to my bed and lie down, pressing the heels of my hands into my eyes.

"How you feeling?" Dorian asks. I grunt in response and he forces a laugh and I would really truly appreciate death right now. "You up for some breakfast? Zero's treating us to French toast from the Inn."

I grunt again. The thought of food makes my stomach churn, but if I'm gonna manage to keep anything down, French toast is it.

"I'll take that as a yes," Dorian says. The sound of him typing on his phone is way louder than it has any right to be.

What if Cauler messaged me? I dig through the tangle of my blankets, twisting my arms all over the place trying to find my phone. I pretty much dislocate both shoulders just to find it on top of my headboard.

No texts from Cauler. Just Delilah asking me to let her know I'm alive. I send her a few vomit emojis and snap Nova a hangover selfie. Everything's awful, but I can pretend.

"Hey, sooo . . . ," Dorian says. I turn my head to look at him, half my face still buried in the pillow. "I probably should've warned you about drinking on medicine."

I blink at him.

"Just 'cause, like," he says quickly. "I mean, we haven't really had a big drinking night since you started taking them, and you were *bad* last night, dude. There's a reason they say not to mix prescription drugs and alcohol. Especially when it's new."

I close my eyes. Press a hand to my forehead. I didn't even think about it. I read the warnings so many times I probably could have recited them by heart, but I've gotten so used to using alcohol in place of the medication, it's like I forgot I was even on it.

"You okay?" he asks.

I close my eyes and huff a laugh. "When have I ever been okay?"

Dorian laughs through his nose. "Relatable."

Zero delivers our breakfast right to our room. He says it's because he wants us to remember him as the best captain we've ever had, but I think it's because he wanted to check up on me.

I feel a thousand times better after eating and showering. At least physically. But I still check my phone every few minutes while Dorian and I play *Borderlands* together. I get a few messages from the boys. The group chat with my sisters goes pretty steady all day. And Nova and I send snaps back and forth like usual.

But no word from Cauler.

God, I feel so pathetic. I could easily message him myself. Say something like, *heyyyy sorry for that total nuclear meltdown yesterday, surprise I am like way depressed!* Or *I'm usually way better at the whole friends with benefits thing, my bad.*

Maybe just . . .

Mickey: Hey.
Sorry about last night.
Thanks for taking care of me.

I toss my phone out of arm's reach and settle in for a long, anxious night.

Jaysen: Hey

Can you come to my room?

Dodge 211

I'll prop the door

I *was* feeling better. Now I kind of feel like I might be sick again.

Dorian's all settled in bed with his laptop, watching Netflix as he falls asleep. I'm half-tempted to ask him what I should do, but I need to figure this out for myself.

Okay. Suck it up. What's the worst that can happen if I go over there? Cauler tells me we're not hooking up anymore? That I scared him away with that mess last night? I'm leaving after next semester anyway. With any luck we'll be drafted to different conferences and only see each other twice a season. By the time he graduates and comes into the league, maybe he'll forget anything ever happened between us.

I take a deep breath, close my eyes, and let it out in a rush.

"I'm going for a walk," I say as I get out of bed and slip into my sneakers.

Dorian pulls out one of his earbuds and gives me a pointed look. "Don't think of me this time. That would be rude to Cauler." He raises an eyebrow and my cheeks flush. Apparently the state I came back in last time I announced I was leaving was a dead giveaway of what I'd been doing.

"I don't know," I say as I pull on my jacket. "Maybe he'd be into it."

"Hmm. Wouldn't that be something?" He puts his earbud back in and goes back to his Netflix. "Well, have fun and be safe."

I roll my eyes. "K, Mom."

I take my time walking over to Cauler's building. It's not a long walk at all, but I drag it out so long, my muscles ache from bracing against the cold by the time I make it to the door. He propped it open with one of his shoes. I sigh as I bend over to pick it up and stretch out my muscles a bit when I stand up.

Still. Stalling.

Get it together, Mickey.

Another deep breath, and I take the stairs two at a time. This building is set up in suites. As in four rooms sharing a short hallway and a bathroom. As in, at any given moment, one of these three doors can open and I will be face-to-face with one of Cauler's suitemates as I knock on his door. At midnight.

I duck my head as I wait for him to answer. Bedsprings creak beyond the door, the sound of bare feet on linoleum. I hold my breath as the door knob turns. My hands feel clammy.

Cauler smells like he just got out of the shower. He's got his glasses on. A long-sleeved T-shirt. He looks good. Really good.

My voice is all kinds of strained when I say, "Hey."

He doesn't say anything. Just steps out of the way to let me in. The first thing I notice is the giant poster of Ashley Graham in a bikini with a fair amount of underboob showing. Besides that . . .

I almost choke on my own saliva.

There's a poster of Nova on the wall. It's smaller than Ashley Graham's, but bigger than the others of singers and rappers and baseball players. She's in a floor-length red dress with a slit all the way up her thigh, leaning forward in a chair with her lips parted in this weird pout.

"Oh my god," I say. I whip my phone out to snap it to Nova.

"My roommate's side," Cauler says. Stating the obvious.

"You never told me he was a Nova fanboy!"

He shrugs, eyes roaming over his roommate's wall. "I'm not in here much."

Cauler's side of the room is pretty bare. There's a Bruins tapestry above his bed. Our practice and game schedule for next semester pinned to his corkboard. Something that looks like an autographed set list next to that. No other touches of his personality to be seen.

It makes it a little easier, being in his room. Alone with him.

We've been alone plenty of times now. But it was always my room, my home ground. This is different, and not just because I'm afraid of what he's gonna say.

Cauler sits on the edge of his bed and puts his forearms on his knees. Hands clasped together. Looking at the floor. The pose of a person who's just been given the most harrowing news of their life.

"So," he says. "Last night."

I sigh heavily. Turn away from him, pushing both hands into my hair.

Here we go.

I sink into his roommate's desk chair. "I'm sorry," I say. Don't give myself the chance to wall up. "I've been taking this new medicine. Shouldn't've been drinking. Thanks for . . ." I swallow against the tightness in my throat. "Thanks for getting me back to my room."

He looks up at me, slowly rubbing his hands together now. I can hear the faint click of his tongue piercing against his teeth for a few seconds before he says, "Remember the things you were saying?"

"Unfortunately."

"Wanna talk about it?"

I sigh again, leaning the chair back on two legs and staring at a point above Cauler's head. I don't want to talk about it. Talking brings up emotions, and emotions in this situation would be very, very bad. But he obviously wants to talk about it.

"What do you want me to say?" I ask. It's a total fuckboy response, but it's all I can manage.

"I want you to tell me what you want," he says without hesitation. His face is the blankest I have ever seen it. I don't like it. He's usually so expressive. I hate that it's my fault he looks like this. "I know you were flirting with Sierra last night, and that's whatever. But if that's how it's going to be, I need you to tell me now so I can decide what to do with it."

I swallow, hard, moving my eyes down to the floor. The small garbage can next to his roommate's desk is overflowing with balled-up papers. His comforter hangs half off the bed, a pile of laundry on the end of the mattress. Meanwhile, Cauler's side is immaculate. It makes me think about what his room at home might look like. If it's just as clean because he lived in Green Bay the past couple years. If he made a mess of it this summer.

"What I want doesn't matter," I say. My voice is choked. I press a fist to my lips and take a deep breath. "Even what we're doing now is dangerous. People take pictures of us and put them online, what if someone sees us—" I cut myself off and clear the emotion out of my throat.

"So do you want to stop, then?" He's stopped fidgeting, sitting completely still as his eyes burn right through me, unblinking. I shift uncomfortably, the chair creaking beneath me.

Stopping would be for the best. No more hickeys to explain away, for one. No chance of someone getting a poorly timed picture of us being careless on campus.

I rub the back of my neck, avert my gaze to Cauler's open closet and its row of mostly black shirts. "I mean . . . no."

Cauler doesn't say anything. I can see him looking at me out of the corner of my eye, but I can't bring myself to look back at him. I cross my arms, slouch down in the seat. Click my tongue against the roof of my mouth just to fill some of the awkward silence.

It lasts a few good . . . long . . . seconds, before Cauler huffs this kind of disbelieving laugh and shakes his head. He rubs his eyes and looks so tired when he says, "Jesus, Terzo."

My pulse spikes. I sit up straight. "What? Now what?"

He shakes his head. "You're such a . . . little shit." He says it like a groan. Like I am causing him physical pain.

"Why is it all on me anyway?" I ask. "You said you know what you want, so why don't you tell me?"

He drags his hands down his face and sits up, planting his feet flat on the floor. He looks me dead-on and says, "I don't want to be just an option for you. I'm not asking for some strict commitment or to be boyfriends or anything. Just, if you're gonna start messing around with someone else, I'm not sticking around for it."

I finally meet his eyes, chewing on the inside of my cheek. It's a simple request, and an easy one to agree to. But part of me is a little disappointed that he *didn't* ask for a strict commitment. I mean, I'd probably say no. It's too risky, too likely to end painfully for both of us. But I can dream, right?

"That's fine," I say.

He studies me for a second, his face unreadable. He takes in a sharp breath and says, "Wanna stay tonight?"

"What about your roommate?" I ask.

Cauler rolls his eyes. "He tried to bring a fucking Ouija board in here with a bunch of his friends, so I kicked him out. Told him not to come back till he's sure he's not possessed."

"Seriously?"

"Yeah. I guess he thought since I listen to screamo and wear black clothes, I'd be chill with it? I don't know."

"So you planning on a single next year, then?"

"Nah. Going for a triple with Barbie and Doll Face."

"Oh." I swear my heart sinks all the way to my toes. The three of them sharing a room. Without me. While I'm off living with one of my veteran teammates in a city that's to be determined. I stand up before I can fall into that spiral and take off my jacket. "Yeah, I'll stay."

He pulls his legs up onto his bed and makes room for me. I kick my shoes off in the middle of the room and settle in beside him.

This will have to be enough.

I WAKE UP in Cauler's bed.

I don't know where I am at first, hit by a brief moment

of half-asleep panic before everything from last night comes together.

Cauler's still asleep, his back pressed to the wall and one of his arms draped over my waist. My sweatpants bunch around my calf where my leg is pinned between his. His lips are parted just a little in his sleep, and he looks so damn soft I could die.

And I'm not looking for anything. I'm really not. But I'm not ready for this to end.

I close my eyes and settle back into the pillow to get more sleep, but a second later, Cauler's saying, "Hey."

His voice is rough in the morning. It's appalling how freaking hot he is.

"Hey," I say.

He stretches around me, making that soft straining noise people make when they do their morning stretch. It's adorable. When he relaxes again, his face presses closer to mine.

"I'd kiss you," he says, "but your breath smells horrible."

"I mean, you didn't offer me a toothbrush last night."

"Those are like ten bucks apiece at the bookstore, man, I don't stock up."

"I guess I'll try not to breathe, then."

He smiles, eyes closed. "That might be for the best."

What would be for the best would be going back to my own room. Taking a shower and brushing my teeth. Emailing the counseling office and getting another appointment set up.

Getting my life together.

"It smells like dirty socks in here," I say.

"Like I said. Your breath is terrible."

"Fuck you, it doesn't smell like feet."

He chuckles. It's the kind of sound that's gonna repeat in my head until it drives me nuts. "My roommate does laundry, like, once a month," he says.

I throw a panicked look over to his roommate's side at the mention of him, but the bed's empty.

"I texted him," Cauler says. "He's not coming back till after brunch. I swear, if he brings a ghost back with him . . ."

I let out a sigh of relief and roll onto my back, stretching my arms above my head until my back arches off the bed. Cauler trails his fingertips over my ribs lightly enough to give me chills.

"Y'know," he starts, pausing to yawn. "Drug interaction or not, it's good to see you get a little emotional sometimes."

I turn my head to the side to give him a look. "I feel mildly offended? Either way, that's all you're gonna get. I have a set limit of one emotion per week."

"I'll mark it on my calendar." His hand is warm on my bare skin.

This is nothing. This means nothing. He doesn't even like me, let alone *like* me. This is only happening because I was the closest available, moderately attractive guy who gave off some pretty transparent gay vibes.

This is nothing.

His fingers flex against my hip. His breath sounds unsteady. His eyes are closed. "Question. Don't think too much into it."

Oh god, here we go.

"What are your plans for break?" he asks.

My tongue sticks to the roof of my mouth when I open it, because oh my god? Is this going where I think it's going?

"I usually go to Nova's," I say slowly. "But she's in Milan or something."

"Raleigh, then?"

I laugh bitterly. "I don't remember the last time I spent Christmas with my family."

I don't say it for the sad look he gives me, but thankfully he doesn't dwell on it. "Soooo . . . why don't you come to Boston?"

I push up onto my elbow to look down at him. "Boston? Like with you?"

"Yeah, I mean." He shrugs a shoulder and avoids looking me in the eye. "My family's pretty hospitable. I don't got five sisters like you, but I have a lot of cousins. Both sides cram into my parents' house, and there's chaos and way too much food and alcohol and card games. I hear my ex-uncle'll be there, so that'll be interesting."

"Why's your ex-uncle coming?"

"He's not officially an ex yet and his kids'll be there, so he thinks it's his right to tag along. My aunt filed for divorce, but it's not finalized yet. Shae gets into it with him. Entertaining as hell."

"Sounds tiring."

"Most things are tiring to you."

Talking about being tired triggers a massive yawn that Cauler covers with his hand to block my morning breath. We both laugh sleepily.

"What'll your family say about you consorting with the enemy?" I ask.

"Ehh, they'll see how tiny you are in real life and realize you're no threat."

"You're no Zdeno Chara yourself."

"Six inches make a big difference, Terzo. Bet you didn't know you got this weird-looking cowlick up here." He twirls some of the hair on top of my head around his finger and my heart fills my entire chest. "I got a perfect view."

"Shut up."

He laughs. Pulls me in closer, closing his eyes, looking like he's gonna fall right back to sleep. I have this acute awareness of every point of contact between us.

"So?" he asks.

I take a slow breath in until my lungs can't hold any more air. I hold it for a few long seconds, and close my eyes on the exhale. "Ah, I don't know. Sleeping on the dock for a few days in the dead of winter sounds kind of appealing. The dining hall will be closed, so I'll get to practice my ice fishing. I didn't do Boy Scouts or learn how to start a fire, so I'll have to fucking . . . Sméagol that shit. And—" I open my eyes to find Cauler grinning at me. "You're not stopping me."

"It's nice hearing you talk when you're not being a total shithead."

Don't think too much into it.

"You call that not being a shithead?" I ask.

"No, that was you being a *little shit.*"

I roll my eyes, groaning. "I'm gonna regret this."

He squeezes my hip. "That mean you'll come?"

"I suppose."

He was complaining about my breath a few minutes ago, but that doesn't stop him from kissing me now.

TWENTY-FOUR

Finals are over, and there is nothing I can do now but obsessively refresh until my grades are posted. I feel pretty alright about biology, and I know I got a perfect score on my Italian exam, but algebra is a toss-up. My final paper for college writing was a mess. I think I'll be good as far as staying above 2.0, but I want to do better than that.

I want to hit Dorian and Cauler levels of academic success. It's not gonna happen in the span of two semesters, but at least it's something to strive for.

Watching Dorian and Barbie load their bags into the Lyft is damn near soul-crushing. This is gonna be an abbreviated break. Not the whole month most of the student body gets. But it feels like I'm seeing them for the last time.

Jesus.

What's it gonna be like to leave them in May?

I don't even want to think about it.

Dorian hugs me tight, saying, "We survived our first semester, dude! We can only go up from here."

Barbie claps me on the back, then thinks better of it and pulls me into a hug. He's so tall, I feel like a toddler in his arms.

Once they're gone, Cauler and I load our own bags into Zero's car. Zero's got one more exam to go before he drives us all to Boston later tonight, so the two of us pass the time in my room.

He's tugging off my jeans when my phone vibrates. I push it off the bed onto the floor and ignore it.

He's pulling his shirt over his head, knees on either side of my hips, when it goes off again, and pushing my hands down into the pillows the third time.

"Something's wrong," he mumbles. "You're not this popular."

"Fuck you. It's probably Dorian updating me. I asked him to check in when he gets to the airport."

"How domestic of you."

We get another minute or two to ourselves before a video call comes through on my laptop, loud and upbeat and intrusive and relentless. We ignore it for a whole minute before Cauler gives up, groans, and rolls off me.

"Go see who it is," he says, burying his face in my pillows.

"I don't wanna," I whine. But the ringing doesn't stop.

"Go." Cauler pushes me toward the edge of the bed and I get up, grumbling as I pull on the nearest pair of sweatpants on the floor. Of course they're Cauler's, long enough that I almost trip over them on my way to the desk.

I run my fingers through my hair and try to make it less obvious what I was just doing as I throw myself into my desk chair. "Shit," I mutter at the sight of Madison's picture on my computer screen. She never initiates contact. I accept the call and it takes a moment of lag before the video connects.

And it's not Madison looking at me.

It's Dad.

The video is frozen on his look of desperation for a second, like he was so sure I wasn't gonna answer. "Hey, bud!" he calls out, and the image jumps and stretches a few times before his face catches up to his words.

I can feel how wide my eyes are. How tightly my jaw clenches even as I try so hard to keep the panic from showing. I haven't talked to him since that game back in November. He's called and texted and I've ignored and ignored and now it's so awkward I kind of want to puke.

I glance at Cauler, almost naked in my bed, lying on his stomach with the pillow bunched under his chin. There's concern on his face that I don't deserve. Not with so many people out there who have much worse parents than me.

"Mickey? You hear me?" Dad asks.

I turn my attention back to him and try to speak, but my voice gets stuck in my throat. I clear it and try again. "Yeah. Hi."

"I'm glad you picked up. It's been a while."

"Yeah."

Dad opens his mouth but doesn't say anything at first, looking like he feels just as uncomfortable as I do. He takes a deep breath, and when he looks down and rubs the back of his neck, I can almost see myself in him. I'm not as good at masking my discomfort as I used to be.

"So . . ." He still doesn't look at me, keeping his eyes down or off to the side, anywhere but my face. "There was a lot I wanted to talk to you about. But I think it'd be better to do it in person. Your sisters are flying out in the morning. How would you feel about joining them?"

I feel repulsed, that's how I feel.

"Little late to buy a ticket," I say.

"I already took care of it. Why do you think I called so much?"

My bed creaks as Cauler sits up, and I look over to see him settle with his back against the wall, head tilted back, staring at Dorian's side of the room. I can't read his face. Is that disappointment or impatience? Maybe he's just hungry.

I don't know him at all. But here I was planning to go meet his family.

I swallow, bite the inside of my cheek.

I'll get to see my sisters. All of them. That's the only positive here.

"How long?" I ask.

"I want you here as long as you can be."

I put my face in my hands and sigh heavily. My chest aches. I can barely process what's happening. Seven-plus years being my freaking long-distance hockey coach and now he's trying to be a dad?

But . . . I want it. I want the chance to have a family again.

I rub my hands over my face. Rake them through my hair. My voice croaks when I say, "Okay."

Dad smiles, his shoulders sagging in relief. As if I even had a choice when he already went and bought a ticket behind my back.

"Great," he says all breathlessly. "Bailey has the flight information. It's an early one. Get some sleep."

He signs off so quick it's like he had his finger hovering over the button this whole time. I stare at the screen for a solid ten seconds before Cauler says, "You okay?"

I push myself to my feet. "Yeah. Sorry."

"Don't be. It's your family."

He watches me as I swap out his pants for my own and finish getting dressed. Doesn't try to interfere, which is good 'cause I can't handle *shit* right now.

"Gonna get my bags outta Zero's car," I say.

"Want help?"

"No." I zip my jacket all the way to my chin. Hide in my hood. Leave him behind. Pull out my phone and immediately message Bailey.

Mickey: This is your fault.

Bailey: Yep.

Mickey: Fuck you bailey.

Bailey: Get over yourself mickey.
You've been ignoring him for weeks.
I was on the phone with him for over an
hour last night with him panicking
about how if he didn't get to talk to you
soon he'd probably never get
a chance to fix things
As if anything needs to be fixed.

Mickey: A lot more than you think

Bailey: Well congrats
now you have a chance to
air out all your petty childish grievances

Mickey: I hate you

Bailey: I know how much you
like to pretend you've had
some horrible life full of
endless suffering but it's
time to grow up mickey.
Mom and dad love you.
That's a lot more than other people get.

Mickey: Real easy for you to say.
Our parents actually raised you.

TWENTY-FIVE

North Carolina is colder than I expected, and all I brought was a Royals windbreaker. I cross my arms and hike my shoulders to my ears, but it doesn't help much. Bailey's wearing gym shorts, and I hope she gets frostbite on her knees. She lived in Raleigh. She should know better.

Madison picks us up from the airport, and as happy as I am to see her again, I can't freaking stand how hyper the three of them get when all I wanna do is put my head against the window and fall asleep. Madison doesn't even need a GPS. She's paying more attention to Delilah in her rearview mirror and Bailey in the passenger seat than the road, but she knows exactly when to turn, exactly when to slow down before a speed trap. She's lived here so long, she probably considers this home more than Buffalo.

I recognize nothing we pass. I might've felt numb to it before the medicine. Now, the sadness that comes over me is so intense I feel sick to my stomach.

It's better, in a way.

Mom and Dad's house is a forty-five-minute drive from the airport in an actual honest-to-god gated community. I mean, there were a couple times in Buffalo when a fan or two would hang around outside our house waiting for auto-graphs, but I didn't think hockey was big enough in North Carolina that they'd need that much security. It's probably just Dad being rich, white, and full of himself.

The house itself is massive, all white stone, big windows, and a front door that looks like it belongs on a palace. The landscaping alone must've cost tens of thousands of dollars, not to mention the Christmas lights that are probably visible from space.

It's overkill, if you ask me.

There's a chime as we walk in the front door, an auto-mated voice echoing through the house announcing *front door open.* The vaulted ceilings and hardwood floors and wide-open spaces make me feel cold and small and the apple cinnamon air freshener reminds me of Cauler and *god* I don't want to be here. I clench my backpack straps and try to breathe.

"Mom and Dad are doing some last-minute grocery shop-ping," Madison says, hanging her keys on a hook by the door.

"And by grocery shopping you mean liquor shopping, right?" Bailey asks.

Madison scoffs. "We have that under control."

"Time to get blackout drunk before they get back?" I cut in. I immediately regret it, even before Bailey rolls her eyes and heads for the curved staircase at the other side of the entryway.

"What's her problem?" Madison asks. She leads us into

the kitchen with all its spotless stainless steel and dark granite countertops.

"She's been like that all morning," Delilah says. She tosses her bags onto the floor by the breakfast nook and goes right to the liquor cabinet. I'm pretty sure it was designed to be a full-blown pantry. I take a bottle from Delilah and a glass from Madison and wander out into the family room. The whole back wall of the house is lined with huge windows overlooking a pool that's been closed for the winter. I have never stuck a toe in that pool. Nothing about this house feels homey or familiar. I could walk into the Vinters' front door right now, kick off my shoes, and go into the fridge like I own the place, but here, I feel like I have to ask permission to get a glass of water. Like the first couple weeks at my billet family's house in Michigan, before I got comfortable.

I ease myself down onto the couch, careful not to crush any of the throw pillows, and twist the cap off the bottle. I don't bother with the glass. Madison and Delilah follow after a few minutes, joining me on the couch with their heels dug in and pillows hugged to their chests, comfortable and belonging as they settle in to drink and watch some reality show. I gulp down as much alcohol as I can stomach in one go.

"Take it easy, Mickey," Delilah says softly. "Remember—"

"Yes," I snap. "I remember." Still, I give her the bottle when she holds out her hand, and she pours me a small glass and places it on a coaster on the coffee table in front of me. Setting my limits.

Bailey comes skulking down the stairs a little while later, sitting across the room with her laptop and headphones, watching lacrosse videos. She's the first one up when the door chimes. My palms start sweating. The soft rumble of Dad's voice carries down the hall, along with another man I barely recognize until Mikayla laughs. That's enough to get me off my feet. I follow my sisters back to the foyer.

Spencer's stuck lugging his own suitcase on top of Mikayla's and a giant bag of wrapped gifts, straining with the weight of it all instead of setting it down. He still manages to look more at ease here than me. Mikayla doles out hugs around her growing baby bump. Nicolette pushes the door open with her foot next, a bunch of plastic grocery bags hanging from her arms. "There's more in the car!" she says when she catches me staring.

If it means avoiding Dad, I'll carry groceries all day. Mom gives me a kiss on the cheek as I pass by her on my way out to the driveway. Her Benz is parked outside the garage, the trunk open and still full of grocery bags.

The garage door is open, showing off a row of sports cars, probably worth enough to get all six of us through college without our scholarships. Even the rental Spencer, Mikayla, and Nicolette showed up in is probably costing them a hundred bucks a day.

One of the first things Cauler said to me is that I'm taking up space at Hartland. Using a full ride I don't need, for a year that doesn't even matter.

I'm going to have to start my own scholarship fund or something to make up for this guilt.

Dad's not in the kitchen when I come back with the groceries, so I help Mom put a few pizzas together for dinner. She starts by asking me about finals and hockey, then eventually moves on to my mental health and medication.

"It takes a while to adjust," she says when I tell her about the drunken meltdown. "If it doesn't work for you, you can always switch to something else. There's plenty of options. Adding therapy would help."

"I know," I say.

"And heavy drinking is one of the worst things you can do when you have depression."

"I know."

She gives me a soft smile, reaching out to brush hair off my forehead. I almost lean into the gesture. I don't remember a time I felt this close to her.

Spencer keeps Dad occupied through dinner, talking about the season so far and trade rumors he hopes actually happen to get the Coyotes in a better position for the spring. I almost butt in to say he should hope for his *own* trade, but then I'd get dragged in. Dad's awkward glances are more than enough for me. Once dinner's done, the cards come out and the liquor cabinet gets broken open for real this time.

I sip on a bottle of pop all night.

I fall asleep on the couch as soon as they turn on a movie and have every intention of sleeping there for the rest of the trip until a hand on my shoulder wakes me. The house is mostly dark except for the green and red coming from the Christmas lights around the windows and the dim glow from the black TV screen that's not actually off. Everyone's gone. Except for Dad standing over me.

"I have a room set up for you," he says softly. I feel like he could've said the same sentence in Spanish and I would've understood it better. There's not an unused room in this house, and even if he forced Mikayla to stay with someone else once Spencer heads back to Arizona, it still wouldn't be my space.

Still, this weird sense of guilt settles in my stomach. I brought up the room situation back in November to hurt him, and apparently it worked.

Bailey would be so pleased right now, seeing me proven wrong about him.

It's a struggle to get to my feet, and I feel weighed down as I follow Dad down a dark hallway, wincing and holding up a hand to block the sudden brightness as he hits the light switch inside the third doorway on the left. It's meant to be an office. I can tell even before my eyes adjust, with the floor-to-ceiling built-in bookshelves and a wall of windows facing the back patio, nothing but sheer curtains for privacy. The double bed pushed into the corner where the two solid walls meet looks completely out of place. The shelves are loaded with all the trophies and medals I've won over the years, and some of my old jerseys are framed on the walls. I know all of it's been stored in boxes until now.

"It's not ideal," Dad says as I silently take it all in. "But I wanted you to have a place of your own."

"Why?" I croak. I needed this years ago, not now.

"I want you to know you'll always have a place here."

My throat closes up and I bite my lip, tucking my chin and keeping my eyes on the ground so he can't see how much this is affecting me. My bag's already on the floor by the bed. Jesus.

Dad bears my silence for a minute before clapping a hand on my shoulder and squeezing. "Get some sleep. I'm making breakfast in the morning."

I give him a nod and wait for the door to close behind him before changing into gym shorts and turning off the lights. I've slept in plenty of unfamiliar beds in my time. Countless hotels and temporary homes. But even in the room made for me in my parents' home, I feel like a guest.

What would it've been like to grow up here? To know the city as well as Madison. To have summers in the pool with my sisters. To always have them within reach.

What would it have been like to grow up with a family?

After an hour lying awake, staring at the ceiling, I grab my phone from beside the pillows and message Bailey.

Mickey: Sorry for being a brat

I don't expect a response till morning, but she answers just a few minutes later.

Bailey: Same
It's just
I talk to dad a lot
And i know he's trying
So it's hard for me to see you
brush him off like that
I get where you're coming from
Just give him a chance to fix it

Mickey: Ok

Bailey: Love you brother

Mickey: You too

CAULER MESSAGES ME in the morning while I'm eating bacon drenched in maple syrup, blessing me with something to focus on instead of my extremely loud family of morning people.

> **Jaysen:** My body hurts

> **Mickey:** Don't look at me

> **Jaysen:** Little shit
> Played more barbarian ping pong
> with my cousins last night

> **Mickey:** ok wtf is barbarian ping pong

> **Jaysen:** I'll show you back on campus
> Start a new party game with the boys

We text back and forth all day, just random little things about what's going on, our family's antics, childhood holiday memories.

It makes me miss him.

That's dangerous.

Dad and I manage to skirt around each other for a couple days, until Spencer flies out to his family and Dad doesn't have his masculinity to lean on in a house full of women. Never mind that every woman in this house could kick my ass.

He sticks to small talk at first. NHL standings, his thoughts on some of the bigger-name players out there this season. Then my grades come in, and I mean, they're decent, but as my parents I guess they're obligated to tell me I could do better.

It's the morning of Christmas Eve when things finally get heavy.

I'm sitting on the couch with a mug of hot cocoa, watching my sisters decorate the tree. I tried to help, but there's too many of them crowding around one another and all the ornaments I put up just got moved as soon as I bent to pick up another one anyway, so I'm fine letting them handle it. I've finally gotten comfortable enough to sit with my feet pulled up onto the couch, which is good because I didn't bring enough heavy socks and this wood floor is *cold*. I pull the sleeves of my hoodie over my hands and hold the mug close to my face, grinning as Nicolette wraps Madison in tinsel and starts taking pictures. Mom and Dad stand off to the side with their arms around each other and mugs in their hands, smiling as they watch.

I almost feel like I'm ten years old again.

Once the tree is decorated to their liking, we all gather in front of it for a picture taken on a timer with Nicolette's camera, Mikayla's arms around my neck and probably the biggest smile I've had on my face in years. I take a few selfies with my sisters and send them to Nova, and she responds with a bunch of crying and heart-eye emojis.

After, we start heading toward the kitchen to get breakfast started, but Dad holds the sleeve of my hoodie to keep me back. "Can we talk?"

I literally feel the blood drain from my face. He sounds so nervous it's like he's the teenager in this situation and not the fifty-two-year-old retired NHL legend.

I run a hand through my hair and toss the other one up like *I guess*. Not like I have a choice. I sink back into the couch and pick up my cocoa again, hiding my mouth behind the oversize mug. Dad sits on the other end of the couch, elbows on his knees, turned slightly toward me. I take a sip and wait for him to find his words.

Maybe Bailey was right. Maybe all my issues really are petty and childish. I'm not the only hockey player out there who left their parents young to play for elite teams. At least I always had a roof over my head.

Dad scratches his jaw and doesn't look me in the eye. "You've grown a lot since August," he says. "Everyone's noticed."

I tap a fingernail against the mug, focusing on the soft ping and saying nothing.

"Not size-wise," he adds quickly. Awkwardly. "As a player."

"I get it," I grumble.

He finally meets my eyes. "And as a person."

I look away, holding the rim of the mug against my bottom lip.

"I'm not going to pretend to really know you." His voice sounds almost choked with emotion, enough that it makes my eyes burn. "I know I've failed in that regard, and I want to do better. But I've seen the way you've changed through interviews, things your sisters say. How you carry yourself. And I'm proud."

My hands are shaking. Why are my hands shaking?

"I could talk about how you've changed on the ice, too, but . . ." He clasps his fingers together. Rolls his thumbs around each other. Sighs. "But that only matters if this is something you want to keep doing."

I blink at him. There's no way he's saying what I think he's saying. "What do you mean?" I ask slowly.

"Do you want to play hockey, Mickey?"

God, I really wish I'd spiked this cocoa. Those are words I never thought I'd hear come out of Dad's mouth. It's never been a question. He carried me on the ice as an infant. Strapped skates to my feet as soon as I was steady on solid ground. Had me out on our pond when I was three. Before my parents even met, it was decided I would play hockey. This is the one thing I have wanted him to ask me from the beginning, and now I have no idea what I'm supposed to say.

"Uh . . ." I swirl what's left of my cocoa, watching it creep up the sides of the mug. "I don't know, I mean . . ."

"This is important, bud." Dad inches closer, and I glance up for a second to see him giving me this sad, serious look. "This isn't something you can go into with uncertainty. There are contracts and millions of dollars involved, you don't get a choice where you end up, and sometimes you don't even get a warning before you're traded across the continent. It's not something you should follow through with unless you're fully in it."

My chest feels like it's caving in, my heart wrung out.

"Then there's this," Dad adds, quiet and cautious as he reaches out to tug on the sleeve of my hoodie. But it's not my hoodie. It's big enough to engulf my hands and hang halfway down my thighs. Because it's Cauler's.

Shit.

It's got his name and number on the back. He left it in my room and I like big sweaters and I didn't even think about it.

Shit shit *shit.*

Dad doesn't seem to notice how wide my eyes have gotten, how I've stopped fidgeting with the mug. He just keeps talking, saying, "After the Royals, you'll probably never play on the same team again. Unless you get really lucky, you'll be hundreds of miles away from each other."

Okay. Yep. This is happening. I set my mug on the coffee table and put my face in my hands. Rub my eyes, push my fingers into my hair. Try not to freak out.

"You'll have to think about it for anyone you end up with. You'll be traveling a lot. If you get traded, it's not just your life that's disrupted. Then there's—"

"Dad." I cannot listen to this anymore. What is happening right now? I keep my elbows on my knees and my hands in my hair and stare at the floor. "It sounds like you're trying to talk me out of it right now."

"No, no, of course not," he says quickly. "There's a lot of great things about going pro, too. I wouldn't trade my experience in the NHL for anything. But. Mickey, your heart's never been in this. I thought if I kept pushing you, you'd eventually learn to like it more, but instead it's done the opposite, and I'm sorry. I'm sorry, Mickey. I just want you to be happy."

"But that's the thing," I say. My voice shakes. "Nothing makes me happy. Not really. It's not even that I don't like hockey, it's just . . . I don't like *anything*. Not enough to matter. All I ever wanted with hockey was a choice. I wanted to come with you when you moved. I didn't care about the best opportunities. I was *ten*. I wanted my family. You could've retired in Buffalo, but you chose to come here and keep playing. You chose to leave me. And when you did finally retire, instead of coming back, you stayed here."

Dad looks down at his hands, his eyes red-rimmed. "I'm sorry," he says.

The words are soft and genuine and *goddammit*. I choke on a sob and drop my face back into my hands. My whole body shakes. I can't breathe. Dad puts a hand on my shoulder and pulls me in until my head is against his chest.

"Whatever you need to do," he says, his chin on top of my head and a hand rubbing my back. The couch dips on my other side. I smell Mom's perfume a second before another set of arms wraps around me. "We'll support it."

"But I don't know what I want," I say. I hear glass clinking in the kitchen. The sizzling sound of something cooking. If I can hear that, my sisters can hear this. I don't have the energy to be embarrassed.

"You have time," Mom says. "You can stay in school. Get a degree. Or play in the NHL and take online classes. Or do none of those things and come live here until you figure it out. There's no rush, *topolino*."

"But what if I take too long and miss the cut? What if I never figure it out?"

"You will," Dad insists. "The most important thing is taking care of yourself."

"We'll get you through this," Mom adds. She kisses me on the shoulder and presses her face against my back, both of them holding me together as I fall apart.

It doesn't erase the years of absence. But in this moment, I wouldn't trade it for anything.

TWENTY-SIX

Campus is quiet.

Classes don't start for another three weeks, and with the snow muffling everything, it feels like I'm the only one here.

It's cold, but I miss the dock. Bundled up in enough layers to make moving inconvenient, I sit on the edge with my legs pulled up and my phone in my lap.

My search history is a mess.

+nhl prospect rankings

+jaysen caulfield

+lgbt pro athletes

+ryan getzlaf playoff slur

+homophobia in nhl

+hartland university marine science

+nhl players with depression

+nhl prospect rankings

+marine science jobs

+marine science degree

+mickey james iii

+mickey james

+jaysen caulfield

+gay hockey players

+online marine science degree

+hartland university online degree

+nhl players with college degrees

+degree or nhl

+nhl draft prospects

Mom and Dad said I have time, but really all I have is till the Draft Combine in June. Six months to figure out the rest of my life.

No pressure.

And then there's Cauler.

I'm surprised Dad didn't make a bigger deal about it. I didn't outright confirm it, but I didn't deny it, either. Sure, he's supported my sisters from the start, but I thought it'd be different for me, being under heavier scrutiny or whatever.

Most rankings still have me at number one, but they're all sure to point out it's a close call and the only thing putting me over Cauler is my availability next season. The ones that put me second, or even lower sometimes, can't get past my size.

None of it's helpful.

I close out of my history and call Nova. She's busy and has her life together and probably isn't gonna answer, but—

"Hey!" Nova sounds so bright and cheery, for a second I forget why I was even calling her.

"Hey, Nova." My voice is rough from all the crying I've been doing lately. My eyes eternally swollen. "Can you do something for me?" We snap often enough that I don't feel bad about skipping the pleasantries.

"Need me to kick someone's ass?"

I roll my eyes. "No, jackass."

She chuckles a little. I hear cars passing in the background. People talking. She breathes heavy like she's walking fast. "What's up? What do you need?"

"I'm about to have this serious talk with Cauler and I need, like, cute penguin pictures on standby if it goes bad. Need to change my coping habits."

"Alright," she says hesitantly. "I'm taking a solo lunch right now, so I'll work on that. You're gonna give me the details later, right?"

"Of course, Nova. Love you."

"Love you, too, babe. Good luck."

I sit in the quiet for another few minutes, head tilted back, breathing in the fresh, cold air. Clearing my head. Letting it wake me up.

We have practice in a few hours. Two games this week. Another four before classes start again.

Six months to let go of everyone's expectations and figure out who I'm going to be. How the *third* on the end of my name has me measure up to the ones before me.

I take one last deep breath, so cold it hurts the inside of my nose, and let it out in a slow sigh before standing up.

Cauler's heading down the dock toward me. I stop after a stutter-step, hands clenching into fists in my pockets. I texted him that we should talk, but I didn't expect him to come searching for me.

He slows when we make eye contact, taking a couple half-steps before stopping a few feet away. We stare at each other, his breath coming out in fast visible puffs like he ran here.

"Hey," he says breathlessly.

"Hey."

"You okay?"

"Yeah, I just . . ." I stop myself. I'm not about to lie right now. I asked him to talk for a reason. "Um . . ." I sigh, shifting uncomfortably. Get it over with. Rip the Band-Aid off. "Look, Cauler. I don't know if you've noticed, but I'm . . ." I laugh bitterly. "I am deeply depressed. Now I'm on medication and I'm still trying to get used to *feeling* things, and honestly a lot of the time, I really hate myself."

I keep my voice surprisingly steady. I am not about to cry here. This is the strongest I have ever felt, being honest with my own mental health.

Cauler just looks at me for a long moment before he says, "What can I do?"

Oh. That's . . . not what I was expecting. I don't even know how to answer that. There's nothing he can do. It's my illness to deal with.

I lift my shoulders and look out over the lake. "Nothing. But . . ."

A cloud of his breath is carried away by the breeze. "Mickey."

I take a deep breath. "Being with you helps. But I'm scared. Everything changes in six months. Who knows where we'll be. Not anywhere near each other. I want you. I want this. But how do we do that when we are who we are?"

I'm shaking when I look over at him. There's pressure building behind my eyes and a weight in my throat. It's so cold I can barely take it anymore, but I don't know what I'm supposed to do here. Dorian wanted the four of us to have lunch together to celebrate making it to our second semester. It's gotta be close to that time now. How do I resolve this before we have to leave?

"Hey." Cauler raises a hand to my face, letting it hover near my jaw, not quite touching. He waits for me to look him in the eye. "Can I?"

I swallow hard. "Yeah."

He traces his cold fingers along my jawline, pushes them into the hair at the nape of my neck, and pulls me against his chest. I melt into him, wrap my arms around his waist and squeeze him tight.

"I don't wanna be just another one of your former team-mates," he says into my hair. "I wanna be able to call you after your games and make fun of the faces you made on the bench or freak out about a sick play you made, and I want you to call and ask about mine and I want to wake up to texts from you. I want to be the one you call when you're having a rough time."

"You'll have to take that one up with Nova," I mutter into his chest.

"I'm not opposed to group video chats."

I huff out a laugh. Cauler loosens his hold on me and pulls back enough for us to look at each other again. He keeps his hands on my shoulders.

"I want this, too," he says. "And I know it's gonna be hard, maybe even impossible, but I want to see where we can take it. There's, like, eight teams within a five-hour drive of here, maybe we'll get lucky and you'll get drafted by one of them. We could see each other sometimes, at least. What do you think?"

He goes quiet, waiting for me to say something.

God, this feels almost exactly like Dad asking me if I

want to play hockey. There's way too much to think about before I can decide on something like that.

Cauler's right. It is going to be damn near impossible, having any kind of relationship with him going forward. Especially when we're both in the NHL. But it'll be completely impossible if we don't try at all.

Even if it only lasts through June, at least it's something.

"Okay," I say. I wipe my nose on the back of my hand and he doesn't even flinch. "Yeah. Let's try it."

He smiles, so soft and beautiful it makes my heart stop for a second or two. I don't think anyone's ever looked at me like that before. If he keeps doing it, this might be easier than I thought.

"Then let's do this right," he says. He steps back enough to hold my hands between us. He lifts one up to brush his lips against my knuckles. My knees feel weak. "Mickey Liam James III. Will you be my boyfriend?"

I'm shaking, and I doubt it's just from the cold. "Yeah," I say, pulling him back to me, rising on my tiptoes to kiss him. Campus is empty. I'm with my favorite person, in my favorite spot at Hartland, kissing as snow starts to fall around us.

This was never how I thought college would go for me. But I wouldn't dare complain.

Cauler breaks our kiss to hug me again, holding me tight until I say, "Alright, can we please go in before my balls freeze off?"

Cauler laughs. I smile.

We walk back to campus to meet Dorian and Barbie with our hands held between us. It feels so nice, I barely notice how cold our fingers are.

EPILOGUE

I twirl my NCAA championship ring around my finger and stand on my toes to see through the crowd. It's hopeless. I'm surrounded by giant-ass hockey players and their mostly equally giant-ass families, and I can't see anything.

"You sure he's here?" Nicolette asks.

"He texted me like five minutes ago saying his bus was pulling in," I say.

Mom pulls on my tie, fixing the knot for the hundredth time in the half hour I've had it on. "Relax, *topolino*. This isn't the last time you'll see Jaysen."

It sure feels like it.

"He probably got an interview request," Dad says, smiling as a man approaches to give him a handshake and then me. I've already shaken hands with so many people I don't know today and the draft hasn't even started.

"Mikayla's on the phone," Madison says. "She says Jordan's had the hiccups for half an hour and she doesn't know what to do."

"Burp her," Mom suggests as she fixes my hair that looks fine as it is. "Or make her laugh. Don't let her eat so fast."

Delilah searches the crowd like me, but she's got the height advantage. "Where's this Alex Nakamoto guy? I want some words with him."

"Leave the poor kid alone," Bailey says. "Not his fault he had a popularity surge."

"Um, yes it is?"

I need to sit down.

"Excuse me, Mr. James?" We all look over as a man with an all-access lanyard steps up to us, eyes on me. "NHL Network wants a word with you."

"Sure." I follow him off to the side, where another guy's being interviewed by TSN a few feet away from Hugh and Alyssa. I'm kinda prepared for them, at least. During the Combine, Cauler and I tried to come up with a bunch of questions we figured they'd ask us and planned out our answers.

I stand with them in front of a backdrop with the NHL Network logo blown up in the center and share a few laughs about the criticism they had for me throughout the season before Alyssa says, "There's been a lot of talk about your improvement with the Royals, mostly where it came from. Last summer most of the talk was that you'd hit your amateur peak and the only way for you to improve would be to play at a higher level. Where do you think it came from?"

I told myself I would be completely honest if they asked me something like this. I've been practicing my answer in my head for weeks. But now that it's finally time to say it, it takes all my power to keep my voice from shaking.

"Well, a lot of it has to do with the guys I shared ice with," I start. "It's hard to be on a line with Luca Cicero and Jaysen Caulfield and stay stagnant as a player. They'd never let that happen, they're all about continuous improvement. And then just the Royals as a whole, they're such an amazing group of guys. I got along with them off the ice great, which makes it a lot easier to mesh well on the ice." I swallow against the nervous lump in my throat. My voice is just a little strained when I add, "But I think the biggest factor was me getting a handle on my own mental health. I was diagnosed with clinical depression, and once I got on medication and started seeing a therapist, I was able to put so much more energy and passion into hockey. I was able to start liking it again, not just seeing it as something I had to do."

Over the cameraman's shoulder, I see Dad smiling crookedly. Mom with her hands clasped in front of her mouth, but her smile still present in her eyes. My sisters, minus Mikayla, watching on with pride.

To their credit, Hugh and Alyssa only look mildly surprised. "What would you say to other players going through similar circumstances?" Hugh asks.

"Honestly, don't be ashamed. A lot more people deal with it than you think, and the best way to cope is to acknowledge it and ask for help. Don't suffer alone."

They move on to more hockey questions, my performance in the Combine, and then another big one. "This is probably one of the more unpredictable drafts we've had in recent memory," Alyssa says. "Most analysts are sure the order of the top three is going to ride on what you intend to do next season. After you won an NCAA Championship with the Royals, there was a lot of speculation on if you'd choose to stick it out in college for another few years. What's the plan?"

"If I'm offered a contract, I'm taking it," I say. No hesitation.

"I'm privileged enough I don't need that full ride, so I'm gonna take online classes and do my field work in the summer and open up a roster spot and scholarship for another player who needs it. I'll miss the guys, I'll miss Hartland, but I want as many other people to have the opportunity to experience that place and that team as possible."

Alyssa's wide-eyed, like she has to change everything she's ever thought about me after a single interview. By the time it's done, my family and I have to practically race to our seats, and I didn't get a chance to see Cauler first.

It's not hard to spot the Royals, a mass of purple along the rail in the three hundred level. Dorian and Zero and Kovy are on their feet, dancing along with the club-like music and laser lights like they're at a rave. Nova and Barbie are next to each other taking a selfie that shows up on my phone a minute later, them making kissy faces surrounded by heart emojis. Jade, Sid, and Karim sit behind them.

I scan the crowd of prospects and their families, looking for Cauler, but I don't see him.

Mickey: Where are youuuuuu

Jaysen: 105 fifth row up
Sorry got pulled into too
many interviews

I find him a second later, sitting with his mom and dad and Shae. He waves at me from across the floor packed with management from all thirty-two teams and I wave back, maybe a little too enthusiastically.

Mickey: You look good

Jaysen: You can barely see me

Mickey: But i still know you look good

He sends back eye roll emojis and then a bunch with their tongues sticking out, and I really hope there's no camera on me right now because I am *blushing*.

Jaysen: My parents wanna
do a big family breakfast with
your family tomorrow

Mickey: You mean i have to
meet your parents with my
whole family with me???
You have met my sisters right.

Jaysen: Yeah
Which means it's only fair

Mickey: I guess i can do that

This is taking forever. My knee starts bouncing and Mom presses her shoulder against me and even though I have been preparing for this night my entire life, I have never been this nervous.

Mickey: I might puke

Jaysen: Save it for gary bettman

Mickey: Omgggg no
Worst nightmare

Jaysen: I'm gonna trip up
the stairs probably so
I'll share the humiliation

Mickey: There is a big
difference between
tripping up some stairs
and puking on the gd commissioner

Jaysen: Idk i bet you'd get
tons of cheers for that

That's when Gary Bettman chooses to make his way onto the stage to his standard chorus of boos. He takes it in stride, used to it by now, smiling as he talks. The massive screen behind him that was playing highlights of the top ten prospects is now switched over to nothing but the draft logo. The longer he talks, the more my anxiety builds.

We got lucky. First two teams up are the Senators and Panthers. Both in the Atlantic division. We'll play each other and our hometown teams at least four times a season. One of us gets Canada's capital and the other gets the Everglades.

Unless something outrageous happens and one of us drops to third and gets sent all the way to LA.

At least they have Dorian.

Jaysen: Loser pays for our next date

Mickey: Hope you've been saving up
I'm craving steak and lobster

"Let's get started," Gary Bettman finally says. My heart plummets. I've been waiting eighteen years for this and here it is. The moment I've been working toward my whole life. Mom takes my sweaty hand and Dad pats my knee. "The first selection of this year's NHL Draft belongs to the Ottawa Senators."

They have three minutes to put their pick in. Three minutes of straight-up agony, trying to keep still as cameras pan over me, trying not to look as sick as I feel. I look at Cauler every few seconds to find him fidgeting with his tie, staring at the screen where they're back to clips of the two of us, chewing his lip. His parents take turns rubbing his arms to calm him.

By the time Ottawa takes the stage, I'm on the verge of cardiac arrest. The owner comes forward to thank their fans for their support and Denver for their hospitality during draft week and I want to *scream.*

Can they just? Get on with it?

Finally. *Finally.*

After eighteen years of anticipation, Ottawa's GM steps up to the mic. "The Ottawa Senators," he says, "are proud to select, from the Hartland University Royals . . ."

I look at Cauler.

He's looking at me.

And that matters far more than the name called first.

THE END

ACKNOWLEDGMENTS

HOCKEY IS AN amazing sport. It takes an outstanding amount of strength and tenacity, and even a bit of grace. This sport has been a major part of my life, growing up in Buffalo during a time when it could be called Hockey Heaven. Unfortunately, hockey culture is known for its toxic masculinity, overwhelming whiteness, homophobia, and inaccessibility. I first and foremost need to thank those organizations putting in the work to make hockey a welcoming place to players like Mickey and Jaysen, Dorian and Barbie: Black Girl Hockey Club, Hockey Diversity Alliance, the You Can Play Team, and Pride Tape.

Thank you so, so much to my incredible agent, Jennifer Azantian, for believing in me through genre changes and always having comforting words when everything gets overwhelming. Thank you to Benjamin Baxter, Brent Taylor, the whole of the ALA family, and to Kim Yau.

To Rachel Murray, for her incredible insight and understanding these characters even better than I do. To Liz Dresner for making this book gorgeous, and Amalas Rosa for bringing my boys to stunning life. To Lelia Mander, Allene Cassagnol, Cynthia Lliguichuzhca, and the rest of the team at Godwin Books / Henry Holt BYR for all their hard work.

Thank you to Rosiee Thor and Marisa Kanter for being my Writer Friends for the past decade (omg!!), and being there for me every step of the way. To Carly Heath for telling me to *let Mickey know things*. To all my fellow #22debuts for letting me lurk, too stunned by all of your greatness to speak up.

To my parents, for always supporting this unrealistic dream of mine, and my sisters for being my closest friends through it all. I hope you see a bit of yourselves in the James sisters. To Gage and Lexi, for putting up with all the times I bailed on plans because *I gotta work*, and all the friends I've made on the DM Ace server for always hyping me up. And to my husband, Rushtin, for loving me through it all.